SOMETIMES DECEIT IS EASIER TO BELIEVE THAN THE TRUTH.

Montana Thomas falls asleep with the woman he loves in his arms but wakes next to her bloody corpse. With the murder weapon in his hand and no memory of what happened, he needs his brother to help him sort through the confusion and grief.

But Dakota is three-thousand miles away and deep into government testing.

The stage has been set and all the players are in motion. All the unknown director has to do is sit back and wait for his true objective to be played out. In an expert game of cat and mouse, the Thomas brothers are subject to manipulation that has no equal. The only people they can trust are each other...if they can survive long enough to find the truth inside the maze of misdirection and deceit.

THROUGH THE GLASS

Book Two Coyote Moon Series Book Two

By
Ann Simko

Lyrical Press, Inc.

New York

Lyrical Press, Incorporated

Through the Glass
13 Digit ISBN: 978-1-61650-219-5
Copyright © 2010, Ann Simko
Edited by Pamela Tyner
Book design by Renee Rocco
Cover Art by Renee Rocco and Dale Rhodes

Lyrical Press, Incorporated
337 Katan Avenue
Staten Island, New York 10308
http://www.lyricalpress.com

PUBLISHER'S NOTE:

This book is a work of fiction. The names, characters, places, and incidents are products of the writer's imagination or have been used fictitiously and are not to be construed as real. Any resemblance to persons, living or dead, actual events, locale or organizations is entirely coincidental.

The publisher does not have any control over and does not assume any responsibility for author or third-party Web sites or their content.

Published in the United States of America by Lyrical Press, Incorporated

First Lyrical Press, Inc electronic publication: June 2010
First Lyrical Press, Inc print publication: September 2010

DEDICATION

To my family, Bob, Noah and Maria, who have put up with my virtual absence for large periods of time. Tap tap tap—
I love you guys.

ACKNOWLEDGEMENTS

Again and always, I want to thank Dale Rhodes for his unfailing support and willingness to read anything I write—even my very ugly first drafts.

To James for his technical support and friendship.

And to everyone who has read this and offered their encouragement—Sonal and Daria I'm looking at you and everyone who helped me at The Next big Writer dot com. Thanks, Sol!

I also wanted to thank my publishers, Renee and Frank Rocco, and my editor, Pamela Tyner—if you saw what she had to work with in its raw form, trust me you would be so impressed! Thank you is not adequate.

CHAPTER 1

The knife slid into the firm flesh of her stomach almost effortlessly. The pain took her breath and stole her voice. The second strike came fast on the heels of the first, never even giving her a chance to scream.

It wasn't supposed to play out this way. Everything had worked out as she'd planned up until now. She knew she'd flirted with danger, but never saw this coming. Even as she choked on her own blood, she hoped she was wrong. She couldn't be dying. She was only twenty-six.

This was not supposed to happen. Murdered in her own bed, dead—this was not what she'd planned.

* * * *

It had been a long time since Montana had been with a woman. Because of the way he looked, people assumed he could have any woman he wanted, and he probably could, but in reality, women scared the hell out of him. They always had. So secure in their own feelings, or so it seemed to him, looking from the outside in. It scared him to get that close, to expose that much and not be able to take it back. Vulnerable and exposed, that's how women made him feel. Naked flesh didn't concern him nearly as much as naked feelings.

He never understood how other men could separate intimacy and sex. To him they were one and the same. The physical and the emotional coiled and entwined around one another. The two could not be separated. Not for him, never for him. It was one of the reasons he chose his lovers carefully, but despite that care he always paid a price in the end. That was the reason he spent much of his life alone. The price in the end was too high.

But not tonight. Tonight he was not alone. He slid his hands along Linney's side, enjoying the way her skin felt. Like warm silk beneath the rough calluses of his fingers. He felt her shiver under his touch. Tilting her head back, she asked for a kiss, and he did not disappoint her. He pulled her close and covered her mouth with his. Her lips parted for him, and he explored the velvet lining with his tongue. God, she felt right, they felt right together. Passion welled with the sheer intensity of the feelings she brought to life inside of him. He wanted to act on them, but knew she needed sleep.

She turned in his arms and snuggled into the curve of his shoulder, her small, warm hands running lightly along his ribs, his hip, traveling back up to rest below his stomach. Her hands touching the scars on his body, each one with its own story. Stories he would rather leave in the past. She seemed to know that and never asked how they got there. He loved her for that alone. The others always wanted the stories, they wanted something he could never give them, a piece of his soul. Someday he would tell her, he would tell her everything. But not tonight. Tonight he simply wanted to be here with her, no past, no future, just now. She understood that as well.

"Mmm, I think you wore me out," she whispered, her voice drugged with sleep and sex.

He rested his chin on top of her head, smoothed her honey-blond hair out of his face and wrapped his arms around her. He grabbed the blankets they'd kicked off and pulled them up to cover them both.

"Cold?" he asked.

"Hmm? No, you're a human blast furnace." He felt her smile.

"And you are beautiful," he told her. It wasn't an empty compliment. If he could have thought of something more profound, he would have said the words, but he wasn't a poet. He made a living dealing with the worst humanity had to offer. He was used to the ugly things in life, so the beautiful ones meant all the more to him.

She laughed at the compliment and raised herself up on one elbow so their faces were level.

"Uh uh." She shook her head, her fingers lightly tracing the contours of his face. "You're the beautiful one and not only here." She placed her hand over his heart. "But here too, my pretty boy." She smiled as she teased him. It was a private joke they shared from the first time they met almost two months ago. She told him, when he asked her out to dinner, that she didn't date men who were prettier than her. The blush her comment caused endeared him to her, or so she said, and she broke her own rule.

"My pretty boy," she repeated. "My pretty Montana Thomas. I think I could fall in love with you."

Montana closed his eyes at the words and found what passed for a smile on his lips. He had fallen and fallen hard. He was just afraid to admit it to himself, let alone her, but the feeling was undeniable.

He tightened his grip around her and hoped she understood his silence. Grateful when he heard the slow measured breathing that signified her sliding into sleep, he found the courage to say the words aloud.

"I love you, Linney," he whispered into her hair, secure that she slept and the words went unheard by anyone but him. "I love you," he repeated.

As sleep claimed him, Montana thought he might actually be happy. He couldn't tell for sure, the feeling was one not completely familiar to him, but one he might like getting used to.

Montana fell asleep with the only woman he had dared to utter those words to, snuggled and wrapped sweetly around him. It was all he needed at that moment.

A moment he took, folded up, and hid deep within the very core of him. A moment he would take out and unfold time and time again whenever he tried to figure out exactly what the hell went wrong.

CHAPTER 2

The voice on the phone that woke Ito St. James at six that morning was filled with fear, confusion and self-doubt. The voice belonged to Montana even if it didn't sound like his friend in the least.

"Ito? I need your help."

The simple request brought Ito from sleep to full wakefulness in mere moments. Montana sounded on the edge and in the next few words he tumbled over the precipice.

"I killed her, I think I killed her." Montana's voice cracked, and Ito heard the grief and disbelief just beneath the surface.

Ito understood Montana. He knew what the man feared, the things that scared him. Those things were precious few and right now Montana was scared.

"Montana?" Ito stood, getting dressed as he spoke. "What are you talking about? Where are you?"

There was a slight pause on the other end of the line as if Montana had to think about the answer. "Uh, Lincoln County lock-up, I think. Ito, she's dead. I had the knife in my hands. Her blood... Ito..."

"Montana, get it together, man, you're not making any sense. Who's dead?"

"Linney, Ito, they say I killed Linney."

"What do you mean, 'they say'?"

"I can't remember. I fell asleep, I woke up… She was dead…her blood… Ito?"

"I'm on my way. Do you have a lawyer?"

"I called you." Montana's voice was thick and trembling.

Ito had seen his friend through a lot, but nothing like this. Montana was losing it and obviously in shock. Ito had no clue what was going on, but he was going to find out. He owed his friend that much and more. Montana had been Ito's commanding officer in the brotherhood of the Rangers. There, all that mattered was trust; it was imperative, without it, survival could not be possible. *Survive* was exactly what Montana and Ito had done. The bond they had formed in the process was tighter than most families, and family was not something you messed with, not in Montana's world and certainly not in Ito's.

"All right, listen to me. You say nothing until I get there. Understand? I'll call Damien Knight and then I'm coming to see you. You hang, Montana, okay? I'm on my way, do you hear?" Silence greeted him. "Montana, you hear?" he asked again, his voice taking on the authoritative tone he hoped would make it through the shock and reach the disciplined Ranger underneath.

"Yeah, yes," Montana answered, his voice just a bit more controlled. "I understand. Ito?"

"Yeah?"

"Hurry, okay?"

"I am on wings, my man. Hang tight."

Ito hung up and stood perfectly still. He tried to recall the last time he had heard Montana like this. Never. That's what concerned him more than anything. Montana was not someone you worried about, he was not someone who asked for help. Montana Thomas was who you went to *for* help. What the hell happened to turn that around?

When Montana had approached Ito about the possibility of starting a business in the field of private investigations, he didn't have to think about an answer. Employed in a dead-end job as a security guard for a high-end jewelry store and bored out of his mind, Ito quit and never looked back. Five years later, Big Sky Investigations was firmly established and actually seeing a profit. Life was good, but life had a way of throwing curve balls at you when you least expected it.

With concern weighing heavily on him, Ito finished dressing and picked the phone back up. He might not know what to do to help Montana, but he knew someone who did.

* * * *

Damien Knight did not appreciate being pulled out of bed on a weekend, until he put his irritation on hold long enough to listen to what Ito had to tell him.

Montana had worked at the same law firm with him, but concentrated on corporate law while Damien worked the criminal side of the fence. By all rights they shouldn't have been friends. They irritated the hell out of each other on a regular basis, but despite that Damien admired the man. That, and when Montana had gone into the PI business, he always made it a point to direct his clients Damien's way if they were in need of criminal defense.

So when Ito woke him up a mere five hours after he had gone to bed, he forgave the intrusion when he found out exactly who was in need of his help.

"What do you mean they're holding him on murder charges?" Damien asked. He sat on the edge of the bed talking softly so as not to disturb his wife. When she grabbed the pillow and put it over her head, he realized the phone probably already woke her. He grabbed a pair of jeans from the chair in the corner of the room, left the bedroom and quietly closed the door behind him. With the phone between his shoulder and ear, he hopped on one foot while shoving the other through the leg of his jeans and tried to make sense out of what Ito was telling him.

"I only know what he told me, and he wasn't making much sense."

"You're right, that doesn't sound like Montana." Damien padded barefoot down to the kitchen and put on a pot of coffee, his one and only addiction.

"And that's exactly what worries me. He is totally unhinged, Damien. You know how he feels about Linney, you've seen them together. If she is dead…" Ito left the sentence unfinished. Damien knew his friend well enough to know that if Linney was dead, Montana's heart would be damaged beyond all possible hope of repair.

"He doesn't remember anything?"

"He says no. Something is wrong here, and I don't mean the obvious. You know Montana didn't kill that girl."

Damien took a travel mug from the cabinet and poured a cup of strong black coffee, then made a mental checklist of what he needed to do. "Right now I don't know anything. I need to make some phone calls. How long will it take you to get to where they're holding him?"

"Thirty minutes."

Damien thought about that. "That should be good. Let me do my thing, then I'm going to grab a quick shower and a plane. You go be with him, I'll be there in two, three hours tops."

"I'm not a lawyer, what if they don't let me in?" Ito asked.

"Trust me, when I get done with them, you won't have a problem."

"Damien, I never heard him like this before, do you understand what I'm telling you?"

"Yeah, I understand. Ito, I'll get him out of this, I swear." Damien heard Ito disconnect the line without another word and hoped to hell he could make good on his promise.

Considering his usual clientele, Damien knew the number for the Lincoln County correctional facility in Lincoln, Nevada by heart.

"Time to work the magic," he said to the still ringing line.

Damien Knight was something of a celebrity in Denver. There had been a murder case a few years back, a man accused of killing his neighbor in a dispute over where said neighbor's dog did his business. The circumstantial evidence was overwhelming. Events leading up to the murder were convincing. Witnessed accounts of verbal assaults and one attempt at trying to poison the dog were all admitted by the defendant. The dog leash used to strangle the man had the neighbor's DNA all over it. Open and shut case, or so it seemed until Damien came into the picture.

Not only had the police failed to Mirandize the man, but the evidence had been contaminated at the crime scene, making most of it inadmissible in court. Damien had no doubt the man had indeed killed his neighbor, but the case never saw the inside of a courtroom. It was dismissed by a federal court judge who called Damien a disgrace to the profession. Damien just cashed his client's check for half a million dollars. After all, what price can you put on freedom? It wasn't false vanity. He was simply that good and saw no reason to be modest about it.

But this was different. As he sat in first class accommodations on his way to Carson City, he wondered what Montana had gotten himself involved in. He'd never represented a friend before, maybe because friends were not something he had in surplus, but he knew Montana wouldn't hesitate if Damien needed his help. There weren't many people he could say that about.

He remembered the last time he had seen Montana. Last week he'd brought Linney out to Denver. That in itself was unusual, Montana didn't see most of the women he dated more than once or twice. This one was different. Anyone looking at Montana knew the boy was officially off the market. Damien wondered if the petite blonde knew how lucky she was. Montana Thomas was stupid in love with her.

They splurged and went out to a five-star restaurant, Damien and Kathy, Montana and Lindsay. Linney, she liked to be called Linney. Kathy remarked on the drive home how they had held hands across the table and Montana's eyes never left the girl's.

"Do you think she's the one?" Kathy had asked him.

Yeah, he did.

Damien realized he knew almost nothing about Linney Keller. He closed his eyes and tried to catch some much-needed sleep before the plane landed. He needed to be sharp, he needed everything he had for Montana. From the conversation he'd had on the phone with the DA, things did not look good. Montana had all but confessed to the murder, but after the initial shock had worn off and he'd spoken to Ito, he refused to utter another word. The DA wouldn't go into details with Damien over the phone. He needed to talk to Montana.

CHAPTER 3

The limo pulled up to the police department in Caliente. If there had been anyone on the street to take notice, it would have caused quite a stir. Not too many limos showing up in Caliente. Damien checked his hair and tie in the mirror, grabbed the alligator leather briefcase from the seat beside him, and got out. He walked to the driver's window and waited for the man to power it down, then flipped him a bill.

"I expect you to pick me up when I call for you."

The driver glanced at the hundred-dollar tip before folding it and sliding it in his jacket. He gave Damien a small salute off the polished rim of his hat and a nod, then drove out the circular drive.

Before Damien pulled open the glass door, he saw Ito get out of a white Humvee parked across the street and walk in his direction. Even from a distance, Ito's half Japanese, half African-American heritage was evident. Damien always thought he was one of the most unique looking individuals he had ever met.

"They wouldn't let me see him," Ito told him. At six-foot-five and an easy two-fifty, Ito could usually intimidate anyone just by his presence, but apparently the Caliente Police Department missed that memo. The man had a good six inches on Damien, and he was pissed. That should have been enough to have Damien take a step back, but then he hated to be predictable.

"You told them you were with me?"

Ito nodded. "Didn't seem to impress them."

That concerned Damien. It meant Montana was still under interrogation. They should be keeping him secluded, but not questioning him without representation. It also meant they thought they had a solid case against him.

Damien pulled open the door and strode up to the glass window just inside the foyer. The bored sergeant looked up from his paperwork and gave him an irritated scowl.

"Damien Knight, representing Montana Thomas." Damien flashed his ID to the sergeant, who spent all of half a second glancing at the two men in front of him before calling up for confirmation.

Damien tried for intimidation. "Why wasn't my associate allowed in to see our client?"

"Because your associate isn't legal representation. He's the accused's business partner," the sarge said with a smug look on his face. "Only legal representatives are allowed in on homicides. You know that."

He did, but it didn't mean he had to like it. "True." Damien tried one last bluff. He wanted Ito with him. If Montana was as unhinged as he thought, Ito might be the only one who could get Montana to keep it together. "But as of this morning, Mr. St. James works for me. He is my legal assistant, and legal assistants *are* allowed in with legal representatives."

The cop knew it was bullshit, the look on his face said as much, but he let them in. After twenty minutes of signing in and searches through personal belongings, Damien and Ito finally stood outside the holding room where they were keeping Montana. Twelve hours had passed since the police found him sitting over Linney's bloody corpse.

Montana sat behind a simple wooden table, his hands cuffed behind his back, his ankles shackled together. He was still covered in the girl's blood, now dried to a dull brown, the clothes they had obviously allowed him to put on at the scene, smeared with it. Damien looked him over with shock and concern. He also saw what he was looking for: leverage. Some of the blood on Montana's face was his own. One eye was bruised and half-swollen shut, his lip split, and fresh blood ran down his chin to catch in the collar of the once white t-shirt he wore.

The detective in the room noticed where Damien's attention had been drawn. "He resisted arrest."

"Yeah, I just bet he did," Ito said.

Montana looked exhausted. He hadn't moved or even acknowledged Damien's or Ito's presence until Ito spoke. A flicker of life came to Montana's eyes at the sound of his friend's voice, and he seemed to notice them for the first time.

"Ito? Damien?" He sounded like he didn't trust his own eyes.

"Yeah, man, it's me." Ito sat across from Montana.

"Why hasn't my client been cleaned up? This is outrageous, he's in need of medical treatment," Damien said. He took the camera he was entitled to bring with him and began snapping pictures of Montana's injuries.

"Your client brutally murdered a young woman a little over twelve hours ago." The lead detective slapped exquisitely clear photographs down in front of Montana. He closed his eyes and turned his head away. It was obvious he had been made to look at them before.

"Fifty-six separate stab wounds. What the hell did she do to piss you off? Yell out another guy's name at an inappropriate moment?"

"Excuse me, detective." Damien turned Montana's face toward him for a better view of his injuries. Montana jerked away from his touch. "Did my client confess to this crime?"

"He might as well have. He was found next to her mutilated body with the murder weapon in his hand and covered in her blood." The detective put his face in Montana's. "They had to take her away in *pieces*, counselor," he said to Damien, but still looked at Montana. "So don't talk to me about his rights."

"I want him cleaned up, his injuries treated, and the cuffs off."

The detective laughed. "Would you like the wine list as well?"

"In case you haven't noticed, I am not in a humorous mood. You have someone get my client his basic human rights, or I will have your department brought up on police brutality charges so fast you won't have time to collect your severance pay."

The detective turned barely-contained rage in Damien's direction, but the man never even flinched. He stood, took keys off his belt and unlocked the cuffs at Montana's wrists.

"I'll see what I can do about those human rights, counselor," he said. "You have thirty minutes with your client. Keep in mind there is an armed police officer right outside this door. The slightest hint of trouble out of that piece of shit and you can take his *rights* and shove them."

Damien waited for the door to the interrogation room to close before turning his full attention toward Montana. "You doing okay?" he asked.

Montana brought his hands in front of him and rubbed his wrists. They were red, raw, bruised and swollen from cuffs cinched too tight.

"Linney's dead," he said, as if he'd just heard the news. His face betrayed nothing of what might be going on behind those black eyes.

"Montana, what happened?" Ito asked.

"Ito, did you know Linney's dead?" He seemed to realize Ito was in the room for the first time.

"Yeah, man, I know." Ito reached across and gently touched Montana's hand.

"You need to talk to me, Montana," Damien said. He wanted to go slow and give Montana the time he needed, but he didn't have that luxury. He could see his friend was in shock, but that was going to have to wait. "Take me back to yesterday," Damien prompted. "You were with Lindsay?"

Montana nodded and wiped the blood from his chin. "Yeah, she wanted to go to La Playa's." He actually managed to smile at the memory. "Mexican food is her favorite, *was*, was her favorite." The smile died before it had a chance to ever really live. "We went out to dinner, took a walk in the desert, watched the sunset."

Damien silently observed as Montana's eyes moved back and forth, his face creased in concentration as if he was trying to make sense of something insensible.

"We went back to her place afterward."

"Did you have a fight? Anything happen at dinner, or after in the desert?" Damien asked.

Montana shook his head. "No, we had a good time. We never fought. I can't even remember having a disagreement with her." He put his head in his hands. When he looked back up at Damien, the grief showed in his eyes. It was the first time Damien felt that Montana was truly with him in the room.

"We had dinner, we went for a walk. I took her back to her apartment, and we made love. I fell asleep with her in my arms, and when I woke up she was dead and I was holding the knife that killed her. I swear to whatever you hold holy, that's all I remember." He put his head back down in his hands as if the mental pictures were too much for him to handle.

Damien wanted to tell him it would be all right, but he knew if he did, Montana would lose it. He kept his tone neutral and professional. "Did they take any blood from you after they processed you?"

Montana nodded. "Yeah, urine too."

"Good. I need a list of everything you had to eat or drink in the last twenty-four hours." Damien pushed a legal pad in front of Montana. "Are they going to find any drugs, Montana?"

He gave Damien a look as if to say he should know better.

"I'm sorry, man, but I wouldn't be doing my job if I didn't ask."

"Alcohol only," Montana told him. "We had a bottle of wine with dinner. I was well under the legal limit when I left the restaurant, let alone by the time we made it back to her place. All I know is I didn't kill her, I loved her. I never got the chance to tell her that, but I did, I loved her. Why would I kill her?" He looked at Damien and then at Ito as if he expected them to give him the answer. "Tell me you believe me."

"I wouldn't be here if I thought you did," Damien said.

"You know you don't need to ask," Ito said.

"Maybe, but I need to hear it anyway."

"You didn't kill Linney, Montana," Ito told him. "But trust me, as sure as the sun rises in the morning, I am going to find out who did."

Montana looked relieved at the words and gave them both a nod. His face creased in concern once more.

"Dakota," he said, looking at Ito. "I need you to get to Dakota. I don't want him finding out about this from the news."

"Done," Ito said.

The door to the interrogation room opened, and Damien turned an irritated eye toward the intrusion. It was nowhere near thirty minutes. Irritation turned to relief as he recognized the huge man lumbering through the doorway.

"God damn! You tell me who hit you, boy, and I swear his badge is history." Cal Tremont, Caliente's local law, planted his hands on the table and peered at Montana's face. "I was out of town and just heard. What the hell are they talking about—murder! I know you, Montana Thomas, you kill on occasion, but murder?"

"Thanks for the vote of confidence." Montana gave Cal a little smile.

"He didn't murder anyone, Cal," Damien said.

"Well, hell, you don't need to tell me that, but I saw the reports."

Cal got Montana's attention. "You landed in a pile of it this time, boy. I'll do what I can, but my hands are pretty well tied."

Montana closed his eyes and nodded. He looked beaten. Damien didn't like that. Montana was a fighter, one of the strongest people he knew. To see him like this, exhausted and defeated, did not sit well with him. He needed Montana with him, if he gave up on himself, Damien had no chance to try to fight for him.

As Cal took a seat next to Montana and began asking questions that he had no doubt answered a dozen times over in the last twelve hours, Damien turned to Ito.

"Do you know where to find Dakota?" he asked in a low voice.

"That I do. What are you thinking?"

Damien sighed and ran a hand through his hair. "I'm thinking I need facts, Ito. Right now all I have is a very dead girl and Montana holding the murder weapon. What I don't have is motive. His memory loss is not going to help. It's been used before."

"He ain't using it, pal." Ito bristled at the implication. "If he says he can't remember, he can't remember."

"Down, boy. I'm on your side, remember? I'm just saying we need more."

"Then I will find you more," Ito said with dead certainty.

Damien had no doubt that if anyone could prove Montana's innocence in the face of overwhelming evidence, it would be the man sitting beside him.

"Right now I'll settle for you finding Dakota. Montana needs him. Keep in touch."

Ito nodded to Damien and stood, interrupting Cal. Walking around the table and ignoring the fact that Montana still wore the blood of a dead girl, he waited for him to stand and pulled the man to him in a fierce embrace.

"I need to go see Doctor Dakota, you hang tight—hear?" Pulling back, Ito put his hands on Montana's shoulders and bent down slightly to look him in the eye. "We will get you out of this, understand?"

Montana shook his head. "Doesn't matter, she'll still be dead. Nothing will change that. Linney's dead, that's the one thing I can't seem to get around." He squeezed his eyes shut. "I can still see her, the look on her face right before she fell asleep in my arms." He opened his eyes again and begged Ito to answer him. "Why don't I remember? I should have been there for her, I should have protected her." Confusion made it through the exhaustion and gave his face a macabre look. "I slept while someone did *that* to her." He motioned to the pictures still lying on the table. "You get Dakota, you find out who did this, and then do me one last favor—you kill the bastard. But don't ask me to care about what happens after that."

"Montana." Ito shook his head. "I care what happens, Dakota cares, hell, even Cal cares, though I doubt he would admit that. Now you do *me* one favor. Do not give up on yourself. I know all you see is the dark right now, my friend, but I swear to you that the dawn is coming. All you have to do is hang on until the light finds a way to break through the night. Can you do that? Can you do that for all of us?"

Montana seemed to consider the request and turned to Damien. "I wasn't sure when they hauled me in, but I am now. I did not kill Linney. I don't particularly care if you can prove me innocent or not, but I do care if you find out who did this to her and why. I will help you any way I can to find that out. It's the best I can promise."

"I can work with that," Damien said. Turning to Cal, he made one request. "Can you keep him out of the general population? He helped put a lot of those guys where they are. I'm thinking they will not be grateful."

Cal shook his head. "I said I would do what I can. But this is out of my hands. He'll stay here until he's arraigned. Hopefully he'll swing bail."

"He'll make bail," Damien said with conviction. "He's not a flight risk."

"Going to be expensive," Cal said.

"He'll make bail," Damien said again.

The door opened, this time their thirty minutes was up. Two armed guards came in and cuffed Montana once more, ran a chain through the cuffs, pulled it around his waist, and locked it all together.

"Time to get cleaned up," one of the guards said, and glanced at Damien. "Wouldn't want to infringe on any rights, now would we?"

The second guard took his night-stick and pushed Montana in the back to get him moving. He wasn't expecting it, and with his ankles still shackled he would have tripped and fallen face-first if Cal hadn't been there to catch him.

Once he was sure Montana was on his feet, he turned on the guard. Cal grabbed the stick and whipped it across the back of the man's knees. He stepped away as the guard went down hard, and then lay on the ground moaning in pain.

"Son-of-a-bitch!" he yelled at Cal. "What the fuck was that for?"

"That was a warning." Cal pulled the man to his feet and smoothed his uniform down. "I know you'll be more careful about how you treat this prisoner in the future, won't you, Officer Griffin? Because if I hear even a rumor that he has been mistreated, whether it is true or not, you will not be a happy man, trust me on that."

Officer Griffin looked confused and more than a little pissed off. "You can't threaten me," he said, trying to reclaim his dignity.

"I think I just did." Cal looked down at the much smaller man. "Now, you will take this man to get cleaned up, and I will be listening to the rumors."

They watched as both officers helped Montana shuffle out the door. He never looked back.

When the door closed, Damien looked at Cal. "Is he safe?"

Cal shrugged. "I don't know, but Montana is more than capable of taking care of himself."

"Maybe," Damien agreed. "But the man who just left here does not in the least resemble the Montana Thomas I know."

Damien grabbed his briefcase and notes, left the briefing room, and for the first time in his career wondered exactly where the hell he was going to pull a miracle out of to save his friend not only from a murder charge, but from himself.

CHAPTER 4

Doctor Dakota Thomas watched the clear amber-colored liquid slowly drip into his veins. He wasn't sick, he wasn't hurt, he was simply doing his job.

"How you doing, Dakota?" The female voice came through the intercom into the sealed bio-chamber where Dakota lay surrounded by a medical staff in biohazard suits.

"So far so good, Maggs."

"Okay, just checking. Your temp is starting to spike, and your heart rate bumped up ten BPM in the last few seconds."

Dakota looked above him at the monitors displaying his vital signs. "Yeah, and it's probably going to get worse before it gets better. We expected that, didn't we?"

Maggie looked at Dakota through the glass wall separating them and tried to smile. "Yeah, but this makes me nervous. It's not like anyone has ever done this before, you know."

Dakota laughed. That wasn't exactly true. He had done this before, not under the same conditions, but he had been infected with a version of the avian influenza virus about two years ago and thanks to an infusion of a very special serum, he had survived. That infusion had left him with a unique immune system. One that seemed to fight off anything they threw at him.

As far as he knew, only one other person in the world had the same invincible immune system. Michael Ricco inadvertently saved his life, and now Ricco and he were repaying the debt they felt they owed society. Well, not exactly owed, not in Dakota's case anyway. More like compelled by guilt to comply with the government's less than subtle requests.

He'd quit his job as an ER physician in his little hometown of Caliente, Nevada, gave up every personal freedom imaginable, and moved across the country to Maryland to become nothing more than a glorified guinea pig for USAMRIID, the United States Army Medical Research Institute for Infectious Diseases.

It wasn't all that bad. In between raging fevers and puking his guts out, he got the warm fuzzy feeling of knowing he was helping humanity.

"Relax, Maggie." Dakota smiled and blew her a kiss through the window. However, the truth of the matter was that forty minutes into the infusion he wasn't feeling that great. He expected it, but he always hoped the next time would be different. It never was.

This time they'd infected him with a variant of the strain of the avian flu he'd already been exposed to, hoping he would have some sort of natural immunity against it. Nothing ever worked out like they thought it would.

"Dak, your temp just jumped to a hundred and three. I'm shutting it down." Maggie motioned to the medical staff inside with Dakota to disconnect him from the infusion.

Dakota shook his head and coughed. "Maggs, stop panicking. Look, shutting it down now won't make a bit of difference, you know that. Just give it time."

"I don't like it."

"You never do." Dakota closed his eyes as his vision blurred. He wished this wasn't familiar, but unfortunately he knew what came next. In the beginning it had taken a day or two for the symptoms to kick in, but the more they exposed him to, the quicker his immune system jumped into high gear. Now it took only minutes for the symptoms to appear, and when they did, they took him down hard.

The only thing that kept him doing this was the fact that they had nearly perfected a vaccine for the avian virus with his help; but seeing how viruses have a nasty habit of mutating and changing when you figure them out, Dakota figured he had great job security. Right now, though, his job pretty much sucked.

Before he could give any warning to the people surrounding him, his stomach clenched. Rolling to his side, Dakota puked on one of the medics in a biohazard suit, and then promptly passed out.

* * * *

Dakota opened his eyes, recognized the pale yellow walls of the hospital containment unit, and slowly took stock.

Dodged another bullet.

He smiled at the thought and stretched. They still had him hooked up to an IV and the monitor, but the numbers he saw told him he was stable.

"Hey."

Dakota turned toward the voice, realizing for the first time, he wasn't alone. He smiled at Michael Ricco sitting in an uncomfortable-looking chair next to his bed.

"Hey yourself. What'd you do, pull the short straw for babysitting duty?"

Ricco grinned, looking very young as he did so, even though Dakota knew better. Michael Ricco was a human anomaly. Somehow, through a series of inhuman experiments performed on him, the gene that controls aging had been turned off, or radically slowed down. At nearly one-hundred-and-thirteen-years old, he barely looked twenty.

"Volunteered," Ricco said. "Maggie was worried about you. You started seizing after you passed out, and they had a little trouble getting you stable."

Dakota waved off his concern. "Your wife worries too much," Dakota said, referring to Ricco's very new marriage.

"That she does," Ricco agreed. Ricco had spent most his life being a guinea pig; all that was required of him at USAMRIID was to give a little of his blood every now and then for development into a serum, the same serum that had saved Dakota's life two years ago. "I just made her go get some sleep, but that's not the only reason I'm here."

Dakota hitched himself up on his elbows and pushed the pillows behind his head. He narrowed his eyes at Ricco. "What's the other reason?" He wasn't sure he wanted to hear it. If they sent Ricco to bargain for them, it was guaranteed not to be something he liked.

"How you feeling?"

"Stop stalling, Ricco. What's up?"

"You have a visitor."

That got Dakota's attention. Visitors were not only discouraged, they were simply not allowed. Security was something the facility did not take lightly.

"Ito is here," Ricco explained.

It took Dakota all of two seconds to realize the implications of Ito St. James not only flying cross-country, but convincing the army to let him in, and none of them were good.

"What's happened?" he asked. "It's Montana, isn't it?"

Ricco locked eyes with Dakota and gave him a nod. "Yeah, it's Montana," he confirmed.

Dakota licked his lips and asked the question he dreaded. "Is he dead?"

"No, not dead. In jail."

Relief flooded through Dakota. "Jesus, Ricco! Don't do that to me. Montana's been in jail before. Jesus, what's all the drama for? Why is Ito here?"

"Dakota, he's been arrested for murder. Apparently, there was a girl…"

Dakota's mind went into search mode. A girl? There was always a girl where Montana was concerned. Then he remembered—Montana had called and told him about the woman he was seeing. He could tell from Montana's voice that this one was different.

"Linney?" he asked Ricco. "Linney's dead?"

"Yeah, I think that was her name. Montana's been charged with her murder. It doesn't look good. The evidence is pretty damning."

"I'm out of here." Dakota whipped the covers off, stood, and pulled the monitor leads off his chest, causing alarms to sound. He shut the monitor off, and then took a piece of gauze from a tray near his bed and pulled the IV catheter from his vein.

"Kind of thought you'd feel that way." Ricco reached under his chair, took a satchel he'd brought with him and placed it on the bed. "I took the liberty of packing for you. It wasn't easy, but arrangements have been made."

Dakota knew what it must have taken to have him released in the middle of research. "I owe you, Michael. Thanks."

Ricco shook his head. "No, you don't, just go and get Montana out of the mess he fell into, that's all I need. Tell him we're there for him, will you do that?"

"You know it."

Ricco stood. "Get dressed, you need to be cleared by medical first, but then you're as free as you get, considering the army owns your ass." He smiled and started for the door. "Ito is waiting with a plane to take you back to Nevada."

Dakota couldn't help but smile. Despite the reason that precipitated it, he was going back. After everything, he still considered Nevada home. Ito was waiting for him and he was going *home*.

* * * *

Medical didn't want to clear him. He still ran a low-grade fever and his lungs sounded congested. Dakota didn't care, he knew by the time he landed in Nevada he would be fine.

"Clear me and let me go, or you can forget about any further cooperation from me as far as this program is concerned," he said, pulling his shirt back on and buttoning it up.

Maggie pushed off the counter she leaned against and walked toward Dakota. "I can't allow you to be jeopardized," she said.

"No, you can't allow this program to be jeopardized and without me and Ricco, there is no program. So either plan on pumping dear hubby full of the shit you've been filling me with or you can kiss your nice cushy job bye-bye."

"You know I won't do that," she said. "Don't you think he's been through enough?"

"I'm leaving, Maggie, clearance or no. You can't stop me." Dakota walked to the door and pulled on the handle, only to find it locked. He turned to Maggie, confused and angry.

"Actually, we can," she said.

"You promised me when we started this whole thing, I could leave any time."

"As long as it was safe for you to do so, right now it's not." Maggie ran a hand through her thick, dark hair and let out a frustrated breath. "Dakota, you're a physician, for God's sake. Just stop and think for one minute. Less than six hours ago, you were infected with an extremely contagious agent. Can you, in good conscience, expose yourself to the general public knowing you could be a threat?"

Dakota looked at Maggie, free of any mask or protective clothing. "Doesn't seem to bother you any to be exposed to me."

"I'm not the one getting on a plane with a hundred other people. Look, I'm not saying you can't leave, I'm only asking you to give us some time. A couple days just to make sure your immune system has a handle on this virus."

"You know as well as I do that by the time that plane lands in Nevada, I'll be fine," Dakota argued.

"No, I don't know that and neither do you. Whatever Michael's serum did to you, it's not predictable. Sometimes you bounce right back, other times, it takes weeks for the symptoms to even show themselves, and let's not forget the time your own system attacked itself. You almost died, Dakota, and would have if not for Michael and his serum. We have nothing but unknowns here. I cannot in good faith let that loose on the general population. Can you?"

"You're asking me to abandon my brother," Dakota said.

"All I'm asking for is some time. I talked to Ito, Montana's not going anywhere. They haven't even arraigned him yet. One day is not going to matter in the grand scheme of things."

"It might." Dakota walked away from the door and sat back on the exam table. She was right. God, he hated it, but she was right. "Don't take this the wrong way, but fuck you, Maggie." Dakota wiped a thin sheen of sweat off his face with the back of one hand and looked up at her, defeated.

Maggie smiled. "I will expect a full apology for that when you get clearance."

"One day?" Dakota asked.

"Don't pin me down on this. Most likely one day, but it depends on you." Turning back to the medics who had examined Dakota, Maggie gave them instructions. "Take him back to medical. I want him monitored and labs drawn every two hours. Let me know any changes, understood?"

They nodded, and Maggie hit a button on the console behind her, unlocking the door. The medics began ushering Dakota away, when he turned back to face her.

"I want to see Ito. Can you do that for me at least?" he asked, his eyes all but pleading with her.

She looked at him for a moment, and then nodded. "Yeah, I can do that."

"Thanks, Maggie."

"And I'll see what information I can find out for you concerning Montana."

"I'd appreciate that."

"He saved my husband's life. He gave him a chance to be a human being again instead of somebody's lab rat. I owe him more than you know. If this facility can help, I'll do everything in my power to do so."

"Spoken like a true bureaucrat," Dakota said, but he smiled just the same. He left with the medics and tried to convince himself that Maggie would hold up her end of the deal when the time came.

CHAPTER 5

Montana tried to ignore the two armed guards who pointed loaded weapons at him as he showered. He was given nothing remotely resembling privacy. He knew that was one privilege he would not have for a long time to come. They had him strip, took his clothes, and watched as he washed Linney's blood off his body.

His movements slow and methodical, he took the soap they gave him and scrubbed until it hurt. He scrubbed until the water ran clear and the last of Linney he would ever touch swirled down the drain.

He shut the water off, caught the threadbare towel they threw at him and dried off as best he could. After wrapping the soaked piece of cloth around his waist, Montana waited for the guards to direct him.

"This way, lover boy," guard number one told him and gave him a nudge with the gun. Out of reflex, Montana caught the barrel of the rifle and pushed it away.

Guard number two took the opportunity to bring his baton down hard on the back of Montana's neck. Montana collapsed, with guard number one's foot on his head and the barrel of the rifle in his ear. "Give me a reason," he said.

Montana didn't.

They hauled him to his feet and pushed him forward.

Montana stumbled, but they kept him standing. Somewhere along the way, they gave him a bright orange jumpsuit and soft slipper-like shoes with no laces. He offered them no resistance, he just kept moving in the direction they steered him. With one final push, they let go and Montana heard the clang of steel on steel as the cell door shut closed behind him.

He clutched the clothes to his chest, sat down on the narrow cot that served as a bed, and focused. His new home measured approximately twelve feet by eight feet and consisted of the cot, a sink and a toilet. He knew what he had to do and was a little surprised at the ease in doing it. He took everything that had happened in the last few hours, closed his eyes, and shoved it all down inside of him. He buried it into the deepest recesses and let his demons watch over the feelings for the time being. He could not afford to feel yet. Feeling things here could cost him his life.

He opened his eyes and slipped on the veil of someone he used to be, someone he thought he would never have to be again. The stranger's face was disturbingly comfortable. He scanned his surroundings and stood. He dropped the towel and ignored the taunts and catcalls from the cells opposite his. Taking no care to hide himself in the shadows, he dressed.

Nothing but the present existed for him. Montana felt centered, more in control than only moments ago. He lay down on the thin substitute for a mattress and gave his body what it demanded: sleep. He was exhausted beyond measure, he knew that. Without sleep, he would make mistakes, and that was not an option. He crossed his arms over his chest, and out of necessity and demand, his mind shut down and he slept.

Too bad his subconscious couldn't give a rat's ass about control. Or that it amused his demons to torment him when he was defenseless against the assault.

He didn't want to think about Linney, but his thoughts wouldn't leave him alone. What started out as intrusion of memories turned into dreams. Just on this side of sleep, Montana's mind played back to the first time he met her, then as dreams morphed from reality, to the last time he remembered being with her.

* * * *

Keys and coat in hand, he closed the door behind him and was about to lock up for the evening when she came running around the corner.

"Oh, no! No, no, no, you can't leave. I sat out in my car for the last two hours, working up the nerve to come in here. If you leave now, I'm not sure I'll ever be this brave again." The words came out in a rush with barely a breath between them.

He suppressed a smile and looked down at her. He couldn't help but look down at her. She stood all of five feet-three and looked up at his face with quiet desperation. No tears, he had to give her credit for that.

"And what exactly is it you needed to work up your courage for?" he asked her.

She took a breath and told him. "I want to hire you. Montana Thomas, right? Big Sky Detective Agency?" She held out a page ripped from the phone book showing his ad.

"I am." He gave her a smile then. "And you are?"

"Oh! I'm Lindsay Keller. Linney. Everyone calls me Linney." She held a hand out to shake his, then remembered she was holding the ad and went to shove it back in her coat pocket. In the process her purse slipped off her shoulder. As she attempted to catch it she dropped her keys, tried to grab them and ended up tipping her purse over. It landed upside-down on the ground next to her feet.

The tears did come then.

"God, what a klutz," she admonished herself as she shoved things back in her purse. Montana heard the catch in her voice and bent down to help her.

"I'm sorry," she said. Giving up the mess on the floor, she just sat there with her head bowed, her honey-blond hair obscuring her face. "I'm such a mess. I'm usually a lot more put together than this, please believe me."

He pushed her hair out of her face to see her better. "Hey, it's okay. Why don't you come in and we can talk."

"You were leaving." She picked her things up and shoved them carelessly back into her purse, suddenly angry. Montana couldn't decide who she was angrier at, him or herself.

He stood and helped her to her feet. "I wasn't going anywhere special." He shrugged, took his keys, unlocked the office door, and motioned her inside. She hesitated for a second, as if weighing her options, then walked through the door and sat in the chair opposite the big oak desk that dominated the room.

He slowly closed the door and took his time walking around to sit at the desk. Even in the dim light of the hallway, he had seen the bruises. They were artfully concealed with makeup, but he had seen them nonetheless.

"What can I do for you, Ms. Keller?" Montana asked, steepling his hands and looking at her over his fingertips.

"Linney, please, it's Linney." She gave him a smile, shy all of a sudden.

"Okay, Linney. What has you working up your nerve for two hours? Why do you want to hire me?"

"All right, but just listen, because if you start asking questions I don't think I can do this. Let me get it all out, and then you can ask anything you want."

"Fair enough." He spread his hands, giving her the go-ahead, sat back and waited.

"I read about you—you and your partner. You used to be Army Rangers, so I thought you would be able to handle Stone."

"Stone?"

She rolled her eyes, reminding him of her request.

"Stone," she repeated. "Stone Kale, my boyfriend. I won't go into all the ugly little details. I'm sure you've heard the same story a hundred times, how things were so great in the beginning, and then turned ugly."

She sighed and bowed her head. Montana was certain when she raised it again to look at him there would be tears in her eyes, but he was wrong. Her eyes were dry, if anything they were hostile, but the hostility wasn't aimed at him.

"I need your help, Mr. Thomas. I want to hire you to help me prove that Stone hurts me, that he lets his so-called friends hurt me—rape me."

Montana kept what he felt out of his eyes and off his face. "Sounds more like a job for the police than a private investigator, Ms. Keller."

She shook her head in frustration. "Don't you think I've tried that route? God! Why do you think I'm here? The police can't help me. They say I have no proof. I have filed PFAs and documented everything he does, but Stone has connections—and not legal ones, if you get my drift. He's in commerce, technically, but he makes his real money in drugs. He makes a fortune importing and exporting them overseas. I didn't know that when I met him. By the time I found out, it was too late. He already owned me."

Montana wanted to break the bastard's face.

"Just so I'm clear on this. Your boyfriend, who happens to be a drug runner, beats you and gives you to his buddies for their entertainment purposes, and the police can't help you and you want me to get proof so you can do what? Press charges?"

She narrowed her eyes at Montana and stood abruptly. "I knew this was a mistake. Sorry to have bothered you, Mr. Thomas."

Montana moved quickly, getting to the door before her. Placing a hand on it, he prevented her from opening it.

"I didn't say I wouldn't help you. I'm just trying to understand, why me, why now?"

She turned her face up to his, her eyes flat and emotionless. "Because, Mr. Thomas, if I can't find someone to help me, one of two things is going to happen in the very near future. One is I will kill the bastard before he touches me again."

"And two?" Montana asked.

"He will kill me before I get the chance. Neither one of those scenarios particularly appeals to me."

Montana saw the truth behind her words. He knew how the police operated. He could practically hear the words they told her, and if this Stone was as connected as she suggested, the second picture she painted for him was the most likely.

"Don't leave," he said. "I want to hear more."

"Does that mean you'll help me?"

"It means I want to hear more, and then yes, I'll help you."

The look of relief on her face practically melted him.

* * * *

The images in his head speeded up, giving him little vignettes of their relationship. The first time he had the nerve to ask her out to dinner, she didn't think he was serious, and then when she did, she wanted to know why. She told him he was too pretty to date.

The way she made little noises in her throat when he kissed her. The way she felt beneath him, the way they fit together so perfectly. Her smell, her shape, everything about her was as if she had been created just for him.

He could see her smiling up at him as they made love, he reached out to brush the hair from her eyes and left a red streak across her face. He looked at his hand, and saw it covered in blood.

He jumped off her and away from the bed they had shared. Linney lay in a pool of her own blood, and Montana found a gore-covered knife gripped tightly in his fist.

Memory turned to confusion, dream to nightmare. Sleep to sudden, abrupt awakening.

Clarity took a moment in coming. Lying perfectly still, trying to get his breathing under control, Montana searched for some point of reference. His brain finally came back online as he took in the bars and sparse surroundings. He willed the still vivid images of Linney, both dead and alive, down to a place where he would deal with them later. He wiped sweat off his face and realized his hands were shaking.

"What's the matter, sweet thang, have a bad dream?"

Montana sat up slowly. The inmate in the cell directly across from his sat on his bunk and smiled at Montana. The grin reminded him of something slimy and cold.

Montana kept his face neutral as he stared at the man. "As a matter of fact, I did. I believe your mama was in it."

The man didn't take the bait. He just laughed. "Well, if that's true I'd be sweating too. My mama was a fucking bitch." The man stood and walked as far as the bars allowed. "I know who you are, bad ass PI. Fucking Army Ranger. Don't mean shit in here. You're fresh meat on a bun, Montana Thomas."

Montana stared at the man, trying to determine if he recognized him. "Do I know you?"

The guy wasn't tall, maybe five-ten, but he was pushing two-hundred pounds. Thick dark hair framed a broad face that spoke of Hispanic origins. The dull eyes and moronic grin suggested the shallow end of the gene pool.

"Doesn't matter, I know you. Can't wait to see you without bars in the way." He walked back to his bunk. Montana heard him laugh quietly. "Sweet dreams, pretty boy."

That got Montana's attention. He stood and walked to the bars.

"You know something," he said, holding onto the cold steel

separating them. He clenched the metal until his hands hurt.

"I know lots of things," the man returned.

"What's your name?"

"Jose, what's it to you?"

Montana thought and came up with nothing. "I don't know any Jose."

Jose chuckled softly under his breath. "Like I said, man, I know you."

Montana started walking back from the bars when Jose spoke again. "Hey, tell me something, was she worth it? I mean, I know she was a good lay and all, but was she worth spending the rest of your life in here for?"

Montana whirled and charged the man only to be brought up short by the bars of his cell. Jose only laughed harder at Montana's frustration and rage.

"Tell me what you know," Montana demanded in a low, lethal voice.

The other man laughed louder. "I don't know a damn thing—pretty boy."

Montana turned the rage inward. It took every ounce of self-control he had, but he let go of the bars and took a step away. He realized that Jose wanted him to lose it, that was the whole point, and he would be damned if he'd give the man the satisfaction.

"Fine," Montana said in a low, controlled voice. "But I'm making you a promise. I find out you do know something—anything—about who killed Linney, and you're a dead man. Remember that, because I sure as hell will."

That stopped the laughter coming from across the isle-way. Montana returned to his cot and lay down with too many thoughts filling his head. Pieces of the puzzle were beginning to fall into place, but huge parts were still missing. How could he not remember what happened? How could he possibly not remember that? It ate at him like a cancer.

Who wanted Linney dead? That was easy. Stone Kale. Montana had that much figured out. The only problem was Linney's apartment showed no sign of a break-in. The only prints found, or so he was told, were his and Linney's. The murder weapon was a butcher knife taken from her kitchen, and again his were the only prints.

Why couldn't he remember? Every time he tried to get a handle on this, it was the one question that kept rearing its ugly little head.

Did he kill her?

No. He had nightmares, violent ones, but he had never acted out in any of them.

Always a first time.

No!

God, the doubt kept coming at him, making him question things he'd always held firmly to. Could the demons he'd fought with nearly all his life have snuck out while he slept?

He squeezed his eyes shut, refusing to accept even the possibility. He wouldn't be able to live with himself if it turned out to be true.

He shouldn't have been tired, but sleep came and took him just the same. There was little else to do until Damien came back. It was either sleep or question the very core of who he always thought he was.

Sleep chose to have pity on him and left him dreamless this time.

CHAPTER 6

Dakota was in what he called his twilight state, somewhere between awake and asleep. His fever had returned a few hours ago, and he was deep within its grasp. He was also pissed as hell.

The night shift had taken over, only one medic watching the monitors. Usually they let him sleep as much as possible during the night if he was stable. The medic's constant visits told him otherwise. His head hurt and his thinking fuzzed with fever, so he just closed his eyes and let them do what they had to. They rarely spoke to him, so the small slap on his face caught him by surprise and got his attention.

"Doctor Dakota."

He felt a weight of no small significance settle on the bed beside him, and he turned his head toward the voice. He blinked his eyes into focus, certain he must be delirious.

"Ito?"

The big man next to him laughed, the sound deep and rumbling, but also warm and filled with welcomed memories. "It is indeed." Ito's hands touched Dakota's face, his brow creased in concern. "I know you're not in the best of shape to be asking this, but time is short, my friend. I can get you out of here, but we need to move now. I need to know if you're up to coming with me, or if you'd rather stay and let these good people do their job and take care of you."

"Ito, we need to hurry," another voice said.

Dakota saw Ricco standing at the doorway.

"What? How?" Dakota ran a hand over his eyes and sat up with a little difficulty. "You can take me to Montana?"

"Dakota." Ricco came and knelt next to Dakota's bed. "I have Maggie's pass, I can get you out of here no questions asked, but we have to move now before she realizes what I'm doing. There's a car waiting at the gate to take you and Ito to a plane. If you want out of here, go now. If not, Ito will stay and wait until medical gives you clearance, but I heard them talking. They'll think of something to keep you here—count on it. They're not about to let you out of their sight, let alone get on a plane unsupervised."

Dakota felt the words as a physical slap, but he supposed he always knew, at some level, he had sold his soul to the devil.

"Michael, you could get into some very hot water when they find out what you've done," Dakota said.

Ricco shrugged and stood, shoving his hands deep into his front pockets. "What are they going to do to me?"

"Why, Michael? Why do this for me? It could hurt things between you and Maggie."

"Because I know what it's like to be kept from family, to be denied simple human freedom. You gave me mine back, now I have a chance to repay that debt to some extent. Montana needs you, I can get you to him—if you want it."

"The medics?" Dakota asked.

"Taken care of, everything is taken care of, but you need to come with us now," Ito told him.

Dakota nodded, swung his legs off the side of the bed, and immediately fell into Ito's arms as dizziness overcame him.

"Are you sure he's all right to travel?" Ito looked over his shoulder at Ricco.

"No, I'm not sure of anything, except we are running out of time.

He doesn't react to things the same way I do. Sometimes he gets really bad, and then the next hour he's fine."

Ito pushed Dakota back on the side of the bed and kept him at arm's length to better look at him. "Maybe this isn't such a good idea," he said.

Dakota pushed sweat-dampened hair out of his eyes and shook his head. "No way, I'm out of here."

"Then we are gone," Ito said, and turned his head to talk to Ricco. "You can still come with us."

Ricco looked down and smiled. "I belong here," he said simply. He held out his hand to Ito. "Here's Maggie's pass. Give it to the guards. They won't question you. I have a change of clothes and some other things you might need in the car."

After helping Dakota stand, Ito reached for the blanket on the bed and wrapped it around the other man's shoulders. Dakota leaned heavily on Ito, but he kept up with the taller man's pace. They met no resistance as they passed the control desk. Dakota had no idea what magic Ricco must had done to accomplish that feat, but he had a feeling the other man was going to pay dearly for it. A part of him felt bad about the trouble he might be causing, but then a memory of what he had gone through to secure Michael Ricco's freedom crossed his mind. He looked at the still vivid scar running the length of his left arm, and that guilt eased up a bit.

"Ricco said he packed some clothes, right?" Dakota asked hopefully.

Ito looked down and realized that not only was Dakota barefoot but besides the blanket all he wore was a thin pair of surgical scrubs, the lead wires that had hooked him up to the monitors still attached, sprouting out of the top of his shirt like wild chest hair.

"I do hope so," Ito said with a smile.

Dakota gave him a nod and concentrated on putting one foot in front of the other. As much as he wanted to be with Montana, hell, just talk to him, the timing could not have been worse.

Ricco was right when he said Dakota didn't respond to things the same way he did. When Ricco had been exposed to an antigen, his body seemed to eradicate it before it got a foothold. He rarely felt sick, but his blood chemistry told a different story. From the records the government had managed to retrieve from the General's abandoned sites, Ricco's immune system attacked any foreign substance as if his life depended on it. The invader wiped out before a normal immune system even knew there was anything wrong. Ricco never felt anything.

The same could not be said of Dakota. Probably because Dakota acquired his immunity through Ricco, or more aptly through a serum made from Ricco's blood. Dakota felt everything. They thought Dakota's immune system, while still amazing, was not nearly as developed as Ricco's. But then Ricco had nearly ninety years to develop his, Dakota only had two. It always looked as if the causative agent would win and Dakota would lose. It was extremely dicey to watch, but he always managed to pull one out of somewhere. His immune system would rev up into overdrive in the ninth hour and he ended up stronger than he started out, but it was hell to get there.

With his immunity complete against the agent he was originally infected with, the powers that be decided to push their luck, not to mention Dakota's, and expose him to a mutated specimen of the same virus to see what his immune system did with it.

What it did, from what Dakota could gather, was scare the hell out of Maggie and the rest of the medical department. Not only did Dakota start seizing with out-of-control fevers, but his lungs filled up with fluid. As they were getting ready to put him on full life support, his body finally decided to respond. Unfortunately the virus was not through with Dakota yet. Delirium, wracking pain, chills and cyclical fevers still plagued him almost twenty-four hours out. Dakota wasn't up to an adventure at the moment. Too bad one was ready for him.

Timing never was one of Dakota's strong suites.

"You doing okay, Doc?" Ito asked.

"Just get me to the car," Dakota said. It was not going to be a fun night.

They reached the last checkpoint and Dakota could see the dark blue government-issued sedan sitting outside the glass doors. All that stood between them and relative freedom was a bored guard who suddenly decided to take an overzealous interest in protocol.

"I thought you were supposed to be in medical, Doctor Thomas?" he said, scrutinizing the pass Ito had given him.

"Do you make it a habit to question your superior's orders, son?" Ito asked.

Dakota watched in admiration as Ito put an irritated look on his face and snatched back the security pass from the guard.

"No, sir," the guard replied uncertainly. "Not usually."

"Then either let us through or call the director herself at this hour and question her orders. Go ahead." Ito picked up the phone and handed it to the guard. "This is one conversation I would love to overhear."

Panic came and went again in a fleeting moment across the guard's face. He took the phone from Ito, placed it back in the cradle, and pushed a button on his console to unlock the glass doors.

"No, sir," he said. "That won't be necessary."

"Smart boy." Ito glared at the man and put an arm around Dakota, nearly dragging him through the doorway.

"Damn, you're good." Dakota grinned. "I mean it, I would have pissed myself if I were that guard with you in my face."

"Just keep moving, Doc." Ito's grip tightened on Dakota's arm. It was the only outward sign of nerves Dakota could detect from him. "We aren't home free yet."

As they reached the doors, Dakota looked up and saw the guard through the reflection in the glass. The man had decided to go with his gut. Dakota watched him pick up the phone and push a single button. He turned to Ito, who had been watching as well.

"Move," Ito told him. He pushed the door open a second before the guard automatically locked it from where he sat, the phone still cradled between his shoulder and ear. Ito all but carried Dakota to the waiting car.

Dakota risked a glance over his shoulder and saw the guard pull a gun from the holster at his hip.

"Uh oh," Dakota said.

"Get in," Ito said, pushing him toward the passenger side. Dakota hoped like hell the car was unlocked.

They had about three seconds on the guard; it was all they needed, barely.

"Stop, hold it right there!" the guard yelled from behind them. Dakota opened the door and threw himself inside just as Ito put the car in gear and tore out of the parking lot with the passenger door still ajar. It slammed shut as Ito rounded a corner with tires squealing.

"Guess you weren't that intimidating after all." Dakota looked in the side mirror as the guard took a stance and squeezed off several shots in their direction. He knew the man wasn't trying to hurt them, only disable the car. One or two rounds hit the back panel with a muffled *thud*, but Ito had put enough distance between them and the compound that the guard had little chance of hitting anything of vital importance.

"Damn it! I was hoping we would have a bit more time," Ito said. Once they got on the main road, he slowed their speed so they wouldn't attract unwanted attention. "We expected they would find out sooner or later. I was kind of hoping for later."

"Yeah, well, it's me. Count on nothing ever turning out the way you would expect it to." Dakota slowly hitched himself up until he was sitting straight in the seat. The adrenaline in his system let him forget how lousy he felt for the moment.

Ito laughed. "Never fear, Doctor Dakota, there is always a backup plan. My car is in the woods a few miles from here. I took a taxi to the base. No one knows what my vehicle looks like, and it isn't registered under my name. They'll be looking for this car, not the one we'll be in. All we have to do is blend in until we get there."

Dakota considered that. "A non-descript, four-door, dark blue sedan with government-issued plates and fresh bullet holes in the trunk. Yeah, we'll blend right in with the woodwork."

Ito kept his thoughts to himself and Dakota let him. He tried to keep his eyes off the side mirror, but found it impossible. After a few minutes he realized he wouldn't be able to spot a tail if one was on their ass and left it up to Ito to get him out of this.

"You know, even if we do manage to get back on the road without them trailing us, they know where we're going. I don't want to get you in trouble, Ito. You have your license to think about, and you need to be there for Montana if they won't let me be."

Ito gave him a sideways glance before looking back at the road. "You listen to me, Dakota. They do not own you. I think you forgot that somewhere along the way. You do what you do for them out of compassion and they use it. You are not property to be manipulated. Yes, they know where we're going, and I ask you, what will they do when they find us there?"

Dakota gave Ito a confused look. It had been such a long time since he'd thought of his own personal life that he forgot he had one.

"They can't dictate where you go and what you do. Not in the face of the local police. They fear the world finding out their dirty little secret more than they fear you leaving. When it all comes right down to it, they're not that different from the man who held Ricco all those years. They like to think they are and hide behind their fancy facility and so-called humane treatment of you and Ricco, but look what happened when you pushed them just a little."

Dakota considered Ito's words and a part of him couldn't help but agree. Even Ricco told him the program was not likely to let him go. But the other part, the part that despite the hell he went through every time they put that needle in his arm, was fascinated by what they had achieved with his help. Who knew what they could do in the future? Dakota knew he was doing great things, things that would make a real difference to the way people lived their lives. As a physician, all he could do was fight the ravages of disease and injury, flailing impotently in a war he would never win. As a medical guinea pig, he had a real chance of eradicating the littlest killers and making a difference in his lifetime. The promise of doing that was what kept him doing this. It was his choice, he had to believe that. They were not just using him.

Then an image of the guard drawing his gun and firing on him, supposedly at Maggie's orders, came to mind and he knew Ito was right. Despite Dakota's reasons for doing what he did, the government had their own agenda. Dakota was only a means to an end for them. He would be deluding himself if he thought any differently.

"I know," Dakota said. "But it was my choice. It might have evolved since this all started, but it was always my choice. They have their reasons and so do I, so I guess we both have hidden agendas."

Leaning his head back against the seat, Dakota sighed and ran a hand over his eyes. The adrenaline faded and exhaustion weighed heavily on him.

"Do one thing for me, Ito, just one thing. Get me to Montana. Let me see him, he needs to know I'm there for him. What happens after that will happen. Neither one of us can stop that. It's bigger than you know. Get me to Montana, then you get him out."

"I can get you out too," Ito said, still looking at the road.

Dakota took a deep breath and for a moment was tempted to let him try. "It's okay, man. They might not be going about it for all the right reasons, but it's the results that matter in the end and I want to be a part of it. Can you understand that?"

"If it's what you want, I'll try," Ito said, but his voice told Dakota differently. Ito most definitely did not understand.

That might end up being a problem, but Dakota didn't have the energy to deal with it. Feeling the last final push of the virus still alive inside him, he knew he had no choice. For about the next five or six hours, he would have to trust Ito to keep him safe because nothing Dakota did was going to change the fact that a part of him could never go back to who and what he was. That was the part Ito would never understand. Dakota had come to accept that he had changed; at the moment it was not only inconvenient but also felt like shit. That was the part he could live without. Too bad he couldn't pick and choose what he wanted to keep and what he wanted to pitch.

Sometimes it was the choices you didn't make that were the truly important ones.

CHAPTER 7

"You stole from me, Michael. That is a betrayal of trust I'm not sure I can get over." Maggie paced in front of her husband.

Michael sat on the end of the bed and simply watched her. He knew she needed to get the rant out of her system. When she did, he would explain himself. Until then, anything he said would be a waste of breath.

"I mean it's bad enough that you involved a civilian in this, but you *know* what we are in the middle of. Keeping him here was to protect him, not punish him! God, Michael, you of all people should understand that, and then to go through my things while I slept…" Maggie shook her head as the words trailed off. "I just can't believe you did that." Running her hands through her hair, she kicked off her shoes and moved to sit next to him on the bed.

"Maggs." Michael tried to take her hand but Maggie kept them clasped firmly in her lap, her eyes focused somewhere ahead of her, anywhere but on her husband. "I'm sorry," he said, and he was, but for the trouble he caused her, not for helping Dakota get out. "But be careful if you want to bring up issues of trust."

That got Maggie's attention and brought her eyes to Michael's face. "What are you talking about?"

"I was there two years ago. I was standing right next to you when you promised Dakota that he could leave anytime for any reason. As I remember, that promise didn't have conditions on it."

"Oh, come on, Michael! I know you are not that naive, so don't for one second try to pull the innocent farm-boy routine on me. I know better. Dakota knew what he was doing when he signed on. He understood the implications of going through with the research, the importance of it!" Maggie jumped off the bed and paced again in front of Michael. Her Irish heritage showing itself in the quick-fire temper she tried so hard to keep under wraps most of the time.

So caught up in her tirade and so certain that Michael was to blame for the mess she was in with her superiors, she failed to notice that her husband had suddenly gone pale. Sweat beaded on his forehead. An aching twinge that had started earlier that day down his left arm became more than an annoying inconvenience and blossomed into real discomfort.

Michael Ricco was no stranger to pain; he had lived most of his life with it as a constant companion. The last two years, however, showed him nothing but a peace he thought he'd never know again. Michael Ricco had achieved something he thought beyond his reach—happiness. Maggie had given him that, she reminded him of the good things in life, the things he had forgotten.

When the pain had started that morning, it caused him little concern. He ignored it and went about his day. When Maggie learned what he had done and hauled him into their private quarters, it got worse. He did his best to try to ignore it now, but it was getting difficult to do so.

"He took you at your word, Maggie. You know that. You're deluding yourself if you believe otherwise." Michael's right hand went to his left shoulder and tried to ease the ache there, but it had now spread across his chest, the pressure making it difficult to breathe.

"He's a grown man," Maggie continued.

Michael suppressed a groan as he answered. "A grown man who still believes in the truth despite what he thinks. He's an idealist, you know that, you counted on that. Now here you are, treating him no better than the General treated me—like a specimen, not a person. It's the one thing he feared most. I couldn't let that happen, don't you see?"

His chest felt as if a vise had been placed around it, the pressure nearly unbearable, even for him. This time the groan could not be contained. Michael winced and would have pitched forward off the edge of the bed if not for Maggie. Annoyance and anger turned to concern and fear in an instant.

"Michael, what is it?" Her hands went to his face as he fought for the breath to tell her.

He wanted to say it was nothing, but he knew it would be a lie. He felt it deep inside of him, as if all the years he had cheated death had suddenly caught up with him in an instant.

Michael caught her hands and looked at her. "Let Dakota go, Maggie. He'll come back when he can. Trust that."

"Just be quiet," she told him. She pushed him back until he was lying on the bed, then moved to her desk and picked up the phone.

"This is Maggie Riley. I need medical in my quarters, stat," she said, managing to keep her voice steady. "It's my husband, it's Michael." Her voice broke, and he saw the tears stream down her face, the emotions he knew she tried to keep in check finally overwhelming her.

He watched her with a detached giddiness he knew had no place here. His life with her was good, and he had no desire to leave it. But sometimes he grew tired of the days that stretched out before him. Despite everything that had happened to him, he still believed in God. He knew his family waited for him in heaven and he very much wanted to see them again. A part of him wanted that very badly, but when he saw the tears in Maggie's eyes he realized how selfish his wishes were. He also realized how little he had to say on the matter of whether he lived or finally died.

He tried to concentrate past the crushing pain, and grabbed his wife's hand to make sure he had her attention.

"I love you, Maggs," he told her right before the world tunneled to nothing more than a narrow beam of light, then blinked out in an instant, leaving him free of the pain but balancing precariously on the edge of life itself.

* * * *

Despite Damien's considerable arguments that Montana was not a flight risk, and a respectable citizen who had fought to put criminals behind bars, the judge denied bail and threatened Damien with contempt if he uttered one more word.

Damien, furious from the unbelievable injustice handed out to Montana, held his tongue. He would be no use to Montana behind bars with him, and he had no doubt that the judge would do exactly that and slap him with a contempt charge if he so much as sneezed in his courtroom.

"Something is wrong here," Damien whispered to Montana as the guards came to cuff his wrists and take him back to the federal lock-up which would be his home while he awaited trial. "There is no reason for you to be denied bail. Something is wrong."

Montana said nothing. He allowed the guards to lead him away without any emotion or even a glance at Damien.

"Keep your eyes open," Damien told him. "This does not feel right to me."

He watched Montana disappear through the courtroom door and knew exactly where he needed to start looking. There were pieces missing to the puzzle.

Normally Damien liked puzzles. They were methodical and logical, just like him. All the edge pieces forming a neat border, patterns and colors matching up, the pieces meshing together. Individually, the pieces meant nothing, an insensible jumble, but in the right order, with a little time and patience, a perfect picture emerged. It was a thing of beauty.

This puzzle was anything but logical. He couldn't even seem to get the boundaries together. He knew why: he had started in the middle, with Montana and the girl. He needed to take a step back and look beyond them. Damien needed to look at Lindsay Keller's life with Harry AKA "Stone" Kale, and see where it led him. He had a feeling his boundaries were all about to come together.

Damien walked out to his rental car, got in and punched a number on his cellphone. Ito answered on the second ring.

"How are things on your end?" he asked without benefit of a greeting. "Did you find Dakota?"

"That I did."

"Any problems?"

Ito laughed softly. "Depends on what you mean by problems."

"Don't play with me, Ito. It hasn't been a good day. They denied bail."

Damien heard Ito sigh on the other end of the line. "Well, then I guess you don't want to hear that the government is very possessive of their new toy."

"I thought you said you had Dakota?"

"I did. I do. I didn't say they let him go willingly."

"Jesus fricking Christ, Ito! I do not need this type of complication."

"It's yours free of charge."

"You forget I do not have a sense of humor," Damien told him.

"I wasn't being funny. It's all right, I have it under control."

"Where are you now?"

"On the interstate on the way to the airport. Arrangements have been made."

"I thought they didn't want to let him go?" Damien asked, confused.

"We had some help. It's a private flight, not impossible to follow but it should buy us some time. Can you pick us up at Alamo landing field? I'll call you when we get there."

Damien sighed, not at all happy about what Ito was telling him. It had all spiraled out of his control. "Yeah, sure. I have some things to do, but I'll wait for your call. I'll see about getting Dakota in to see Montana."

"You might want to wait on that. The doc is a little under the weather right now."

"Ito, you are not making me smile, here."

"Sorry, but it is what it is. I'll call you."

The line disconnected and Damien stared at the phone, trying to decide what he needed to do first.

Linney Keller, she was the key to all of this. He needed to get to know her almost as intimately as Montana. Ito had given Damien the key to their agency, and he knew it was the perfect place to begin his search. It was where Montana had first met the woman. Knowing Montana as he did, Damien was certain that the man had done a very detailed search before even agreeing to take her on as a client.

Damien pulled up in front of the stylish three-story brick office building. He had never seen Montana's and Ito's place of business. There had never been the need before. Fumbling for the right key, Damien opened the front door and had no problem finding the office among the half-dozen or so other businesses that shared the space with them.

Big Sky Investigations announced its presence with a beautifully embossed wooden plaque outside the door. Done in several different types of wood, the artist had managed to capture the majesty, beauty and vastness that embodied the spirit of the state of Montana. It depicted the simple skyline of the Rocky Mountains shown in silhouette against a setting sun. The name of the agency also was the logo for the state. Big sky country. Nothing could describe it better. Montana has a lot of sky, a lot of land, and very few people per square acre. The people who lived there liked it that way. Not exactly

Damien's taste, but it suited Montana perfectly. The man craved space and seclusion almost as strongly as Damien craved the fast-paced life in Denver. He never understood why Montana chose to leave a well-paying job for something as unconventional as private investigation.

Despite their years of friendship, Damien realized there was quite a lot about Montana Thomas he did not understand. He had remained an enigma, sharing precious little with anyone. It didn't help the situation he found himself in now.

He let himself inside and immediately felt his friend's presence. Everything was in complete order. A calming palette of light grays and a combination of different hues of blue greeted him. He knew Montana had chosen the color scheme. It was an exact duplicate of his old office in Denver.

He located the filing cabinets and was a little surprised at the amount of clients listed. Thanks to Montana's meticulous sense of order, he found the file on Lindsay Ann Keller within minutes. He spread the thin folder out on the large oak desk dominating the room, sat behind it, and began to read.

Lindsay Keller was twenty-six years old, born December second, nineteen-eighty-four, the only child of Barbara and John Keller from Lubbock, Texas, both deceased. Not a very lucky family line.

She moved out west about a year ago for a "fresh start" according to friends she had left behind. Instead she ended up meeting Harold "Stone" Kale. Kale owned the building she moved into.

Damien read Montana's notes.

Normally Kale has little or no interaction with his building's tenants; he has building managers to handle that. But according to Scott Jefferies, the building manager where Lindsay Keller lives, Kale happened to be there to approve some high-end repairs the day Lindsay moved in. Jefferies stated the man was "obsessed with the girl." He demanded her name and number from Jefferies, a direct violation of signed tenant rights.

"He threatened me with my job and then my life if I didn't give him the information."

When asked why he didn't see the need to go to the police about Kale's actions, Jefferies just laughed.

"The cops aren't going to be there when he sends his goons in to kill me."

Jefferies was hesitant to divulge any more information than he already had, but told me Keller started seeing Kale that night and could not be found without his company from then on.

According to Ms. Keller, Stone Kale was a perfect gentleman for the first six months they saw each other. He took her on exotic trips, bought her expensive gifts, and lavished her with praise and attention. All in all, he managed to turn the head of a young girl from Texas.

And then she discovered exactly what Kale did for a living. It was not an accident; it was almost as if he wanted her to know so he could hold it over her head, in her own words "own her".

Once she knew about the drug trade, the gloves came off and according to Keller, Stone showed his true colors. The first time he raped her, she ran. He found her and beat her, threatened that the next time she left him it would be worse.

She ran again. When he found her that time he didn't touch her. Instead he threw her to his associates, like raw meat to a pack of wolves.

Damien looked at the margin and saw several names listed there in red ink, the strokes so heavy the paper had ripped through in places. He read them with great interest.

Derrick

Andrew

Jose

Jorge

Montana had circled the names and had questionable locations listed for each of the four. The one that interested Damien the most was the listing for Jose. The possible location for that one happened to be Lincoln County Correctional Facility. The same location a certain federal court judge had just mandated Montana to remain at while awaiting trial.

"Son-of-a-bitch!" Damien looked at the name again and shook his head. "This whole thing is wrong."

Working on a hunch, Damien pulled up the number for the lab in Carson City. It was where all the specimens were sent from suspects arrested in Lincoln County. Punching in the number, he waited while it rang and hoped for one small piece of luck to come his way. He figured he was about due.

"Carson City Crime Lab. This is Macy. Can I help you?"

Damien smiled at the familiar voice. "How's my favorite redhead?"

A low, sultry laugh greeted him on the other end of the line. "Well, well, well, if it isn't the Knight-rider."

"It's been awhile, Mace, how you doing?"

"Good. What do you need, Damien?"

"Ah, Mace, that crushes me. What makes you think I didn't call just to flirt?"

"Because I've known you too long, I know you are hopelessly in love with your wife and I'm smart."

Damien chuckled and propped his feet on the polished wood of the desk. Montana would have been pissed at such an indiscretion, but he figured since he was trying to save the guy's ass, he was allowed.

"Still seeing that loser, Jared, Jimmy, whaeverthehell his name is?"

"It's Jerome, and no, I'm not seeing him, I married him."

"Oh! Bullet to the brain." Damien laughed.

"Okay, we've done the prerequisite niceties, and I'm backed up to my various unpleasant body parts with work, so cut to the chase, Damien. What do you need?"

"Darling, you have no unpleasant body parts, but I won't waste your extremely valuable time. I'm looking for some lab results on a client."

"Name, date of acquirement, and specimen," Macy asked. Damien could hear her keyboard through the line.

"Thomas, Montana, Lee. Blood and urine for tox screen. You should have received the specimens day before last."

"'Kay, hang on, let me check. That should have been processed by now, but I don't think it's been sent out yet."

Perfect.

"Yeah, here it is." Damien could hear her working the keyboard and waited. "Thomas, Montana, Lee. Tox screen shows the presence of Rohypnol, Ketamine and Epinephrine and small amounts of ethanol. Urine tox shows the same."

Damien's feet came down off the desk. No games now.

"You sure you have the right specimen? Montana Thomas."

"Yeah, slick, I know how to do my job." Macy sounded irritated at the implication. "Your boy liked to party."

"Yeah, I'm sorry, Mace. It just caught me off guard. You have been, as always, incredibly helpful."

"Uh huh, sure. And now you will hang up without listening to me and call me only when you need me again."

"Hmm? Yeah, sure. Hey, thanks, Mace." Damien hung up, looking at the list of drugs he had written down. A list of drugs found in Montana's system. Damien sat back in the leather chair and thought about what he had just learned.

One dead girl affiliated with a nasty drug trafficker who used her for his own personal kicks. One friend with no memory but caught with the murder weapon in his hand, and the girl it killed next to him. Rohypnol, the infamous "date rape" drug known for its amnesiac quality, found in his client's system along with Ketamine, an extremely powerful disassociative drug, known on the streets as Special K. Usually cut with epinephrine to make it more stable. All found in Montana's blood. All denied to have been taken by Montana.

The last puzzle piece: a known associate of the victim's boyfriend was being held in the same correctional facility as his client. One thing Damien knew for sure—Stone Kale either killed Linney or had someone else do the dirty work for him and framed Montana for the crime. What he didn't know was how. How did those drugs end up in Montana's system? The lack of memory could now be explained, the Rohypnol would have erased everything that happened while it was active. The Ketamine would have radically altered whatever he did remember, making it unreliable.

Not enough answers and too many questions. Maybe the girl might be willing to talk to him. Who says the dead can't talk?

He searched Montana's desk drawers for a phone book. When he found one, he let his fingers do the walking until he found the number he needed, then he flipped his cellphone open, punched it in, and waited for it to be answered.

"Lincoln County Pathology."

"Deacon?"

"Yeah, who am I talking to?"

"Not sure if you'll remember me. Damien Knight. We worked a case together a few years ago. The guy arrested for murdering his wife—turned out she killed herself and framed him with previously planted evidence."

The line was quiet for a minute. "Oh, yeah, yeah! I gotcha' now, sure, Damien Knight. Man, I sat in on that trial. You smoked in cross."

"Maybe, but it was the evidence you gathered from the wife's body that gave me what I needed to prove my case."

"Damn, that was sweet. I'm thinking you're not making a social call here. Am I right?"

"Perceptive as usual."

"You don't need to schmooze me, man. What can I do for you?"

Damien wasted no more time with foreplay. "You had a female vic brought in two days ago. Lindsay Keller. Fifty-six stab wounds. You do the 'top yet?"

"Yeah. Well, not me, but the pathologist. Just finished up. I heard you were defending her killer."

"I'm defending the man accused of her murder. Big difference. Can you give me the results of the 'top?"

"Now, you know I can't do that. Against all types of rules and things."

"How much lab techs make these days, Deacon? I could have a little of my appreciation sent your way by day's end."

Damien waited out the silence on the other end of the phone.

"If anyone asks, I will deny talking to you, man. Okay, listen, 'cause I am not repeating myself. Cause of death was exsanguination. Chic was stabbed a total of fifty-six separate times, probably bled to death before whoever did it was done."

"Tox screen?"

"Clean, but she was raped."

"Pre or post mortem?" Damien asked.

"Pre, I got two DNA contributions in the vaginal vault."

"Two?"

"Yup. One we identified as your man. The other I don't have a name to go with the face yet—so to speak."

Damien dragged a hand through his hair. "You sure it was rape? Couldn't have been rough sex?"

"Well, anything's possible, I guess, but the coroner is officially calling it rape."

"Anything else I should know?"

"Nope, that's the highlights. Hey, I could lose my job if anyone finds out I told you this."

"I'll be sure to make it worth your while, and thanks."

Damien hit the end button and thought about the new information he had just found out.

"Sweet Jesus, Montana. What the hell did you find yourself in the middle of?"

CHAPTER 8

Maggie Riley-Ricco sat in a chair next to her husband's bed and held his hand. It felt so cold. This could not be happening, she told herself again, but no amount of denial would grant her another moment with him. Damn it! Life was a cruel, heartless bitch.

Two years simply was not enough time. He shouldn't have been hers to begin with, she knew that, but it didn't make it any easier to let him go. By some cosmic short circuit, Michael Ricco and Margaret Riley found one another.

At first he had been an oddity, nothing more than what the government intended—a specimen in a gilded cage. Between Dakota Thomas and Michael they learned amazing things. Medical research jumped ahead fifty, maybe a hundred years. They developed vaccines that could be used to save countless lives. It was, she supposed, what the General, the psycho who gave up everything, even his name, thought he was doing when he'd held Michael prisoner.

The General used Michael Ricco and others like him as pawns to perform numerous inhumane experiments, all in the name of science. The problem with that, Michael and the others never gave their permission. They were taken, used, and killed in the name of science. Collateral damage. According to the General they were doing a great service for their fellow man.

Michael's escape ended with the General's capture and an end to the program. Michael had volunteered, this time, to let the government use what the General had done to him. This time there was no pain, he only gave them his blood.

Somewhere along the line, Maggie fell in love with the farm-boy from Virginia. The last two years brought her more happiness than she thought she deserved. Michael learned how to smile again. He told her he loved her, and she believed him. She loved him more than she thought she could love anyone, and now he was leaving her.

He lifted a hand and wiped a tear from her cheek.

"Don't cry," he told her.

His voice was so weak, he sounded nothing like her Michael. As soft-spoken as he normally was, his words were never empty. She knew when he spoke it was always worth your while to listen. She'd learned more from listening to Michael Ricco in the last two years than she'd learned in her entire time before knowing him.

She sniffled and tried to smile. The result, she knew, was a little scary. "Sorry, can't seem to help it."

Maggie could hear his breathing getting worse, but Michael refused to let them do anything more for him. They put him on a morphine drip to deal with the pain, but that was all he would allow.

"Margaret, a word please," Doctor Eugene Connelly, the program's medical director, asked to speak to her away from Michael. It was always Margaret with him, never Maggie, never ever Maggs. It was Margaret. She didn't want to leave Michael, but she needed to hear what the doctor had to say.

She stood and leaned over, placing a whisper-light kiss on Michael's lips.

"Be right back," she told him. He gave her a small nod and closed his eyes. God, he looked so tired. She walked over to where Eugene waited for her, out of Michael's hearing.

Shoving his hands deep into his lab coat pockets, Eugene looked directly into her eyes. "We've done everything we can for him, Margaret. I'm sorry, but it's just not going to be enough."

She knew it was true, but shook her head in a gesture of denial. "No, I mean his immune system could still kick in, right? Dakota's always does just when we count him out."

The doctor shook his head. "This is not about his immune system. This is about a one-hundred-and-twelve-year-old heart calling it quits. His body's letting him know it's had enough. He's in full-blown congestive heart failure, Margaret. We've made him comfortable, but I can't fix this. He is working on a ten percent ejection fraction. His heart is failing."

The tears came in earnest now and she didn't care who saw them. "How long?"

Eugene shrugged. "I can't tell you that, but not long, his body can't take much more."

"You won't let him suffer?"

"No, he's had too much suffering in his life, the least we can do is make sure he has none when he dies."

She looked away and nodded. "Thank you for that."

"Go be with him, Margaret. Go be with your husband."

Maggie went back to sit with Michael and wait for the last word, the last look, the last moment she would ever spend with him, and felt her heart break in too many pieces to be put back together again.

"Still crying," Michael whispered to her.

She wiped her eyes, took his hand and kissed it. "No, I'm not."

"Liar." He smiled and closed his eyes. "Maggs?" he asked, still keeping his eyes shut. It was difficult for him to even speak now. "I need you to do something for me, a couple of things."

"Anything, name it."

"I want to be buried with my family, in Virginia. Next to my daddy."

"Michael." She shook her head; she knew he was dying, but she couldn't bring herself to talk to him about it. It was too much like giving up.

"No, there's no time for this, Maggs." His voice rose in frustration, and his face scrunched up in pain.

"Do you need something more for pain?" she asked, edging closer to him, afraid every moment might be his last.

He shook his head and controlled his breathing, his face relaxed, as Maggie saw the pain recede for the moment.

"Just listen, okay?" he asked.

"I'm sorry, okay. Virginia, yeah, sweetie, I can do that for you, count on it."

"I know I can count on you, Maggs. This one is a little harder though, but a lot more important." It was getting more difficult for him now, Maggie could see it. He seemed to fight for every word, every breath.

"Anything, Michael."

He opened his eyes and tried to focus on her. "You need to let Dakota go."

"Michael."

"Don't tell me you can't, I know better. Maggie, don't turn him into another lab rat, it will kill him. He's not like me. Let him go. He'll be back when he can, and you'll learn more from him if he wants to come back, not if he has to."

Michael," she said again.

"Call off your dogs, Maggs. Let. Him. Go."

"I don't know if I can," she said honestly.

"Well, convince whoever has the power and let him go. Maggs, please, promise me."

"I promise, Michael." She would have promised him anything at that moment.

He seemed to relax a little at her words. "Good. Okay, one last thing."

"Michael, you need to get some rest." She knew how useless her words sounded, but couldn't help them. He seemed to understand and smiled at her.

"Time enough for rest later, I only want to say one last thing. I need you to remember something for me, never forget it."

"I can do that."

"I love you, Maggie Riley. You have made the last two years easily the best of my life. Don't be sad. I have lived longer than most people have a right to. It's time and I'm more than ready, but I will miss you, love."

"God, Michael, I just got you, it's not fair."

"We had two years we were never meant to have, Maggs. You can only cheat fate for so long."

"I love you, Michael." Maggie looked up as the monitor started to alarm. Michael's heart rate had slowed down. The beats on the monitor became farther apart.

He gave her a nod, the only indication he had heard her, and then his breathing became irregular and his face creased in pain as he struggled for breath.

Before she could ask for help, Eugene was there. He increased the morphine dripping into Michael's veins, and Maggie watched as his face relaxed once more.

"Michael?" she asked, her hand squeezing his a little harder.

He was no longer responding to her.

"I can help him go peacefully," Eugene told her quietly. "No pain, just a gentle nudge over the hump."

"I'm not ready for this, Eugene." Her eyes blurred with tears as the doctor reached up to silence the alarms.

"Maybe not, but he is."

The words hit her and showed her how selfish she was being, but letting him go was more difficult than she could have imagined.

Michael made the decision for her. His heart rate on the monitor slowed dramatically to twenty, then fifteen beats a minute. Maggie looked at Michael's face and saw peace there. The line indicating the function of his failing heart went flat.

Eugene pulled the stethoscope dangling from around his neck and put it in his ears. He placed the diaphragm on Michael's chest and listened for what seemed like a long time. With one hand, he pulled the earpieces free. He looked at Maggie's devastated face and shook his head.

"He's gone," he said, telling her what she already knew.

Maggie held onto Michael's hand and squeezed her eyes shut. What would she do now? How was she going to live the rest of her life without him? She placed a hand on her still flat belly and wondered if she should have told him. She'd planned to tell him about the pregnancy she'd only just discovered, but when she found out what he did with Dakota, the news seemed less important in the light of her anger at him.

Then he had collapsed and *hey honey, guess what? I'm pregnant!* didn't seem appropriate. Now she was left with the prospect of raising their child alone and missing him forever.

She took a deep breath and did what she always did in a crisis: she pulled it all together and did what had to be done. She opened her eyes and stood, still keeping his hand in hers, holding on as long as possible, and spoke to Eugene.

"I need to tell his family," she said. "I want you to make arrangements to have his body sent to Virginia. I'll let you know the details after I speak with his family."

"You can stay here with him for a while if you want," Eugene told her.

Maggie shook her head, bent down and kissed his lips one last time.

"No, Michael's not here anymore, Eugene, and I have work to do."

Anyone else would have thought the words were callous, but the doctor understood and gave her a nod.

"I'll take care of him, Margaret. Let me know where I need to make arrangements."

She nodded, gave Michael one last look, and wiped her tears. She turned to her staff, who waited quietly behind her, and put on her game face. She was met with grief and pain almost as raw as her own. These people were Michael's family too. She might have lost a husband, but they lost a friend, a brother of sorts. She looked at each one of them, acknowledging the loss, and when she came to the last one, she knew there was no more time for the luxury of grief.

"We need to get in touch with the team sent after Dakota," she said.

"Maggs." Tess, her team coordinator, stepped forward. Maggie could tell she picked her words carefully as she spoke. "Look, I don't mean to be indelicate here, but with Michael gone, Dakota is all we have left. Without him there is no program. We need him back. Every moment he's gone we are losing valuable information."

Maggie took one step forward. "Don't you think I know that?" She paused to collect herself. "He's right, you know. If we don't let Dakota go, we're no better than the psychopath who tortured Michael for all those years. I don't know about you, but I sure as hell do not want to leave that as my legacy. I signed on to help people, not hurt them. I promised him, Tess. I'm calling the dogs off. Michael was right, Dakota will come back on his own, but if we force him, we'll be no better than the General. I won't do that to him. Will you?"

"I don't like it," Tess said.

"I don't like a lot of things right now, but it's the right thing to do and you know it. Do it." Maggie left the room and walked calmly to her office down the hall. She kept her steps even, measured. It gave her some illusion of control to keep everything in check, when all she wanted to do was run screaming out of the building, to collapse in hysteria and weep about losing her Michael.

She sat behind her desk and folded her hands in front of her to complete the illusion of control as much as to stop them from shaking. Her husband lay dead down the hall from her, and she was discussing the benefits of human decency in a world where individuals usually looked out only for themselves. Before she met Michael Ricco, she had been one of them. He changed her. He changed everyone he touched. Spend enough time with the man and it was inevitable.

Maggie took a deep breath, then went to fulfill her final promise. She flipped open her roller-deck, found the number she needed, and put a hand on the phone, but before she could pick it up, Eugene appeared in her doorway.

"Are you doing okay?" he asked her.

She tried to smile. "No, Eugene, I most decidedly am not doing okay. But it doesn't matter. Right now I have a mess to clean up and a husband to bury."

"Margaret, I need to do an autopsy on Michael. I'm so sorry to even have to ask it of you, but as legal next of kin, I need you to sign some papers." He stepped up to her desk and handed her the forms.

Maggie took them but didn't look at them. "What? Why?" She shook her head. "No, Eugene, he doesn't deserve that, no autopsy." She tried to hand the papers back to him.

"I'm sorry, but it's not up to you, it's not even up to me. Michael was admitted to my hospital and died less than twenty-four hours later. It is a federal mandate that an autopsy is done to determine cause of death."

"But we know what killed him, you told me, it was his heart," she said, confused.

"I know, but honestly, who can say for sure what finally did him in? The things that were done to him, his body chemistry... Margaret, I hate to sound like a scientist, especially now, but think of what he could teach us through his death. He agreed to be part of this program so that we could learn from him. Don't you think he would want us to learn as much as we can and find out what caused that incredible body of his to finally shut down?"

Maggie looked from the forms in her hands to Eugene. She knew he was right and tried to shelve her personal feelings and do the right thing. *The right thing.* God! She was beginning to hate that phrase.

She took a pen from the ceramic jar on her desk, went through the papers, and one by one signed them. Eugene extended a hand, taking them back.

"You promise me he will be treated with dignity and respect?" she asked, keeping the tears at bay. She had to be strong now, and tears would only make her weak.

"I would have it no other way. I admired the man more than I can say. Trust me to take care of him."

"I'll hold you to that, Eugene. I was just about to call his brother's grandson to tell him. I'll have all the arrangements for you in an hour or two."

"I should have most of the results from the autopsy by then. If you want to talk, you know where to find me." He waited for a response; when none came, he simply gave her a nod and left.

Maggie sat at her desk and tried to remember what life had been like before Michael, and found she couldn't conjure up the feelings. Her eyes drifted to a picture on her desk. Their wedding picture.

She remembered the day with perfect clarity. She'd worn a simple white linen shift. He placed flowers in her hair, honeysuckle because he liked how they smelled. She bought him the only suit he had ever owned, let alone worn.

Not a lot of need for suits on a dairy farm, he reminded her when they went shopping. He didn't complain, he even smiled as she made him try on suit after suit until she finally settled on the very first one.

They both looked so happy in that moment frozen in time. It had taken her so long to find the smile he saw fit to grace her with. So long for her to find a way through the years of indifference and pain, to find the man somewhere underneath. He told her that she saved him from himself, and now he asked her to save Dakota from becoming like he was.

It might get her in trouble with her superiors, but screw them all. She would do it. She would do it for Michael. Just in case Tess had a change of heart, she picked up her phone and dialed her chief of security, somewhere in the air on the way to Nevada.

Jason Peters answered his cellphone on the private flight out of the government airfield in Bethesda.

"Jay? Listen, we have had some developments here. I need you to have the pilot bring you back."

She cut him off as he protested, keeping the news of Michael's death to herself. He would likely have the same reaction as Tess. "Look, I don't want to hear any excuses, I'm giving you a direct order. Come home. As of this moment I am cutting Dakota Thomas free, and before you say another word, yes, I am taking full responsibility for this action so don't fear for your precious job. I'm calling you back, Jay. Come in." Knowing he would do as he was told even if he didn't like it, Maggie hung up and put her head in her hands.

Sudden anger flared to life inside her. Anger at Michael for leaving her to deal with all of this alone. She picked up the wedding portrait and pulled her arm back, intending to fling it against the wall, but found she couldn't do it. Anger circled back to grief once more and she hugged the picture to her chest and let the tears come. Deep, racking sobs shook her body and she felt a loss she was certain had no equal.

"When you get to that heaven of yours," she said through the tears, "you just better tell that Emma you're taken. I don't give a crap about all that *till death do we part* bullshit. You are mine, Michael Ricco, and I do not share well, even with former fiancées." Maggie placed the picture back down in its proper place on the corner of her desk and got it together again.

She picked the phone up and dialed a long distance number to a place she had only visited once before. They had meant to go back but somehow never got around to it.

"Hello?" The voice was accented with a soft Southern twang she found comforting. It was a voice very much like Michael's. Even after all the time spent away from his roots, he had never lost the accent.

"Matthew?"

"Yes? Who is this?"

"Matthew, this is Maggie Riley, Michael's wife."

"Maggie! Oh hell, yeah, I recognize your voice now. How are you? How's Michael?"

"Matthew, I don't know how to tell you this," she began. She wasn't sure she could actually say the words out loud.

Matthew made it easy for her. Maybe he could hear it in her voice, or maybe he knew there would be no other reason for her to call. "Oh, God, Maggie, it's Michael, isn't it? Something has happened to Michael."

Her voice cracked but she kept it together. "I need to bring him home, Matthew. He told me he wanted to come home. Can you help me?"

"I knew something was wrong. He called me last week, told me he wanted to make sure he had a plot next to his daddy when the time came."

Maggie let out a little laugh. "He never told me he called," she said more to herself than to Matthew. How very like him to save her the trouble of making arrangements.

"Bring him home, Maggie," Matthew told her. "Bring him home so we can say goodbye."

Goodbye. Maggie wasn't sure she had the strength to do that, but she had no choice. Michael Ricco, after over ninety years, was finally going home for good.

CHAPTER 9

On the second day after his bail was denied, Montana's cell door clicked open at seven AM along with every other one on the block. Time for breakfast. It wasn't the time that bothered Montana, he had already been awake for hours, but his meals had, up until today, been delivered to his cell. But after his conversation with Jose, Montana had begun to suspect that Stone Kale's influence reached into the legal system, perhaps even as far as a federal court judge.

Montana had sat in on arraignment hearings before, but from the other side of the fence. There was no reason, he could see, for him to have been denied bail. It was obvious that Kale did not intend for Montana to live long enough to make it to trial.

"Come on, lover boy, up and out," the guard told him. "Room service has been discontinued."

Montana knew better than to offer him a comment and stood.

The guard slapped his baton in his hand as if he was waiting for an excuse to use it. "You want to eat? Get moving."

"Don't suppose staying here is an option?"

The guard just laughed.

"Kind of what I thought," Montana said, walking out of the cell and falling into line with the rest of the inmates.

Jose fell in behind him. "Hey, pretty boy," he whispered, and then laughed softly as the guards moved them toward the cafeteria.

Montana kept his eyes forward, his senses on high alert. He harbored no delusions that Jose was the only inmate who had an agenda concerning his future, or more aptly put, his lack of one.

Every time the line slowed down, Jose shoved Montana hard in the back. After the first time, Montana braced himself for it, his temper brewing, but keeping it in check until the timing was better.

As they reached the cafeteria and the food was placed on his tray, Montana could feel the tension around him growing. With tray in hand he turned to find a table but found Jose and a few of his friends instead.

"Whatcha' supposed to be, anyway?" one of Jose's posse asked. "Some kind of Indian or something?"

Jose laughed. Montana was used to the comments over his obvious Native American heritage. He turned and canted his head at Jose, no readable expression on his face. With one slow-motion push, Jose knocked the tray out of Montana's hands, and gasped in mock surprise as the tray and its contents fell, the plastic containers upturning and the sad excuse for breakfast splattering over the floor.

"Oh, man, you gotta' be more careful, they don't hand out seconds." Jose stood in front of Montana, placing his own tray on an empty table.

"What's the problem?" one of the guards asked, glancing over at the disturbance.

Montana let his gaze flick to the guard long enough to gauge a threat or not. Satisfied that the man was more annoyed than angry, he quickly settled his eyes back on Jose once more. That, he decided, was where the real threat lay.

"No problem. The chief here just had a little accident." Jose smiled at the guard, then turned the cheesy grin back to Montana. "Didn't you, chief?" Jose asked, the smile retreating, leaving behind a thin hard mouth with no trace of amusement.

Montana assessed Jose and the two men who flanked him. He had about eight inches and twenty pounds on Jose. The other two were a little bigger, but Montana felt he could take either of them; the three of them combined might prove to be a bit of a challenge, but one he was more than up to.

Concentrating on Jose and ignoring the other two, Montana took a step toward him and looked down, accentuating the difference in their height.

"The choices you make in the next few minutes might be the most important ones you make in the whole of your miserable existence. I suggest you consider what you are about to do carefully, because I will promise you one thing." Montana spoke calmly and slowly as if addressing a small child with a poor attention span. It had the desired effect, as he saw the cockiness dial down a notch in the man's stance. Jose took an involuntary step back as he looked up at Montana in confusion.

"What the hell are you talking about?"

"If you start this, I will go for you, no one else, just you. Do you understand? Stone Kale can't protect you in here, not from me, not for long."

Jose tried to smile again but he lost his edge. He looked to the men on either side of him and gave them a quick, almost hesitant, nod. They stepped in fast, each grabbed Montana by an arm, intending to immobilize him as Jose took a go at him.

As soon as goon number one touched his right arm, Montana went to a dark place. A place he never wanted to visit again, but once there it became easy to drop the veil and just go with it. Here he didn't need to think, he only needed to react.

Sidestepping the man before he had a firm grip on his arm, Montana used his size and strength to his advantage. He turned the man around and pulled his back to him. Montana's bicep slid around the man's throat and squeezed tight.

The second man had a grip on his left arm, but it didn't even slow Montana down. His left arm swung toward the center of his body with the man still clinging to it; he crashed goon number two's head into goon number one, then let both men drop stunned and useless to the floor and centered his attention on Jose. The entire time his gaze never left the smaller man. Montana sensed rather than saw the two guards coming toward him from opposite corners of the lunch room. He knew he didn't have much time and concentrated on getting the job done.

In two steps he was on Jose. The smaller man tried to bluff with posture and attitude, but Montana was past all that. Two quick jabs, one to the gut to immobilize, the other to the face. Blood splattered Montana's face and jumpsuit, the red standing out in stark relief to the bright orange.

Jose rolled in a ball, his hands to his face, blood flowing out through the gaps in his fingers. Montana felt the guards on him now and registered a hard hit to his side with a baton; he ignored it and went for Jose again. He grabbed the man in a chokehold, making it nearly impossible for the guards to get a clean hit on him without first getting Jose. Not caring what the consequences would be, he turned his attention to the attack at his back just long enough to give Jose a message before he let the guards subdue him.

He pushed the fat guard who had hit him with the baton and kicked him to keep him down, then pulled Jose's hands away from his face and whispered into the other man's ear.

"Tell your boss that I will find him, and when I do, I will kill him. And when I'm done with him, if I find you had anything to do with what happened to the woman, I'm coming after you, got that?"

Jose looked straight ahead with wide, fearful eyes. It was clear he very much *got that*. Montana let Jose go and stood, arms outstretched, indicating he was done. He would let them take him now.

The guards, not in the mood for the sudden submission, wanted their own revenge.

"The son-of-a-bitch is crazy, Bobby, let him have it!" The guard Montana had hit stood up, wiping blood from a split lip.

Bobby, the younger of the two guards, held a Taser in one hand. Montana could see he was reluctant to use it. Frustrated that his backup was not as pissed at the sudden disruption of the daily order as he was, the older guard grabbed the Taser.

"Goddammit, Bobby!" The older guard aimed and fired, sending seven-hundred thousand volts of electricity coursing through Montana's body.

Everything seized up at once. In one brief moment before he lost consciousness, before the pain made it through the haze of blackness, Montana found Jose. The look of pure fear on the man's face told him he'd accomplished one thing.

He'd just told Stone Kale he would not go down easy.

CHAPTER 10

Damien Knight sat on the bed in his hotel room and spread the contents of his briefcase out in front of him. He needed to wrap his mind around what was fact and what was presumption.

With a pristine yellow legal pad and a new black pen in hand, he began to take notes. He made two columns, one he labeled *fact*, the other *fiction*.

He knew without a doubt that Montana did not kill Lindsay Keller. He also knew that despite the positive tox screen, Montana, to his knowledge, never used recreational drugs. The memory loss could be attributed to the Rohypnol and Ketamine found in his system.

On the flip side of the coin, his client had been found by police with the murder weapon in his hand, confused and incoherent at the scene. An anonymous cellphone had called it in. Damien listened to the call a dozen times, a nondescript male voice telling the 911 operator that a woman had been killed and then giving the address. That was it, the call lasted all of twenty-five seconds. He had it compared to a tape of Montana's voice and came up empty, no match.

Montana and Linney's prints were the only ones found at her apartment. No forced entry, no witnesses stating they'd seen or heard anything unusual on the night in question.

Damien looked at the photos of both the victim and Montana at the time of his arrest. That's when all the little red flags started to go up.

First, the autopsy report stated that Linney had been raped and had two different DNA contributions present. It made it impossible to tell if Montana had been the rapist or not. He knew it wasn't a possibility, but he tried to leave his personal feelings out of the equation and think like a juror.

The fact that Linney had sex, voluntarily or not, with Montana and another man shortly before her death said one thing to Damien—her killer had raped and then brutally stabbed her to death. There were no defensive wounds on the victim's hands or forearms, but there were bruises around her wrists, suggesting she had been held down or in some other way restrained. The pattern of the bruising indicated that it had been hands that held her, not ropes or tape. It also suggested to Damien that there had been more than one assailant. The thing that Damien could not get around was the utter lack of evidence to that effect.

The more assailants, the better the chance that someone would leave behind some biological evidence, yet Linney's apartment had been clean, everything purposely pointing to Montana as the murderer.

Second, the photographs of Montana shortly after his arrest showed faint ligature marks on his wrists and bruising at his jaw and mouth, all attributed to his resisting arrest. Montana, of course, could remember nothing. But the bruising in the photographs was hours old. How could handcuffs applied far later than that cause the bruising Damien saw? He had an answer to the question but no proof, and that's what pissed him off.

The woman was his wild card in all of this. All he knew about her was a brief impression the night they met and the fact that Montana did not fall easily and he had definitely fallen for the pretty blonde and fallen hard. Maybe that was the problem—Montana hadn't been thinking clearly and didn't watch his back. Linney Keller had a history with Stone Kale and tried to leave him—for Montana. Apparently that didn't sit well with Kale.

A known drug kingpin, Kale seemed to always have his fly zipped and his hands clean. No one could touch him. He had been brought in and cleared so many times it was highly suspected that he had paid connections in the legal system, but no one knew if it was true or not. Damien suspected he had stepped into more than he bargained for when he answered Ito's plea to help Montana. If he couldn't prove Stone Kale killed Linney, Montana wouldn't have to worry about spending the rest of his life in prison, he wouldn't stay alive long enough to stand trial.

The one question Damien didn't have an answer to was why did Stone let Montana live when he killed Linney? Was it just to torture him before he finally did kill him? Damien looked over his list and ran a hand through his hair, then ripped the paper out of the tablet, crumpled it and threw it off the bed. He didn't need facts to clear Montana, he needed a freaking miracle.

Too late to talk to Montana and too early to sleep, Damien wished he was home. He missed his wife. Kathy had the unnerving ability to see through all the bull and get right to the point. More than once it had been her intuition that cleared Damien's clients, not his. Lying back on the bed, he grabbed his cellphone from the bedside table and punched in his home number. It was a crapshoot if she would be home or not, her social life with friends kept her almost as busy as his job kept him. He was convinced the time spent away from each other kept their marriage strong. The phone picked up on the second ring.

"Hey, babe."

"Hey, I was just thinking about you. Miss you."

"Right back atcha'." Damien closed his eyes and tried to picture her—short, curly, black hair that seemed to have a life all its own and stunning blue eyes. Kathy told him on their first date that he was going to marry her. He laughed and silently swore never to call the aggressive wench again. Seven months later the self-proclaimed perennial bachelor watched the most beautiful woman he had ever seen walk toward him down the aisle. Not a day went by that he didn't know he was the luckiest idiot on the planet. Kathy had saved him from a life of mediocrity and introduced him to bliss.

"You sound tired. Bad day?"

He gave her a little laugh. She knew him so well she could judge his mood just by the sound of his voice. "Wish you were here, or better yet, wish I was there," he told her.

"How much trouble is Montana in?"

Damien sighed and rubbed a hand over his closed eyes. He hadn't called with the intent of burdening her with the case but he knew she would ask; maybe that's why he'd called. He needed her.

"That bad, huh?"

"Worse. Kath, I don't know if I can get him out of this one." Damien would admit that to no one but her. His normal bravado was saved for the public and colleagues, never for her.

"If anyone can, it will be you. If not, then it can't be done. You are the best, babe, don't forget that. Montana's counting on it."

"Gee, thanks, no pressure or anything." He laughed, his eyes stilled closed.

"Want to talk about it?"

"You sure you want to hear it? It's not pretty."

"Never is. Let me have it."

He smiled and pictured her curled up in the corner of their sofa with the four-pound Pekingese she insisted was a dog sitting in her lap.

"God, I love you."

"Of course you do. Now start talking so we can figure out how to get Montana out of that place and back home where he belongs."

Slowly, methodically, Damien laid it all out for her, every nasty detail and every theory he had shared with no one yet. Kathy listened and Damien talked. In the back of his mind, he thought maybe with her help he might just find that miracle.

* * * *

Ito watched Dakota turn in his sleep. Despite his service in the army, or maybe because of it, he didn't understand Dakota's involvement with the government. The things they did to the man were inhuman. To Ito, they were no better than the place that held Ricco all those years. The physical changes in Dakota were dramatic. It had been nearly two years since Ito had seen him last. Dakota had lost weight, giving him a lanky, loose-boned look. Ito had always known the man with a smile on his face and a quirky sense of humor. Maybe he had caught him at a bad time, but the doctor looked like he had not smiled in a very long time.

Ito had seen the look before on the faces of rescued prisoners of war. A haunted look that said what words failed to express. Two days' worth of stubble and a nearly relentless fever didn't help, but Ito wondered what the hell they had done to Dakota since he had last seen him.

Still holding the phone, his mind went back over the conversation with Maggie Riley. While Dakota mumbled something incoherent in his sleep, Ito wondered how the hell he was going to find a way to tell him what he'd just learned. But tell him he would—the man deserved to know.

Ito stood and surveyed his surroundings. At first he objected to Dakota's suggestion that they stay in Montana's apartment, but then, realizing that Maggie would find them regardless of where they slept, he relented. Now of course it made no difference.

Montana never made an issue of his talent as an artist, but the fact that his own original watercolors and pencil drawings covered the walls introduced those who knew him to a side he rarely shared with the world. In the foyer was a pencil sketch of Dakota. It captured the essence of the man perfectly. The portrait showed three quarters of Dakota's face, leaving the rest hidden in shadows. A smile played on his lips, and his eyes sparkled with a glint of a joke yet to be shared. It showed Dakota as seen through Montana's eyes.

Another showed a group of soldiers standing in a tight semi-circle, arms around each other's shoulders and smiling. Ito couldn't help but grin. He recognized the faces smiling back at him. There was Bobby, Patrick, Ray, and standing in the back, towering over them all, his own face. Ito was surprised at how young and carefree he looked in the drawing. He wondered if he ever looked that carefree anymore. Ray was gone now, killed while rescuing Dakota from hell on Earth, but Bobby was still alive as was Patrick. Memories encroached for a while until Ito grew uncomfortable with their insistence. Pushing them back to a place where he could tolerate them until he had the luxury to pay them the respect they deserved, he came across one last portrait.

This one was different than the rest. Instead of charcoal, this drawing was done in vibrant yet soft colors and it was the only drawing that showed a woman.

Ito had met Linney once and had no problem recognizing her. Shoulder-length hair the color of honey framed a heart-shaped face with skin smoothed and tanned by the desert heat. She looked out, away from the viewer, and smiled shyly, but it was the eyes that captivated the artist. Montana had captured the sadness buried deep in her soul and brought it to life through her eyes. They showed anyone who cared to look a tortured past with maybe a promise for a happy future. A future that, Ito knew, had been cut brutally short. Ito gently touched the glass-covered picture with a finger, following the curve of the girl's lips, and thought he could see why Montana believed this one was different. He could see it too, through Montana.

"I never met her. She was beautiful," Dakota said from behind him.

"That she was," Ito said with his back still to Dakota. Turning, he saw Dakota sitting up on the couch where he had fallen asleep earlier. "How are you feeling?" he asked. On quick inspection, Dakota's eyes seemed clear and more focused than they had a few hours ago.

"Better." Dakota rubbed the back of his neck, and then scratched at the stubble on his cheek. "Nothing a hot shower and a pot of coffee can't fix."

"Fever gone?"

Dakota rolled his eyes. "I don't need a babysitter, Ito."

"I'll remember that next time you pass out in your own vomit." Ito smiled. "Go take your shower, Dakota. I'll make you some coffee, and then we need to talk."

"That sounds ominous. Maybe the shower can wait. Is it about Montana?"

"Not this time." Ito walked toward Dakota and sat opposite him in a large leather recliner. He had been the bearer of bad news before, but somehow this was different. This was far more personal. "Maggie called," Ito began.

"Well, that didn't take long. How the hell did she get your cellphone number?"

"You lived with those people for two years and you have to ask?" Ito sighed and met Dakota's eyes with a hard stare. "You can relax, they cut you loose."

Ito watched the information sink in. Dakota's eyes narrowed at the realization that the news was not a good thing. "What? Why? What happened? Maggie would never let me go, the program is way too important."

"Michael's dead," Ito said. "Heart failure, last night. It was quick, Maggie said he didn't suffer."

"What? No, he was fine, we just saw him, he can't be dead."

Ito waited until Dakota thought it all through, then stood and walked to the picture window looking out over the desert. It showed the promise of a beautiful day. Rose-colored clouds touched the horizon, while the sky above cleared to a deep lapis blue.

"Damn, Maggs must be a mess. God, Ito, Ricco's dead? I thought he'd outlive all of us."

"You okay?"

Dakota stood and headed for the bathroom. Ito watched him carefully, but Dakota had learned how to guard his emotions well in the last two years. His face was a blank canvas showing Ito nothing, but he could guess at the extent of the man's feelings. He knew Michael Ricco and Dakota shared something Ito could never understand. Dakota had saved Ricco and Ricco in turn had saved Dakota. In the end they both shared the same fate—to be studied, to be specimens, human oddities suitable for the great scientific freak show.

Dakota turned and gave Ito a tired smile, but said nothing. He simply shook his head and walked into his brother's bathroom, shutting the door behind him. Ito heard the shower start. There was nothing more he could do to help Dakota, whatever emotional turmoil the doc was going through, he would have to handle it on his own. Ito's main priority was Montana.

He flipped his cellphone open and punched in Damien's number. He expected voice mail but got the man himself.

"You better have good news for me, because I am not in the mood for any more shit," Damien said on answering.

Ito chuckled. "Roll out on the wrong side of the legal system, counselor?"

"I mean it, Ito, tell me some good news. I'm begging you."

"The good doctor is feeling better and is ready to see Montana," Ito told him.

"Well, Montana might not be ready to see him. I got the call not more than five minutes ago, Montana's been placed in solitary confinement. I'm en route now to find out what happened. Ito, this whole freaking thing is bad."

"Define bad."

"Bad as in Stone Kale had Linney raped and killed in front of Montana, and then framed him for her murder. Bad as in Kale has his lackeys in the same jail as Montana with orders to eliminate him. Bad as in I cannot prove a fucking word I just said. Bad as in Kale's reach might be a lot longer than either one of us want to think about. And bad as in I cannot do a damn thing to protect Montana."

"You're right," Ito conceded. "That is bad. What do you want me to do with Dakota?"

Damien sighed before answering. "I don't know. Hell, bring him. From what I can figure out, there was an altercation. Montana assaulted a guard and another prisoner. I don't know anything more than that. If I can, I'll get Dakota in to see him, but tell him not to count on it. What about the program Dakota works for? Are they still giving him grief over leaving?"

"No, no more problems." Ito didn't see the sense in burdening Damien with problems he could do nothing about. Damien had never met Ricco or knew exactly what Dakota did at AMRIID. He had enough to think about concerning Montana, and Ito decided to leave it that way.

"Well, that's one thing in our favor," Damien said. "Look, I'm pulling into the prison now. Give me about an hour to get things sorted out and talk to Montana. I'll give you a call if I can get Dakota in."

"I will do that. Damien, tell Montana..." Ito paused, unsure of how to finish his sentence. "Tell Montana to do a Branson."

"What?"

"Just tell him, he'll understand."

"Sometimes you guys weird me out, you know?"

Ito laughed. "Do your job, counselor, I'll work on the rest."

"I'm trying my best, man. I'm trying," Damien said.

The line disconnected and for the first time since that frantic call from Montana, Ito wondered if Damien's best would be anywhere near good enough to pull Montana Thomas out of the hole he had fallen into.

CHAPTER 11

Linney stood in front of him, naked and bloody, the blond hair crimson and dripping, the sweet smile in stark contrast to everything else.

"You promised you would keep me safe." Her hands swept over the gaping wounds in her chest and abdomen. "Does this look safe to you?"

Montana tried to go to her, but he couldn't move. A new vision of Linney replaced the one standing in front of him. Linney next to him in bed, her wrists held above her head by many hands, a knife to her throat, her eyes on Montana as another man covered her small body with his own. Tears streaming down her cheeks as she was brutally raped. He could hear the grunts and smell the musky sweat of the man who took her.

Men. There was more than one.

He couldn't help her because they had tied him, beat him and forced him to watch.

"You twitch, I slice her throat."

It was more than a threat, it was a promise.

"Doesn't look much like protection to me," the other Linney told him. She stood over her counterpart, watching her own rape. "*That* looks like me about to die." Stepping back into the shadows, she was replaced by Stone Kale.

Montana watched from the dark. When they were done amusing

themselves with the girl—*the girl*, as if she meant nothing to Montana, as if by neutralizing her identity it would hurt less even here in his nightmares—Kale bent over her and made a show out of kissing her gently. He then looked at Montana and smiled as he brandished a knife.

"You're a dead man," Montana told him.

Kale laughed. "We haven't even gotten to the fun part yet," he said, brushing the edge of the blade lightly along Linney's inner thigh.

Montana wanted to look, he needed to see what happened next, to convince himself beyond any doubt that he hadn't harmed her, but was denied even that small relief.

Images came at him fast and hard, everything hazed in red. He felt the needle pierce his flesh, thought he heard screams, and felt slick, wet warmth cover him, and then nothing.

"A lot of good you were," the naked, bleeding Linney admonished him, leaning down as she placed a bloody kiss on his lips. He hadn't realized he was on the floor until then. "My pretty boy, my big strong soldier." She stood up and turned, but kept her gaze on his. "Fucking useless excuse for a hero. All you did was get me dead." Flipping her blood-drenched hair behind her and splattering him in the process, she faded as she walked away.

Still restrained, Montana desperately tried to move to reach her.

"*Linney!*" He tried to yell after her, but his voice came out only as a whisper.

Clunk, snick, thud.

Montana heard the sounds but couldn't place them.

"Up!"

The voice came to him through a haze, and he realized Linney had gone. He desperately tried to get to a place where he could follow her, explain to her, but the voice was insistent.

"Up!" This time the word was punctuated with a sharp jab to his side.

Montana opened his eyes with a start and tried to orient himself quickly. It took him a moment longer than the guard was willing to wait and a foot kicked him in the back.

"Get up now. You have a visitor."

Pushing the dream down to a place where he could deal with it later, he attempted to sit up. He immediately realized where he was and what had happened. The last few minutes were a little hazy, but from the naked mattress he had been thrown on in the otherwise empty room, he surmised he had been placed in solitary confinement. As he struggled to a sitting position, he realized that despite protocol, he had been shackled after they had subdued him and left that way.

His hands and feet, bound with leather restraints, were numb and tingling. Dizziness attacked unexpectedly, and he nearly fell back to the mattress without his hands for support.

The second guard, hidden behind the first, stepped in, caught him and hauled him to a standing position. Everything ached, he felt as if he had just run a marathon in full pack, in ninety-degree heat.

The second guard bent down to release the restraints around his ankles while the first guard placed a Taser to the side of his neck.

"Don't give me any trouble, pal. Someone wants to talk to you, and I don't want to be the one to tell him he can't."

Montana focused on the chipped, puke-green, concrete wall in front of him and concentrated on his breathing. Air in, air out.

The leather straps tightened momentarily as the guard cinched them to loosen the buckles. Blood revisited his feet, bringing with it excruciating pain as circulation returned. Montana ignored it, keeping his gaze level and his body still. He knew if the guard discharged the Taser where he had it placed on his neck, it would most likely be fatal. He wondered if the guard knew that. From the nervousness the man displayed, Montana didn't think so. He waited until the guard removed the weapon and lowered his eyes. The guard nudged him forward with a cudgel to the small of his back.

He knew better than to say a word, but he couldn't help but wonder who had the clout to get him out of solitary for a visit.

Damien?

Maybe. He'd find out soon enough.

With his hands still bound behind his back, they ushered Montana into the visitors' lounge. The room, usually packed with anxious family members trying hard to ignore the fact that their loved ones were incarcerated and surrounded by armed guards, was eerily quiet. Today the room was empty and silence prevailed.

The guards placed him in a chair next to a table and cuffed his already restrained hands to the back of the metal chair. Outwardly he showed them nothing, his eyes downcast and defeated, head bowed, his hair falling forward, hiding his features. Inside he missed nothing; he knew where each of the guards positioned themselves in relation to him, how they were armed and their individual level of experience. Despite his outwardly calm demeanor, his gut clenched. This wasn't right. Everything about the way they had handled him was wrong.

Jose should never have been allowed to approach him, the guards should have intervened long before they did, and when Montana relented there was no reason to Taser him, let alone place him in solitary. Someone else pulled the strings. The prison guards, maybe even the warden, were just the puppets. He had a good idea who the puppet-master might be. The door to the lounge opened but Montana didn't look up, he knew Damien was not his mysterious visitor.

After weeks of surveillance and images seen through magnification, he had no trouble recognizing Stone Kale as he swaggered into the visitors' lounge. Every muscle in Montana's body tensed, and then, as if on command, he relaxed. Loose and languid, he appraised the man who killed Linney Keller as he took a seat opposite of him. A simple wooden table separated them. Three feet—it might as well have been a thousand miles.

An eerie calm came over Montana as his mind became quiet.

Nothing would be gained by letting his emotions rule the moment. Kale had the advantage—for now. There would come a time when Montana would allow what he now buried to come to the surface, a time when he would let the demons slip off the leash and do as they would.

Not now.

Now he simply listened to his heart beat. He found his center and waited for the show to start.

"How ya doing, sport?" Dressed immaculately in a charcoal gray Armani suit and lavender silk shirt and tie, Kale slicked back his hair and crossed his legs. Leaning forward and inspecting Montana's bruised face closely, he clucked his tongue and shook his head in apparent concern. "Damn, they've been a little rough on you, huh? Well, what can you do? You know, I don't believe we've formally met, outside your surveillance role that is. I'm Stone Kale. I would shake hands, but it seems you are a bit inconvenienced."

"I know who you are," Montana said, his voice low and neutral. "What I don't know is why you're here. What do you want, Kale?"

"What do I want?" he asked Montana. "What do I want?" he seemed to ask himself. "I came here out of the goodness of my heart to offer you shared condolences. We both lost someone we cared deeply about."

Anger, hot and demanding, surged through Montana. It took all the restraint he could call on to maintain the outwardly calm demeanor.

"Who do you own, Kale?" Montana asked. His quiet voice belied the lethal feelings that threatened. "Must be someone big for you to have the balls to come in here like this." Knowing anger was exactly what Kale tried to elicit from him, Montana was determined to show anything but. "No, wait, anyone who murders an unarmed hundred and ten pound woman doesn't have much in the balls department."

Montana raised his head and met Kale's eyes for the first time. What he saw in the other man's eyes was exactly what he was hoping for. Rage, barely contained, simmered behind the blue eyes that stared back at him.

Montana pushed a little harder. "I can't quite figure out how you did it with me there, but little by little the pieces are coming together." Leaning as far forward as his restrained hands allowed, Montana kept his voice deadly quiet and his face free of any emotion. The combination, he had been told, was terrifying to look at. "You're dead," he said and sat back.

He watched Kale blink as the words registered.

"I'm not the one chained to a chair," Kale said. "I'm not the one in a God damn jail cell waiting for trial. *I'm* the one on the outside. *I'm* the one who gets to walk out of here, you cocky bastard." With every word, his voice rose. Kale gripped the table separating them with both hands and leaned toward Montana.

Montana simply smiled.

"And I'm the one she was in love with," Montana said.

Almost before the words were out, Kale lunged. Flipping the table that separated them, he wrapped his hands around Montana's throat as the guards ran toward them. The chair Montana was shackled to flew backward with Montana still attached. Kale straddled him, and squeezed. When the guards tried to pull him off, he satisfied his anger by slamming his fist into Montana's face.

Despite the fact that he was defenseless, Montana smiled.

"Mr. Kale, sir!" The guards pulled Kale off their prisoner and tried to defuse the situation. Kale shook free of their grip and walked a step away as another guard came to Montana and righted his chair.

"You okay?" he asked, inspecting the split lip and bleeding gash on Montana's chin. Montana ignored him, his eyes following Kale's every move.

Kale turned around to face Montana once more. Anger vibrated off him as he fought for control. Pacing in front of Montana, he pushed hair out of his eyes and finally stopped and bent down to stare into

Montana's face.

The guards tensed and moved between their prisoner and Kale. It was obvious to Montana that Kale's influence on them only went so far. He didn't think they were willing to risk having to explain to their superiors why an unauthorized visitor beat a restrained prisoner. A prisoner who should be in solitary confinement.

"You are *nothing!*" Kale yelled. Spittle flew from his lips, and his face blanched with undiluted anger. "Linney belonged with *me!* I came here to tell you that. No one takes what is mine, *no one!* Now neither of us can have her, you son-of-a-bitch!"

"She wasn't a thing to be owned," Montana told him.

"I should have killed you when I had the chance," Kale whispered.

"What, and miss all this fun?"

Kale stepped back, took a breath, then shook his head. "Linney's funeral is today. As her parents are dead, I made sure she had the very best of arrangements. I'll be sure to throw a rose on the casket for you."

The comment nearly took the smile from Montana's face, but he refused to let Kale know the effect the words had on him. He filled his head with an image of Kale's life slipping away slowly, at his hands. No weapon, just his hands; it would be all he needed. It would take a long time, and Montana would enjoy every moment of it.

When he thought he could manage it, he lifted his head and felt blood spill down his chin. He waited until he was sure he had Kale's attention.

"You got some blood on your shirt, might want to change that. It doesn't come out, you know."

The comment took Kale off guard. His face screwed up in confusion, he looked down at his shirt and found Montana's blood speckled across the lavender silk. He brushed at it, causing the speckles to smear into streaks.

Kale seemed to regain control once more and walked toward

Montana, putting the guards on edge. They took a step toward their prisoner.

"Relax, I just want to say a final farewell to my new friend, comfort him in a time of loss."

The guards stood close, not wanting the situation to get out of hand again, as Kale bent down and whispered something in Montana's ear that only he could hear. Montana sat staring straight ahead, giving no indication of what he heard.

Standing back up and giving Montana one final look, Kale turned and left the visitors' lounge. The guards relaxed almost visibly at the man's absence. Montana watched them look at one another nervously.

"This was a bad idea," said the younger guard who had held the Taser on him.

"Shut up and get him back. Clean him up. And you..." The older guard got in Montana's face. "If I hear any shit about police brutality, I will personally give you something to complain about. Get him out of here."

His hands were still restrained but freed from the back of the chair. Montana offered them no resistance. All he could think of was Kale's parting remark. That and the fact that Linney was being put to rest today by the man who had killed her.

Linney was being put in the ground. He would have given anything to be the one in that casket. Anything for Linney to be alive again.

He tried to put the thoughts away, but indulged for just a moment. No one would be able to tell by looking at him that it was the last time the Montana he had been would surface.

That Montana was useless. So he became who he used to be: a man who could kill without thinking twice about it. Someone who could take a life without uttering a single sound, who could tell you the best way to take a life in any given situation and survive at any and all costs. It was a side of himself that Montana despised, but maybe it was the side that might be able to get them both out of this alive.

The only problem—one of them wasn't sure he wanted to bother.

CHAPTER 12

Montana sat on the narrow exam table in the infirmary, his right wrist shackled to the metal table, an armed guard next to him as the male nurse patched him up.

"He's going to need a couple of stitches on his cheek, and that eye is going to swell shut, but nothing's broken as far as I can tell."

"I don't give a fuck, sew him up and hurry." The younger guard seemed nervous and twitchy. He kept looking at the door to the infirmary, his eyes betraying his nerves.

"Hey, I'm not the doc. I can only triage and treat the minor shit. I can't do the sewing."

"Look, I'm not doing any more paperwork today, got it? If you don't fix him, I'm taking him back as is."

The nurse looked at the guard, and then back to Montana. Pulling on a pair of gloves, he opened a tray beneath the counter and took out supplies.

"Sorry about this, man," he said in a low voice to Montana. "I don't have the right type of thread. I'll do what I can, but the sucker's going to leave a scar. I don't have any lidocaine either, going to hurt like a bitch."

"He's tough, Mikey." The older guard nudged Montana's shoulder with the barrel of his weapon. "Ain't ya, chief? Just patch him up, he's pretty enough."

Montana sat unmoving as the nurse wiped the blood from the wound and threaded a curved surgical needle. Twelve times the needle pierced his flesh, pulling the ends together in a gross approximation of what once had been. Through it all Montana stared at the wall. He never made a sound; he made no movement of any kind.

Mikey patted the blood caused by his makeshift repair job away and appraised his work. "I tried to make the stitches small, but it's still going to leave a scar," he said by way of apology. Montana made no reply.

"We done here?" the nervous, younger guard asked.

"Just need to give him a tetanus booster, and then, yeah, all done." The nurse unlocked the medicine cabinet, obtained the vaccine, and paused to answer the ringing phone.

"Clinic," he said, holding the receiver between his shoulder and chin as he drew up the clear fluid into a syringe. Tapping out the air and measuring the correct dose, he paused, his eyes flicking from the guards to Montana and back again. Pushing Montana's sleeve up, he prepped the area with alcohol and injected the booster efficiently into the man's shoulder. He withdrew the needle and pulled down Montana's sleeve all while listening to the person on the other end of the line.

"Yeah, okay, I'll tell them. Yeah, sure." He let the phone slip off his shoulder, catching it and replacing it in the receiver. He placed the used needle into a sharps receptacle, peeled off his bloodied gloves and looked at the guards.

"His lawyer is here, wants to talk to him."

The guards exchanged glances.

"Something wrong?" Mikey asked.

"Nothing you need to worry about." The younger guard looked at his counterpart. "What do we do?"

"We take him to see his lawyer. Wouldn't want to infringe on his rights, now would we?" The older guard unlocked Montana's cuff from the table. Montana slid off and stood, holding his hands behind his back, patiently waiting for them to be restrained once more. His eyes blank and expressionless.

"You sure he didn't get whacked in the head?" the nurse asked, scrutinizing Montana. "The dude don't look right to me."

"He's fine, Mikey, just clumsy and took a header, that's all. Simple accident, right, chief?"

"What if he tells his lawyer? Look, I got a family depending on my paycheck, I can't afford to get fired over this shit." The young guard wiped a thin sheen of sweat from his face with the back of one hand. "I hear his lawyer is some slick guy from Denver, never loses a case."

"Calm your ass down. We do not have a problem here. A prisoner tripped and cut his face. We followed proper protocol and obtained medical treatment for his injuries, even got him all boostered up, didn't we, Mikey? No problems here, right, chief?"

Montana gave no indication of hearing.

"See, the chief understands. Now we'll take him to see his counselor in accordance with his legal rights, and then we'll take him back to his cell. No problems, because the chief knows exactly the consequences if he should cause his lawyer to become unduly concerned over anything."

Montana heard their words, but gave them nothing. His mind quiet, his thoughts calm. This was not the time to act. He would wait. His time would come, he knew that, but not now.

The younger guard gave him a little shove in the small of his back, and Montana moved. He felt centered and, despite the circumstances, completely in control. His hands may have been restrained behind his back and loaded weapons trained on him, but his feet were free. He estimated it would take him three seconds to take both guards down before either of them could fire a round. A hard kick to the side of a kneecap and a quick follow up with a blow to the throat would leave both men incapacitated. Another five seconds to locate the keys to the cuffs, and considering his hands were behind his back, another twenty to set himself free and take the guard's weapon.

But not now.

He would wait.

He would let them take him to Damien and see how the game played itself out.

* * * *

Damien watched as they ushered Montana to the small windowless room. He couldn't understand why they wanted him to meet Montana here, then he caught a glimpse of his face and he understood. They didn't want a room full of visitors and attorneys to witness the man's injuries and start asking questions.

"What the hell happened to my client?" Damien stood and addressed the two guards accompanying Montana.

"He had an accident," the older guard told him. "We had him treated in the infirmary."

"I bet. Montana?"

"I fell." Montana had yet to meet Damien's eyes.

"See, no problems. You let us know when you're finished, counselor, and we'll make sure we escort him back to his cell."

Damien watched the guards leave and lock the door behind them before turning his attention back to Montana.

"Jesus!" Damien sat opposite Montana and looked the man over. His right eye was swollen shut, thick black sutures curved along his jaw up his cheek. It looked red, raw, and painful. "Want to tell me what really happened? Who did this?"

"I fell."

Damien shook his head. "Sure you did. This is getting out of hand, Montana. I know Kale has his people in here with you."

"I can handle it."

Damien raised his brows and looked at his client's face once more. "Not from where I'm sitting. Look, I get that you might not be able to talk to me about this, but just listen. Your tox screen came back positive for Rohypnol and Ketamine."

Damien watched Montana's face carefully and saw the briefest glimmer of interest in the black eyes that stared past him.

"It's why you can't remember anything," Damien continued. "The bastard drugged you, and killed Linney."

Montana shook his head. "No, he was there, but he didn't kill her. He watched, he stood in the shadows and he watched while she was raped and he watched as she was killed."

Damien leaned forward, his arms on the table between them, his face intent. "You remember?"

Montana thought, his face creased in concentration. "Bits and pieces, more like dreams than memories." He turned and focused on Damien for the first time since entering the room. "He was there, Damien. If he was there he had to leave something behind. I need to get out of here. I can prove he did this, but I need out."

Damien sat back and ran a hand through his hair. "I'm working on it, I have a meeting with an appellate court judge later today. Tell me they did this to you, and I can get you out on grounds of abuse."

"They didn't touch me."

"You're not helping, Montana. Who do you think you're protecting?"

"Kale was here."

That took about ten seconds for Damien to process. "What do you mean, Kale was here?"

"About an hour ago." He turned his damaged face to Damien. "A parting gift."

"Kale did this? Where were the guards? Damn it, Montana, it's not enough the son-of-a-bitch has his people inside, he has to come and *see* you? What the hell did he want, what was his point?"

"Relax, Damien."

"Relax? He plans to kill you before you ever get the chance to take the stand. You realize that, don't you?"

"He can try."

"Jesus, enough with the stoic bullshit. The man has his hand in the local police department, maybe even the federal. It's within his power to take you out and cover his ass while he does it. I don't think you understand just how dangerous this guy is."

"He is an egotistical sociopath. He thinks money can buy him anything. He's wrong. He has no discipline, coming here to see me is proof of that. Kale wanted to rub my nose in the fact that he had Linney killed and I am the one he thinks will pay for it. He couldn't stand it that he never confronted me. You see, I took something that he considered his property. Linney wanted out, and I was the one who helped her find the way. Then I had the nerve to love the woman. It was killing his ego that he couldn't confront me, that he couldn't see my reaction. He is dangerous, Damien, but not in the way you mean. I understand him."

"You're underestimating him, Montana."

"Men like him think they are untouchable. Eventually they make mistakes. Kale made several. The first one was abusing Linney. The second was having her killed. The last was involving me. I'm not underestimating him, Damien."

Montana didn't say the words, but Damien knew what he was thinking—Kale was the one underestimating him. Damien heard the unspoken thought clearly and he knew Montana well enough to believe him. Sitting bloodied and beaten, shackled and incarcerated, Damien didn't fear for Montana. Damien wondered if Stone Kale understood the danger *he* was in.

"You're not immortal," Damien reminded him. "Watch your back."

"Always."

"Look, I'm not sure about the timing on this, I'll leave it up to you, but Dakota is here."

"What do you mean here?"

"I mean he's *here*. It took some doing, but I got him a pass. Do you want to see him?"

"What about Ito?"

"He said he had business to attend to, left Dakota with me. Oh, yeah, I have a message for you from Ito. He said to 'do a Branson', whatever that means."

Montana's mouth, the side without the stitches, curved up in what could have been mistaken for a smile. "Tell him I'm working on it."

"So, do I get to know what the hell you two are talking in code about, or as your lawyer am I not privileged to such things?"

The smile vanished. "Dakota will drive you crazy unless you let him in."

Damien shook his head and stood. "See, people like you are the reason I never joined the military. All the cloak and dagger stuff? Not my style. Besides, the wardrobe is hideous." Checking his cufflinks, Damien walked to the door and signaled the guard there. "You sure? I mean, don't take this personally, but you look like shit."

"Dakota's seen me look worse."

Damien shrugged as keys rattled outside the locked door and Dakota was let through. Dakota stopped inside the door and stared. The guard took up residence inside the room.

"Dakota." Montana seemed almost amused at Dakota's reaction.

"Who the hell did *that*?" Dakota asked, coming to the table to get a better look at Montana's face.

"Nice to see you too."

"Screw that. Damn, Montana, who was the sad excuse for a butcher who sewed you up? A seamstress could have done a better job."

Montana shrugged. "I'm in jail for murder, we haven't seen each other in almost two years, and all you care about is my face?"

"Someone has to." Dakota smiled. "How long ago was that done?"

"Maybe ten, fifteen minutes, I guess."

"Good, then I have time." He turned to Damien. "I have a bag in the car, I need it."

The guard intercepted Dakota as he moved around the table to touch Montana.

"Sir, I can't allow any physical contact with the prisoner."

Dakota turned and faced the guard. Glancing at the man's name badge, he cocked his head and pulled out his wallet. "Well, Sergeant Miller, is it? It certainly looks as if someone had physical contact with the prisoner."

"That was an accident, sir."

"I bet. Regardless of how the injury occurred, as a physician I can tell you it has not been treated properly." Dakota pulled his government ID out of his wallet identifying him as a doctor; it also listed several very high-powered government officials as contacts. The move was meant to intimidate, and it was obvious to Damien it worked.

"Now, unless you would like a government-issued medical malpractice lawsuit on your hands, I suggest you bend the rules, Sergeant. I can treat this properly and gratuitously. If you refuse, that wound will become infected, requiring at best weeks' worth of antibiotics, possibly hospitalization, perhaps even surgery. All at the taxpayers' expense. You can pretty much kiss any pay raise coming your way bye-bye."

Sergeant Miller looked at Montana, and then back at Dakota, obviously at a loss. "I'm sorry, sir, but I can't allow it."

"Dakota, let it go," Montana told him.

Dakota turned back toward his brother. Damien didn't know Montana's brother, but he knew human nature. He could sense the helplessness Dakota felt. He tried to take control the only way he knew how, the only way he could.

"Dak, it's okay," Montana said.

"No, it's not," Dakota said. The anger slipped away, leaving behind frustration. Dakota, recognizing a lost cause, slumped into the chair opposite Montana.

The guard sighed, obviously relieved he didn't have to force the issue.

Damien moved next to the door and observed the two brothers. If he'd had any doubts about letting Dakota in to see Montana they were eradicated. Before his brother entered the room, Damien had sensed an almost predatory attitude coming from Montana. His eyes had been hard, showing Damien nothing. All that changed as Montana addressed his brother. The bond between them was nearly tangible.

"I came as soon as I could," Dakota told him.

"I know."

"I'm sorry about Linney. I'm sorry I never got the chance to meet her."

Montana kept his eyes on Dakota as if nothing else mattered. "I know, it's all right. How are you? You're not letting Maggie push you around, are you?"

Dakota brought his eyes to meet his brother's for the first time since he sat down. "Michael's dead."

Montana blinked once. "I'm sorry, Dak."

Damien didn't know who Michael was or the connection he had to Montana, but he could tell the name meant something to him.

"When?"

"Last night." Dakota shook his head. "Not your problem. Hell, what am I doing telling you that? You have your own problems."

"Stop. Michael was family, you had every right to tell me."

Dakota gave him a quick nod, the subject changed at the risk of overwhelming emotions. "What can I do to help? How do I get you out of here?"

Montana narrowed his eyes at the questions. "Nothing."

"Forget that."

"Dakota, listen to me, this is not an option. I wanted to see you, I needed this, but your involvement ends here. You cannot have anything more to do with this, understand?"

"No." Dakota shook his head. "I don't understand. You don't really think I'm going to just sit back and expect the legal system to realize they arrested the wrong guy and ever-so-nicely let you go. No offense," he said as he turned and looked at Damien.

Damien gave him a shrug.

"You can help me best by not giving me anything else to worry about. You would be a liability. I can't protect you in here."

"I don't need protection."

"Go back to Maryland, Dak. Stay out of this." Montana looked at the guard. "You can take me back."

"No way. You do not get to call the shots on this one. Maryland is not an option anymore."

That got Montana's attention. "What do you mean by that?"

"I'm not going back, I'm done with it."

Montana shook his head, his face animated for the first time. "Go back. They can protect you."

Dakota stood and watched the guards move forward and shackle his brother's hands to a chain around his waist. Damien could see the tension in Dakota. He almost expected him to jump the guard.

"Not going to happen."

"Let it alone, Dak," Montana made one last plea, staring directly at Dakota, black eyes peering into green. When he was sure he had his attention he spoke again, the words quiet but precise. "*Wicasa wa wayie k'atach anum wicao.*"

Dakota gave his brother a nod, saying nothing else. But it was the expression on his face that concerned Damien more than anything.

"Montana?" Damien came to his client's side, confused by the meeting's abrupt ending.

"Keep him out of this, Damien. Tell Ito to watch his back."

"What about you?"

"It's under control. I'm good."

"I'll be in touch," Damien said as the guards pushed Montana ahead of them and out of sight.

Dakota stood slightly behind Damien, the anger and frustration replaced by confusion. Or was it understanding? Damien couldn't tell.

"What the hell was that? What did he say to you?"

"That was Sioux, an old Indian proverb," Dakota told him, his eyes still on the door Montana had disappeared through.

"What does it mean?"

Dakota turned and gave Damien his attention for the first time. "The literal translation would be something like, 'Coyote is always out there, and coyote is always hungry.'"

"I don't understand."

"My family is Lakota," Dakota explained. "One story our *santee*, our grandmother, told us was of the coyote. In Lakota lore, coyotes are seen as tricksters. They try to make you forget how dangerous they truly are by acting foolish and making you forget to fear them. The coyote will try and lure you into a sense of security right before it rips your throat out and has you for dinner. Montana was trying to tell me not to trust the coyote."

"Who is the coyote? Kale?"

Dakota shook his head. "I don't think so. Too obvious."

"So someone you trust is not trustworthy?"

"Yeah."

"The coyote is always hungry."

Dakota licked his lips and met Damien's eyes. "Yeah."

CHAPTER 13

The cell door slammed shut with all the finality of a coffin lid falling into place. Solitary confinement again. Montana didn't mind, he liked the quiet. The small windowless room had only enough light for the cameras he knew monitored him. They had taken the restraints off this time.

Gingerly lowering himself to the mattress in the corner, Montana lay down. The sutures in his cheek pulled and throbbed, his chest burned from the Taser discharge, and his throat was raw where Kale had tried to strangle him. But all he could think about was Linney in the ground. She hated the cold and the dark. They had laid her to rest in both. Maybe the quiet wasn't such a good thing after all. Squeezing his eyes shut, he forced images of Linney from his mind.

Instead he thought of what Ito had told him. *Do a Branson.* The three words took him back almost a dozen years.

Ben Branson was one of the most dangerous people Montana ever knew. Washed out as a Ranger, not because he couldn't hack it, but because Branson played only by one set of rules—his own. Attitudes like that never sat well with the army. Branson was labeled as unstable and discharged from the service pending a psychiatric review. Branson had no problem with the discharge, the review board however never got the chance to determine exactly how unstable he was. He took off.

Montana didn't need a review board to tell him Branson was

dangerous. He had trained the man; he knew firsthand what he was capable of. Branson saw no point in keeping the bad guys alive—ever. If Branson had the shot, he took it. To him it was as simple as that. Ethics and morality played no part in his decisions. In a way it freed him from the dilemmas of choosing right over wrong, to Branson his way was always the right way. He had no demons, no nightmares. Montana was willing to bet the man slept like the dead. There were no shades of gray in Branson's world, only black and white.

From a strictly professional point of view, Montana admired the guy's expertise. He was the best. Montana lost track of him after he left the army, heard he made a living as a mercenary. Gun for hire. If you could afford him.

Their lives crossed paths unexpectedly in the summer of '98. Luckily for Montana, Branson didn't care about things like rules and procedures.

It was supposed to be a routine recon mission, in and out. A cartel outside of Bogotá had been pinned down, and Montana and his team were to infiltrate and determine where they were holed up, how many, and how heavily armed. They were not to engage. Orders were very clear on that. Obtain the information and let ATF do the dirty work. Sounded easy enough, right up to the point when the Black Hawk delivering them to the drop zone took a shot and fell out of the air.

Well, one question had an answer: they were heavily armed, at least with RPGs.

Montana came to with the heat of the burning helicopter searing his skin like meat on a grill. Rolling away from the inferno, he could still see the pilot slumped against the control panel as flames licked over his body. Dead, or soon to be dead.

Montana did not come away unscathed. Crushed ribs and a shattered right arm stole his breath. He searched for the rest of his team and counted four of eight thrown clear of the doomed aircraft. He could only make out Ito for sure, the others were just guesses as blood from a gash over his eye blurred his vision.

"Red Wolf One calling Red Wolf Two, mayday, mayday, we are down. Repeat, we are down, over." Montana keyed the radio in his helmet and waited for a reply. All he got was static.

Ito ducked and ran to Montana's side, blood running down his face from a wound on his scalp. Gunfire in staccato bursts cut through the brush around them. "How bad?" he asked, giving Montana a quick once-over.

"I'm good. Who do we have?"

"Bobby, Ray, Patrick, and yours truly."

Ito's information told Montana four of his team didn't make it. "Damn! Injuries?"

"Bobby's bad. Patrick's alive but unconscious. Ray wants to blow something up."

Montana couldn't help but grin. "He might have a chance to do just that." Ito helped him sit and Montana grimaced and coughed up blood. He couldn't seem to get enough air.

"We need to get out of here."

Wiping his mouth with the back of his hand, Montana nodded. "Any ideas?"

"No contact?"

Montana shook his head. "They're either maintaining silence, or the radio's shot. Either way, it's too hot for them to come in. We're not supposed to be here, remember?"

They both ducked and covered as dirt kicked up by a grenade rained down on their position.

"We need to move," Montana said, trying to get to his knees. He didn't make it.

"You can't travel. Moving Bobby will kill him, and Patrick is still out."

Montana leaned back on one elbow, his broken right arm dangling at his side, and looked around him. Ito was right. "Well, that sucks."

Ito smiled, wiping blood out of his eyes. "It does indeed, my friend, it does indeed." He checked the ammo in his belt and gave Montana extra clips he had obviously scavenged from their team members who no longer had use for them. The dead had no worries. For them the battle was over. For Ito and Montana it had just begun.

A voice cutting through the static in Montana's headset drew his attention.

"Black Hawk, do you read?" The voice was a whisper and in perfect unaccented English.

"This is Black Hawk, I read you. Identify yourself." Montana gave Ito a confused look and a shrug.

"I'm right in front of you, Black Hawk. Just keep your finger off the trigger, I'm coming through and I am friendly, repeat, friendly."

The thick jungle in front of the downed helicopter parted, and a single man came through. Dressed in green and brown camouflage and heavily armed, he ran over to Montana and Ito.

"I saw you go down. I don't usually interfere with army business, but what the hell, I'm in the neighborhood. How many dead, how many injured?"

"Who the hell are you?" Montana asked.

"Well, that's gratitude." The man looked at Montana's fatigues with his name and rank across the right breast pocket and laughed. "Major Thomas? Would that be as in Major Montana Thomas?"

"Do I know you?"

"Branson," Ito spoke up. "Thought you were dead."

Branson gave Ito a nasty, crooked smile and a nod. "Lucky for you I'm not. I would love to get all chummy and reminisce with you, but seeing as half the drug cartel of Columbia has you in their sights I suggest we keep conversation to a minimum and haul ass." Branson gave a short whistle, and the brush came alive with half a dozen of his men.

Ito came to Montana's side and hoisted him to his feet.

The last thing Montana remembered was Branson smiling at him. "Imagine that, I get to save *your* ass."

Two days later Montana woke up in a field hospital, and Ito filled him in on what had happened. Ben Branson and his men not only saved their asses, they killed the entire cartel, every man. The money the cartel was rumored to have in their possession was never found and Ben Branson was in the wind. Montana never saw him again. From that day on whenever his team had a risky mission, something that weighed the odds against them coming out alive, when they needed to do the impossible, they would tell each other to do a Branson.

Montana wondered exactly what Branson would do in his situation, and then realized Branson would never have allowed himself to get here in the first place. Survival at all costs. That was fine with him. Montana always thought Branson did what he did because he didn't care if his actions caused his death. A man without fear was a dangerous adversary. It was survival as an act of attrition. If he was still alive at the end of all of this, fine. If he wasn't, that caused him no concern either.

If Ito wanted him to do a Branson, Montana had no problem with that.

CHAPTER 14

Ito parked the white Hummer outside the building Linney Keller lived in, the building she died in. He'd circled the block three times until he found a place large enough to accommodate the vehicle. In a neighborhood dominated by Honda Civics and Toyota Camrys, the Hummer stood out like a pimple on a prom queen. That was fine with Ito, he didn't believe in being something he wasn't, and subtle was one thing he would never be.

Earlier, Ito spent a good part of the morning doing his homework. The little things always made all the difference. The things that don't stand out in the middle of a field waving a red flag.

Since moving forward on the case was getting him nowhere, Ito decided to look back instead. Scott Jefferies, the manager of Linney's building, knew something he didn't see fit to share. Ito thought that was terribly unfair of him and wanted to give the man a chance to change his mind.

Nice middle-class neighborhood. Ito sat in the Hummer for over an hour and watched. Ten in the morning and all the good people were deep in whatever it was that kept them in their nice middle-class neighborhood. No foot traffic and only a few cars passing by on the street.

Ito knew Jefferies was home. He'd called with the premise of looking at a vacant unit; not Linney's, not enough time to paint over all that blood. The police had released the apartment, having scoured it for evidence, but Ito wasn't interested in that. He looked over the information he'd collected on Scott Robert Jefferies and the list of indiscretions the man had compiled during his life. They were mostly unimpressive. Originally from Philadelphia, Jefferies was a small time player. Misdemeanors filled his rap sheet, petty shit that Ito couldn't have cared less about. It was his association with Stone Kale and Linney Keller that interested Ito.

He opened a duffle bag on the seat next to him and pulled out a Kimber .45 semi-automatic. He untucked his shirt to hide the weapon, straightened in the seat, and pushed the gun into the waistband of his pants. He reached into the duffle again, took out a roll of duct tape, and finally exited the Hummer.

Ito knew from Damien's notes where Jefferies lived. Inside the foyer, first floor, first door on the left. He thought he would have to buzz to be let in the secured building, but obviously Jefferies had been expecting him. Figuring the one bedroom units went for over a grand a month, Ito could understand his enthusiasm.

Ito stood outside the door for a moment and heard Lynyrd Skynyrd blaring through to the hallway. *Sweet Home Alabama.* He rapped on the door, the music went quiet, and soft footfalls could be heard rushing forward and pausing. Ito made sure Jefferies got an eyeful as he peered out the peephole.

The door opened slowly, and Jefferies poked his head out. "Mr. St. James?"

"Not quite what you were expecting?" A grin split Ito's face as he pushed Jefferies back into the apartment. He saw no need to continue the game.

Ito shouldered his way through the opening and backed the man up, kicking the door shut behind him, then pulled the Kimber free.

Jefferies's eyes widened when he saw the gun, and he backpedaled to a desk at the side of the entrance. He pulled open a drawer in the desk and pulled out a small caliber handgun. Ito cut him off before he could even bring it up to aim. Ito grabbed him by the back of the shirt and spun him around, hooked his free arm under the man's chin and lifted. Jeffries kicked and thrashed, the weapon dropping from his grip, his feet a good four inches off the ground, harsh rasping noises coming from his throat. Ito squeezed just a little and held it until the thrashing stopped.

Deprived of blood, Jefferies's brain shut down and his body went limp in Ito's arm. It was an effective way to subdue your enemy, only problem was, sometimes it did more than subdue. This wasn't one of those times.

Ito sat on Jefferies's couch and waited for him to wake up. He watched as the man's head lifted off his chest. Jefferies looked confused, but when he saw Ito things seemed to come together for him. He tried to back away from Ito and panicked when he found he couldn't move. Ito had made good use of his time and the duct tape.

Secured to his desk chair, Jefferies pulled against the tape that held him. "What is this! Who are you? Look, if it's money you want, that's not a problem. What's your pleasure, man? Ruppies, K, Meth? Come on, we can do business, there's no reason for the drama."

Jefferies babbled and Ito let him wind down before coming to stand over him. He didn't say anything, he just stood and stared. Jefferies started to sweat, one thin trickle rolling down his temple.

"What, man, what! What do you want?"

"Who killed the girl?"

"The girl? What girl? Oh, geeze, Kale's chick? How the hell should I know?"

Ito nodded as if in agreement with the man, and then reached out and pushed his thumb just under the mandibular joint, pressing on the nerve there. Jefferies bucked and tried to move away from the pain, but the tape held.

"Fuck! Man, stop, stop!"

"The girl." Ito released the pressure.

"I don't know!"

"Twenty-six nerves come together right about here." Ito placed his finger under Jefferies's clavicle, the brachial plexus, the hub of nerve central, and caressed the spot. "That..." Ito patted the spot on Jefferies's cheek where he had dug his thumb. "Was foreplay."

"Jesus, he'll kill me. He's a freaking psycho, man!"

Ito squatted down in front of Jefferies so he could look him in the eye. Jefferies reminded Ito of an animal caught in a snare trying to decide if it should gnaw off its own foot or die in the trap.

"He's not here," Ito reminded him. "I am."

Jefferies stared at Ito's index finger poised over the soft skin. "Kale didn't touch her," he said, his eyes never leaving the finger resting lightly on his chest.

"Keep talking."

"What the fuck do you want? I told you Kale didn't kill her, that's what you asked. Now let me the fuck up!"

"Now see, that's where we run into a problem, because I have this feeling that you know a whole lot more than you're sharing with me. Someone killed that girl and it wasn't my good friend. No forced entry means *someone* had a key. So, I asked myself who would have a key to an apartment besides the person living there? I'm sure you see the logic here, right?"

Ito shook his head, brought the Kimber up and tapped his chin with the barrel.

"So this is my dilemma. I know you let *someone* in her apartment that night, or at the very least gave someone the key. You have knowledge I need, and I sure would be indebted if you would share that knowledge." Ito pushed very lightly into the tender flesh, just enough to give promise of what was to come.

Jefferies paled and his mouth opened in an 'O' but no sound

escaped. He needed air in his lungs to make sounds; he had none—the pain had stolen it.

Ito kept the pressure up while he talked. "That's only about half a pound per square inch, I'm not even trying." Ito could tell by the look in the man's eyes he had decided to gnaw.

He released the pressure.

Jefferies coughed and gulped air back into his lungs. "Damn, just stop, stop! What, do you guys have like a club or something? Psychos 'R Us? Jesus!"

He took a moment to get it together and Ito let him.

"Okay, Kale had a thing for the chick, not that I blame him, she was slamming. But he took it a little far, you know?" When Ito said nothing, Jefferies swallowed and continued. "Then she found out about the psycho side and decided she wanted out. But he wouldn't let her go. I would see her come home with bruises, crying. Kale wanted me to put cameras in her apartment so he could watch her."

"Did you?"

"I told him no, no way. That's when he sent his muscle to pay me a visit."

"You put the cameras in, you parasite."

"Hey, I got a kid, man. They never touched me, but I have a three-year-old daughter, she lives with her mother. They told me what they would do to her. I believed them, so yeah, I put the cameras in. Those little spy things they use for undercover work."

"Who did you give the key to?"

"Look, I saw her go up with the guy, her new boyfriend, big guy, dark hair. About an hour later Kale shows up at my door with six of his guys."

Ito leaned forward, all amusement gone from his expression. His hand curled in the material of Jefferies's shirt. "You gave him the key."

"Yes! Hell yes, I gave him the key. You don't know the son-of-a-bitch, he would have taken the key anyway and still had his goons hurt my little girl."

Ito released him and wiped his hand on his pants as if he had just touched something vile. "What about the cameras? Do the police know about them? Where are the tapes?"

"Kale had me take them down before he called 911."

"Where are the tapes?" Ito fought for control. If the cameras were rolling when Kale had the girl killed, he had evidence.

"Kale. Kale took them. I swear he had a hard-on just thinking about them."

"Did you see them?"

"No, no way, I mean, I saw the blood, the freak butchered that girl."

"And you gave him the key." Ito stood and walked to the door. He had what he came for and now felt in need of a shower.

"Hey! Wait." Jefferies pulled against the tape. "I gave you what you wanted, man. Come on, you can't leave me like this. He'll kill me and my little girl if he finds out I talked to you! Cut me free."

"You're a smart guy," Ito told him. "Figure it out."

Before he left, Ito walked over to the stereo and turned Lynyrd Skynyrd back on. He jacked the volume up, and left Scott Jefferies screaming at him through the closed door.

He walked with deliberate calm to the Hummer. Sliding into the driver's seat, he took the Kimber and the duct tape and placed them back inside the duffle, then sat with his hands on the steering wheel.

He knew Kale wouldn't destroy the tapes, his ego wouldn't allow it. All Ito had to do was get them and he'd have the proof he needed to get Montana out.

Kale had a virtual army at his disposal. Ito had a gun-shy doctor and a lawyer.

He ruled Damien out immediately. His reputation could not be in question if he was to help Montana. Dakota was going to be a problem.

Ito wished he had left him in Maryland, but he would deal with the good doctor even if he had to hog-tie him. Ito was not about to save one Thomas brother at the expense of the other. Dakota didn't know it yet, but the game was over for him.

Damien should still be babysitting Dakota, and Ito needed to figure out exactly how he was going to pay Stone Kale a visit and still be breathing at the end of the day. He turned the key, and the Hummer roared to life. Ito pulled into the street and headed back to Montana's apartment.

He wondered as he looked out at peaceful suburbia if any of these people knew the devil that walked among them. Probably not. Devils seldom wore their horns in public.

CHAPTER 15

Dakota asked Damien to drop him off at Montana's apartment. Damien was reluctant, but did as he was asked.

"Ito told me to keep an eye on you."

"What's Ito afraid I'm going to do, Damien? I know you have a hell of a lot more important things to do than Ito's bidding, and I can't help but take offense that I'm someone who needs looking after."

"I think he's just worried about you."

Dakota felt the slightest hesitation on Damien's part and gave him his most trusting smile. "Look, Ito should be back soon. I'm beat, I'll probably just crash, okay?"

"I do have a meeting in about thirty minutes." Damien glanced at his watch, and Dakota got out on the passenger side of Damien's rental car.

"Go to your meeting, I'm going to order pizza and sleep." Dakota shut the door.

Damien powered down the window to continue talking to him. "You sure? I mean, you seemed a little out of it after Montana left, after he talked to you."

"So, I won't trust anyone, come on, I won't talk to anyone. I swear I'll wait for Ito."

"You have my cellphone number, call if you need anything."

Dakota started walking away and gave Damien a wave over his shoulder as he jogged the few stairs up to Montana's apartment. Working the key in the lock, he heard the rental car drive away and waited for four beats of his heart to turn and make sure Damien had left.

When he was sure he was alone, he switched from the laid-back attitude he'd showed Damien to hyper-mode. Every nerve tingled along his spine.

The coyote was hungry.

He hadn't been entirely honest with Damien. The story he told him was true enough if taken literally. He knew what Montana meant, but kept that part of it to himself. It was true Montana told him not to trust anyone, that even friends could be enemies. But what he didn't share with Damien was the rest of Montana's message. It was the reason he had spoken in Sioux, he didn't want Damien to know.

Montana told Dakota not to trust anyone, he also told him to run, that his life was in danger. Their grandfather lived in secrecy and privacy somewhere in the mountains of Montana, in his own way, that's where Montana told Dakota to go.

Find the coyote. Trust no one and find the coyote.

That was what Montana told him. Coyote was the term they used for their grandfather. Montana wanted him to run and hide in the mountains with their extended family, to stay safe. To hide from Kale.

Dakota slipped inside Montana's apartment and after closing the door behind him went from window to window and pulled the shades. Then he got to work. Dakota was not about to hide away while Montana's life was in the balance. He wasn't exactly keen on becoming a walking target, either.

He rummaged through Montana's belongings, thinking his brother would forgive the intrusion. It took him a few minutes of searching, but Montana was methodical and Dakota knew him well. Next to his bed in a side table drawer, Dakota found what he was looking for: a Colt

Python .357 magnum with a four-inch barrel. Taking the weapon and extra ammo clips, he grabbed his bag from the foot of the bed, checked the contents, and realized he was painfully short on one important thing—money. All he needed was enough to buy one item and he would be set. Searching through drawers and coat pockets, Dakota managed to procure twenty dollars from Montana's apartment.

He glanced at his watch, Ito would be back soon. He had to move. No note, no explanation, Dakota grabbed his bag and Montana's keys from the rack near the door, shut the lights off, locked the apartment behind him, and walked away.

Montana paid to have his vehicles housed in a locked garage behind the apartment. Dakota found the key to the garage and walked to his transportation. It was a good thing Montana was behind bars, because if he knew what Dakota was about to do, he would be seriously pissed. There in the dimly lit building were two of Montana's most treasured possessions. One was the black Jeep Wrangler, gleaming like new. Dakota considered that for a moment, then walked past it in preference of the vehicle parked next to it.

He grabbed his sunglasses from his bag and slung it across his shoulder. Dakota straddled the sleek Harley-Davidson Sportster 883L and donned the glasses, he powered open the garage door, and kicked the puppy to life.

The engine purred like a well-fed cat. Dakota powered the door shut behind him and eased onto the street until he got a feel for the bike. He tried to keep a low profile until he cleared town, waited for the open highway to pull the throttle back and let her rip. At about eighty MPH, with the wind slicing through his hair and billowing his jacket out around him, Dakota bent low over the handlebars and found a smile on his face for the first time in a long time.

For the moment, his life belonged to no one but himself. No one monitoring him. No one looking at him through the glass. Now there was just the feel of the powerful engine between his legs, the wind in his face, and a complete feeling of freedom. He could go anywhere, do anything, because for that moment Dakota truly was in the wind.

In the bottom of the bag Ricco had packed for him was a credit card in his name with no spending limit. It was tempting, but credit cards could be traced. The twenty he'd found in Montana's apartment wouldn't last long, but if he could get where he was headed, he might have a solution to his money problem as well.

The thought of Ricco had grief surfacing and Dakota indulged in the feeling. Michael Ricco had every reason to let his past rule him, instead Ricco tried to use what had been done to him to help those who had unknowingly abandoned him to the hands of a madman for most of his life. Ricco had to be one of the bravest men Dakota ever knew. He'd influenced Dakota's choices in his own life. Ricco gave him the chance to disappear from the government's radar and lead a normal life. But after what Ricco had been through, and still having enough humanity left in his soul to do what good he could, Dakota had no other option but to join him. They had become far more than friends. Dakota considered Ricco family, and now he was gone. Dakota never got the chance to say goodbye. He pulled into the last Walmart before hitting the open desert, and told himself when he had the time he would rectify that. Michael deserved that much at least.

There was no sense dwelling on things he couldn't control, so he put the thoughts out of his head. Dakota parked the bike as far away from any other vehicle as possible and entered the supercenter. It took him a minute to get his bearings, then he found what he was looking for in the electronics department. He took the disposable cellphone and a Coke from a small refrigerator next to the register to a self-checkout, paid in cash, and walked back to the bike. His throat was dry and the Coke went down smooth. He threw the empty bottle in a garbage can near the cart holder and straddled the bike. Even though he knew it would be nearly impossible to trace the call, he decided to activate the phone from the parking lot just in case.

He punched in the private number instead of the office number. When the call was answered on the third ring, he knew he'd guessed correctly.

"Maggie."

It took her a minute to place the voice. "Dakota?"

"I'm so sorry."

"About what, Dak? Leaving, or Michael? Neither one is something you need to feel sorry about."

She sounded tired to Dakota. "He was family, Maggie, you know that."

"I do, and now I'm the one who's sorry. I haven't exactly been on top of things lately." He heard her sigh, and then her voice took on the authoritative tone he knew so well. "Where are you, Dakota? I've been trying to find you."

Dakota's brow creased at the question. "Ito said you cut me loose, Maggs. I took him at his word."

"We did. Dakota, there is something you need to know."

"I'm not coming back, Maggs. I called to say I'm sorry about Michael and to tell you that I'm not coming back, I'm done with the program." Dakota pulled the phone away from his ear intending to disconnect the call when he heard Maggie pleading with him on the other end of the line.

"Dakota, don't hang up, please, just listen to me, that's all. Just listen!"

He put the phone back to his ear and let her wonder if he was still there for a moment.

"Dakota?" He could hear the panic in her voice.

"I'm here."

"Look, don't hang up, please. I need to talk to you, I swear it's important."

"I'm listening."

She let out a sigh of relief. "I'm not sure how to say this."

"Maggie, if you're trying to trace my call, I'll save you some time, I'm not where I intend to be in about an hour. Tell me what's on your mind or I'm hanging up."

"Dakota, they did an autopsy on Michael. I got the final results today."

That took him by surprise. Not the fact that they did an autopsy on Michael. As a scientist, it would have been fascinating to see what kept him alive all these years and then find out exactly what caused him to die. What surprised him was that Maggie thought it important that he know about it, that she had tried to get hold of him to specifically inform him of the results.

"I thought he died of heart failure, that's what Ito told me."

"Well, technically I guess he did, but Dakota, the lab reports suggest something you need to know. When they messed with Michael's immune system all those years ago, they had no idea what they were dealing with. It seems that when they altered his genetic blueprint, they also altered how his immune system reacts to pathogens. It was the experiments that kept Michael alive."

Dakota shook his head, not fully grasping what Maggie was telling him.

"His body needed something to fight against. *That's* what kept him alive all these years. His immune system was the way it was because it was constantly battling something. The General had no clue, but he was the one responsible for Michael's longevity. When we took him in, we promised him no more experiments."

"He had nothing to fight against," Dakota said more to himself than Maggie. He already knew why she had been so desperate to talk to him, but he let her say it anyway.

"All the colds, the pneumonia he had last year, his immune system was trying to give itself *something* to fight. But after a lifetime exposed to far worse stuff, it just wasn't enough. We killed him, Dakota. It wasn't intentional, but in taking away the pain we ended up killing him."

"You gave him peace, Maggs. He loved you, don't forget that."

"Dak, do you understand what I'm trying to tell you? You could be the same way. You need to come back so we can get a handle on this thing. Maybe it happened the way it did to Michael because of how long he was exposed to the experiments. It might be different with you, but we can't be sure until we study it closer. You need to come in, Dakota. For your own sake you need to come in, and the sooner the better."

Dakota sat on his brother's Harley in the middle of a Walmart parking lot and pondered his future. The day was cool for Nevada with temperatures in the low eighties and a fragrant breeze coming out of the desert. He closed his eyes and leaned his head back, taking a long, deep breath and enjoyed the opportunity to do exactly as he pleased—for the moment at least.

"Dakota, are you listening to me?"

"Yeah, Maggs, I'm listening. I'll let you know." He heard Maggie calling his name as he disconnected the call. He knew they would be looking for him again, but time for once was in his favor. He didn't think for one minute he could drop off the radar forever. They would find him eventually. The trick was to keep them looking in another direction until he was ready to be found. Right now there were more important things he needed to worry about.

Dakota thought about Michael Ricco again and the blood they shared. It saved his life once. He wondered if it might end up killing him as well.

CHAPTER 16

The Nevada desert at twilight is a testament to survival at its most deceptively beautiful. Deep within the *Pehute* Wilderness, nestled in the arms of the Black Rock Playas, exist some of the most exquisite natural formations ever to be seen. Man was not a frequent visitor here, and that was what Dakota counted on as he pressed the bike higher up into the hills. He only had a quarter of a tank of gas left. If it ran out before he made his destination, he risked a long cold night with nothing but the bedroll strapped to the back of the bike and half a bottle of water stashed in the bottom of his bag. He really needed to plan these mad dashes for freedom better.

He wasn't even sure he was headed in the right direction. He had only been to the remote cabin once before and it had been more than eight years ago. Dakota had not grown up with his father, he had only recently become acquainted with the man. A year after they had met, David invited Dakota to the cabin for a little R&R. The week had brought him closer to a man who was all but a stranger and left him with a feeling that he had family out there other than Montana. His brother was a little slower in warming to the fact.

David told him anytime he wanted to get away he was welcome to use the cabin. Dakota never had an opportunity to take his father up on the offer, until now. Considering his brother was in jail for a murder he didn't commit, and the real killer wasn't content with that, Dakota felt now was a good time to disappear. He needed to think. Kale was looking to kill him, Maggie was looking to save him, and Ito was going to beat his ass if he got his hands on him. Not to mention what Montana would do when he found out he took his bike.

No one besides Dakota and David knew about the cabin and seeing how there was no official connection between him and his father, it was as hidden and safe a location as possible. Now all he had to do was find it—in the dark—with only his memory to guide him. Nothing looked familiar. The years had changed the landscape. Landmarks he remembered were either gone or overgrown. Dwindling daylight and lengthening shadows didn't help.

He turned off the main road and, accelerating up a steep incline on what was nothing more than a rock-strewn path, Dakota pulled the throttle trying to use the daylight left to him. He saw the rock directly in his path too late to do anything about it.

Dakota leaned his weight to the left trying to dodge it, but his front wheel took a direct hit. It crumpled, lifting the rear tire off the ground and catapulting Dakota over the handlebars. He let go, doing an impressive mid-air flip, and landed on his back with a muffled *thud* on hard-packed dirt. With the wind knocked out of him, Dakota looked up in time to see the five-hundred-pound motorcycle falling out of the sky to land on top of him.

The engine stalled and the sounds of the night seemed to hold their collective breath, or maybe he had gone deaf. When everything stopped moving, the pain finally registered. His breath came back in rasping gulps, and a searing heat scorched his left leg. Dakota looked to find his leg pinned under the exhaust pipe, the heat burning through his jeans. The acrid stench of spilt fuel and oil reached him, the quiet ticking of the cooling engine loud in his ears. By some fickle whim of fate, the bike had landed with the handle bars twisted beneath it leaving a space small enough for Dakota's leg. It hurt like hell, but he didn't think it was broken.

He sat up, wrestled with the bike, and managed to get enough leverage to pull himself out from beneath it. The wrecked bike lay beside him as he panted and tried to get his bearings. The sounds of the night returned. A coyote sang somewhere out in the distance. Dakota's calf from ankle to knee burned and ached, his jeans scorched and black. The skin beneath, he guessed, would look much the same.

Damn, Montana was going to kill him about the bike.

He rolled to his knees, planted his right foot on the ground, and tried to stand. He didn't get far. His head began to spin, and his vision blurred as a new pain blossomed behind his eyes. Dakota found himself on his back again with the sky looking down, mocking his failure. He touched the back of his head, his fingers came away bright with blood.

Well, that can't be good.

He must have hit his head harder than he thought. His vision darkened and thoughts scrambled, but before the night closed in on him he swore he saw someone looking down at him shaking their head. Dakota blinked and tried to bring the image into focus, but the only thought that came to him made no sense.

The Indians had found him.

With that thought burrowing into his head, he let the swirling darkness claim him.

Like he had a choice.

* * * *

Dakota looked up at an old Indian and thought he still must be dreaming. Deeply lined crevices marked a leathery face the approximate color and texture of tree bark. Long, white hair pulled back into a braid dangled over one shoulder. Dakota put one hand to his head and the pounding in his skull. The face in front of him smiled, and suddenly he knew who he looked at.

"Walter?" he asked, naming his grandfather.

"You looked like you could use a hand," Walter said.

"How? How did you know I was here? Where did you come from?"

Walter laughed. "The entire mountain knew you were here. Nice take-off, by the way, landing could use some work, though."

Dakota sat up, still holding his head, and gave his grandfather a rueful grin. "No kidding. Hey, is this David's cabin? I found it?"

"Well, technically I found you first, but you weren't that far from it. I came here to commune with the spirits. Your *santee* passed into their world. I thought I would find peace and solace. I found you instead."

"*Santee* died? Ah, Grandfather, I'm sorry." It had been two years since Dakota last saw his grandmother. The excuses didn't matter. His *santee* was gone.

Walter shrugged. "It was her time. She was ready for the journey and it seems the time of her passing was fortuitous for you. I would not have been here otherwise."

Dakota suppressed a groan as he sat on the side of the bed and took stock. Besides the killer headache, his left leg throbbed. He touched the back of his head and felt sticky blood there.

"How long have I been out?"

"Not long, just got you here. Didn't get to look you over, but it's safe to say you hit your head."

Dakota smiled through the drill hammer behind his eyes. He never could figure out when his grandfather was joking. Considered a shaman of his tribal community, Walter Willowcreek also possessed a medical degree from Harvard. Dakota could not have ended up in better hands.

"I was just about to see to your leg."

Dakota swung his injured leg back on the bed and hitched himself up so his back rested against the pine headboard.

"Where's the bike?" Dakota asked. If he was followed and the bike was found, it wouldn't be long until the cabin was located. The last thing Dakota wanted was to put Walter in harm's way.

"Last I heard, you were out East, some research facility." Walter took a pair of scissors from the top of the bedside table and sliced Dakota's jeans length-wise next to the scorched area.

"The bike, Walter." Dakota groaned as his grandfather gently peeled the material from the wound beneath it.

"Hid it. Didn't figure you were up here on vacation."

The denim had melted, fusing with the flesh. Walter debreded the wound. When he removed the scorched material, burnt flesh came away with it.

"Damn!" Dakota said between his teeth and pressed himself back against the headboard.

The wound showed the shape of the exhaust pipe, bleeding freely now that it was open. Walter took a pitcher of water and poured it over the burn. Dakota's hands bunched around the sheets as he tried not to yell out loud.

Walter inspected the wound and nodded. "Not too bad, second degree burn. Probably why it hurts. If it was third degree you wouldn't feel a thing. You're lucky, could've broken your leg."

Dakota wiped sweat from his upper lip, feeling more than a little queasy. "That's me, lucky."

Walter took supplies from a bag at the foot of the bed.

"You look like you were expecting me."

"No, not you in particular, but you never know what you might wander into. I happened to wander into my idiot grandson taking a street bike off-road. Like I said, you're lucky." He opened a jar of green goo and scooped out a generous handful. Dakota smelled the vile concoction from where he sat.

"Whoa, wait, just what the hell is that?"

Walter, seeing no need to explain himself, smeared the stuff over the wound. After the initial stinging, the pain disappeared. Every bunched muscle in Dakota's body relaxed as the pain backed down.

Dakota let out a breath. "God, now if you could only do that for my head."

Walter smiled and retrieved the singing kettle on the stove. Dakota scooted down until his head rested on the pillow. He closed his eyes and tried to will the headache to go away. The smell of sweet lavender and eucalyptus had him opening them again.

"This might help." Walter placed a warm cloth steeped in the fragment brew across Dakota's eyes, and the pain retreated. A contented sigh escaped his lips as he sank deeper into the pillows.

"What's going on, Dakota?" Walter asked. "I don't see or hear from you in nearly two years and now, when I know you should be somewhere else, I find you deep in the heart of the playas riding your brother's motorcycle. What are you running from?"

Speaking into the comfort and darkness provided by the cloth over his eyes, Dakota started at the beginning, wherever that might be. He wasn't sure anymore. He knew Walter would end up finding out everything anyway, so he left out nothing.

Knowing his grandfather's love for isolation, he started with a question of his own. "Have you seen the news lately, read a paper more recent than three months old?"

Walter shook his head. "No, but I feel now as if I should have. Tell me what could have caused you to run to the mountains, and why is your brother not with you?"

"Montana's in trouble, Grandfather," Dakota began. "And I haven't a clue how to get him out."

Walter Willowcreek pulled a hand-carved stool next to the bed and began wrapping the burn on Dakota's leg.

"Tell me," he said.

Dakota started talking and as he did, he realized he had done what Montana asked of him. He had found the coyote, or rather the coyote had found him.

CHAPTER 17

Ito knew something was wrong from the moment he got out of the Hummer outside Montana's apartment. If he had any, the hairs on the back of his neck would have been standing on end. His suspicions were confirmed when he saw the door jamb splintered, the door swinging on broken hinges.

He'd holstered the Kimber after leaving the Hummer, but now drew it as he entered Montana's home. Both hands on the weapon, Ito chambered a round and slid a finger into the trigger housing as he sidestepped into the front foyer. Nothing had been spared—furniture toppled; cushions slashed, their stuffing billowing out the wounds like rising dough; lamps smashed; carpets shredded; desk drawers emptied of their contents and then destroyed. Even the drawings and paintings on the walls did not escape the fury.

Ito stepped on glass and looked down. The drawing Montana had done of his Rangers lay beneath his feet. The glass shattered, the drawing itself torn, and a bloody handprint trailed down the webbed glass.

If Dakota ever was in the apartment, Ito didn't believe he was still there. Gone, of his free will or someone else's. Ito looked for some sign of what might have happened to him. He bent down to examine the damaged drawing closer, concern for Dakota foremost in his mind.

"Drop the gun."

Ito held his hands out to his side and slowly let the gun clatter to the floor. The man was to his left and obviously had seen him coming in from the street. A rookie mistake: he never cleared the room. All Ito could see was the Glock off to his side, pointed at his head.

"You prone your black ass now, boy, or I'll sure as shit shoot you dead."

Ito did as he was told and lay on the glass-littered wooden floor.

"Spread 'em."

He felt a knee in the center of his back and the cold barrel of the gun at his temple. He spread eagle on the floor and felt another set of hands search his body. So there were two of them.

"He's clean," the one on his back proclaimed, pulling Ito's wallet from his back pocket.

"Get up," the other one told him.

Ito slowly got to his feet and placed his hands on his head, lacing fingers together. These boys seemed nervous enough without giving them something else to worry about. Ito turned and saw the men for the first time. He recognized the Nevada State Police ID they both wore around their necks.

"You're cops."

"Yeah, and you're in a lot of trouble, Mr. St. James. What are you doing with the piece?"

Ito creased his brow in confusion. Nothing about this felt right. Neither man wore a uniform. Jeans and t-shirts were not the norm for on-duty officers, even in Nevada. They both oozed nerves like water from a broken radiator. The trooper who was now riffling through his wallet wiped sweat from his upper lip with the back of one hand. Ito saw the fleshy part of it was cut and bleeding. If they were investigating a break-in, they shouldn't have touched anything. Yet the man had a cut hand and there was blood on the glass at his feet. Ito also noticed the hand that wasn't cut was sheathed in a black leather glove as were his partners'.

"I'm licensed to carry. My permit's there." Ito motioned to the wallet the cop still held.

After a few moments he found it and showed it to his partner. "He's telling the truth. He's a PI, Thomas's partner."

Both troopers exchanged glances, their guns still trained on Ito. He watched them carefully. "Can we relax now?" Ito asked. "Or are you still going to shoot my black ass?"

The troopers relaxed their stance and pulled their weapons off him, but it took longer than he thought it should have.

"What happened here?" Ito asked, taking his wallet back from the trooper with the bloody hand. He glanced at the name badge. *Zack Carver.* The other man's badge had flipped over so Ito couldn't read his name.

"A break-in. We got a report of a break-in. We were just checking it out. You surprised us, thought the place was empty."

"I didn't see a squad car, and you're not dressed for the job."

"We're not on duty," Trooper Carver told him. "We heard the dispatch on the scanner. We were in the area, thought we'd check it out."

"How dedicated. You didn't happen to find anyone?"

The other trooper shook his head, holding his weapon down at his thigh. Ito noticed his finger still wrapped around the trigger. He didn't like that.

"No," the trooper said. "We were told that the occupant's brother has been staying here. You don't know where he is, do you?"

Ito shook his head, taking everything in. Carver had maneuvered himself slightly behind Ito, his weapon also out. Carver was jittery and sweating freely, he looked like he was ready to jump out of his skin. Ito felt the most immediate danger coming from him.

"Last I knew he was right here. Kind of concerns me that he's not."

"Do you know where he might have gone?"

"Not his babysitter." Ito kept his eyes on Carver. The man kept looking to his partner for some sort of signal, and Ito sensed something was about to go down. He had no idea what was going on, but he was willing to bet his left ball that these guys were dirty. The blood told Ito they had been the ones who had tossed the place, and he didn't think robbery was a motive. They were here on someone else's bidding, and their interest in Dakota concerned Ito.

Without waiting for things to circle the drain, Ito took one quick step to the side, and then to the back. He spun Carver around, bringing the smaller man in front of him, his hand curled around the one holding the gun. He squeezed the fingers wrapped around the grip and felt them snap one by one. Carver released the weapon and would have cradled his broken hand if Ito had let him.

"God! Jesus!" Carver screamed as his partner drew on Ito. But with Carver in front of him, it would be impossible to get a clear shot.

"Let him go!" the other trooper told him. "Drop the weapon and let him go!"

"I have a better idea." Without waiting for a reply or giving the other man time to react, Ito shot him in the right knee. The man dropped the weapon and rolled to his side, keening in agony. Ito pushed Carver down next to his partner and retrieved both troopers' guns. He snapped the ID badges from around their necks and kept the Kimber trained on them. The IDs looked real enough, the Nevada state seal in holographic relief showed on both. Zack Carver's partner's name was Lewis Ward.

Squatting to be on eye level with both men, Ito crossed his arms over his knees, the Kimber dangling by his side.

"Who sent you?"

Ward held his leg, rolling from side to side, his face contorted with a mixture of rage and pain. "God damn! You're under arrest."

"Yeah, sure. When you take me in you can explain what you were really doing here. Want to bet your ass on that scanner report, boys? I suggest you start talking or sure as shit I'm going to shoot your white ass. Who sent you?"

Carver cowered next to Ward, but found enough courage to yell in Ito's face. "Screw you, asshole."

Ito shrugged and brought the Kimber up and shot Carver in the foot.

"Fuck!" Carver started crying.

"If I have to ask again, I go for the hand."

"We're here on a call, I swear," Carver said.

"You sure?" Ito asked. He pulled his cellphone out of his pocket and flipped it open. He punched in 911 and turned the phone around so both men could read it. "You want to know what I think? I think if I hit send and report a break-in at this address, it's going to be the first they've heard about it. They will send a *real* unit and you will have some *splaining* to do!" Ito laughed at his own Ricky Ricardo imitation, his finger poised over the send button.

"Kale! It was Kale!"

"Shut up, Zack," his partner warned.

"How many does he own?" Ito asked, meaning the state police. Carver understood him perfectly.

"I don't know, four others besides us that I know of. He doesn't tell us anything. He just gives us orders and then pays us."

"Jesus, Zack!"

"God, my foot!"

"Keep talking." Ito pinned Zack's hand against the wall and brought the Kimber up.

"Fuck, man, fuck, put the gun down. He wants the brother. The guy is not right in the head. He told us to come here and kill the brother and toss the place."

"Dakota's not here?" The revelation confirmed what Ito already knew.

"Do you see him? No, he's not here! Christ, I think I'm bleeding to death."

"You should be so lucky. Why does he want Dakota dead?"

"How the hell should I know what the freaking psycho wants?"

"He wants to make the other one suffer." Ward, both hands holding his shattered knee, found his voice. "The one in jail."

"Killing the girl wasn't enough?"

Ward actually managed to laugh. "Nothing is enough with Kale. He'll kill you too."

Ito gave the man a big toothy grin. "I doubt that."

Ito stood and glared at the two men at his feet. "You sold yourselves to the devil. To protect and serve, don't believe *to murder* is in that oath. I would love to stick around and see how you explain all this to your boss, but I have work to do. You can tell Kale one thing for me, though."

Ward looked up at Ito. "Yeah, what?"

"You tell him he fucked with the wrong boy. You tell him if he wants the Thomas brothers, he needs to go through me first." Ito bent down to be on eye level with Ward. "I promise you that ain't going to happen."

Ito turned to leave, then paused in the hallway. He bent over and retrieved the drawing of the Rangers. Shaking the broken glass free of the picture, he rolled it and walked out, leaving the two dirty troopers to decide what to do next. Ito had no problem deciding what his plans for the future were.

Back at the Hummer, Ito sat and thought. There was nothing he could do to help Montana, he would have to trust Damien to that task. Dakota was missing and that fact ate at him. He could only hope that Dakota knew Kale was looking for him as well and went to ground, but he would feel a whole lot better if he knew where the colossal pain in the ass was.

The only way to keep both Dakota and Montana breathing was to get to Kale. Kale had the tapes and Kale pulled the strings. Ito decided Stone Kale was nothing more than a spoiled child who needed manners beaten into him. Ito knew he was the perfect choice to do the beating.

He put the key into the ignition, and the Hummer's engine roared to life. Ito found a smile on his face. It had been a long time since he looked forward to doing a job. This one was going to be fun.

CHAPTER 18

Cal Tremont always thought it odd that an authentic Irish pub existed in the heart of Nevada, but perhaps even stranger was the fact that the owner was Russian. Victor Marusko had married into the Irish family. When his wife inherited the pub after her parents died, he figured, what the hell. It was paid for and sure beat working construction. When his wife died ten years ago, he took over management completely. The name however was a local staple. O'Reilly's it was christened and O'Reilly's it would stay.

Cal frequented the fine establishment with the predictability of the setting sun. Victor always had a black and tan already built and waiting for him when he walked in.

"My friend!" Victor spread his hands in greeting as Cal opened the door and took his usual seat. Third stool from the end of the bar. "I be worried, you not here yesterday. Something wrong? I had to drink your beer myself, no sense in wasting." Victor laughed. After all these years, he'd never lost his accent.

"No one's more sorry about that than me, Vic." Cal raised his drink in salute and took a long swallow while looking around the dimly lit tavern. He licked the foam from his upper lip and saw who he was looking for. Drink in hand, Cal approached the lone man sitting at the table shrouded in shadows deep in the corner.

He sat down without a word or invitation. Cal had known this man all his life. Not once in all that time did he think he would be having this conversation.

Gabe Garrett raised his eyes as Cal sat. He didn't seem overly surprised at the sheriff's presence there. But the man didn't look good. His eyes were shadowed, his cheeks gaunt. Something ate at Gabe and Cal knew exactly what.

"Was wondering when you would get to this."

Cal took a long, slow pull off his beer and leaned back. The mahogany captain's chair creaked and groaned under Cal's bulk. He stared back at Gabe and took a moment to soak up the atmosphere. The hazy bar smelling of smoke and stale beer was his favorite place in the world. Now it would forever be tainted with the memory of what he was about to do. At his age, Cal didn't have many friends left, and he was about to lose one.

"We've known each other a long time, Gabe. We've watched each other's kids grow up. You helped me bury Margie. I never would have figured you to sell out."

"You don't understand."

"Then explain it to me. Real simple so someone stupid like me can get it. I want you to sit there and tell me how you could run that prison for the last twenty-five years, how someone I was proud to call friend could do this. Explain that to me, Gabe."

"I had no idea how far into the system Kale infiltrated. I swear I didn't, you have to believe me."

"Save it. What do you expect from me, sympathy? You've known Montana Thomas since he was born. You know that boy didn't kill anyone, now you offer him up as a sacrificial lamb? Have you seen him? Have you seen what's been happening in your house?"

"Don't you think it's been killing me? I haven't slept in days, Cal. Kale owns half my staff. He's threatened my boy. He told me he had connections where he's going to school out in California. Said he would make it look like a drug overdose. I believed him."

"You could have come to me."

Gabe put his hands on his head and spoke to the table. "I don't know what to do anymore."

"They'll kill Montana if he stays where he is. You have to know that."

Lifting his head, Gabe pleaded with Cal. "What if I came to you now? What would you tell me to do? Can you promise me my boy won't be harmed, can you do that, Cal?"

"Can you live with yourself if you stand by and let Lilly's boy get killed?" Cal asked.

Gabe continued to stare at Cal, his eyes shifting from left to right, trying to figure it all out. "What do you want me to do?"

"Transfer Montana. He needs to be somewhere Kale has no control over. The federal pen in Carson City."

"I can't." Gabe shook his head. "You don't understand."

Cal sat forward, slamming his glass on the table between them. The beer sloshed over the rim and onto his hand. "Don't tell me I don't God damn understand. I'm seeing things a hell of a lot clearer than you lately. You get Montana out of your house before Kale decides to stop playing with him. If that boy dies, his blood is on your hands. Don't you for one minute think our friendship will stretch that far. Make it happen."

Cal threw some cash on the bar. "Gabe's tab is on me tonight."

Victor smiled as he wiped down the bar. "Ah, yes, my friend. See you tomorrow?"

"Don't waste any beer on my account."

"Oh, I will miss you then."

"Not as much as I'll miss you."

As he left the bar, Cal didn't bother looking back at Gabe. He didn't need to. Gabe would do what he asked, Cal had that effect on people. He only hoped he wasn't too late. He was giving Montana a chance, the only one he was likely to get. It was up to him to take advantage of it, but knowing Montana as he did, Cal's main concern was how many people were going to get in that boy's way when he did.

CHAPTER 19

Dakota finished his tale. He sat on the edge of the bed trying to ignore the pain in his leg and head. His grandfather stood and walked over to an exquisite walnut roll top desk in the corner of the room. He tapped fragrant tobacco into the bowl of a well-used pipe, and came to sit next to Dakota once more. Walter took a lighter and puffed until the leaves glowed red, inhaled deeply, and exhaled smoke. Only then did he center his gaze back on his grandson.

Dakota waited patiently. He knew his grandfather well enough to understand he never did anything in a hurry, and not without a great deal of thought.

"Do you know this man, this Stone Kale?" he asked finally.

Dakota shook his head. "Never heard of him before."

"You know for a fact that he was the one to kill this woman?"

"I only know what Ito told me, and I *know* Montana didn't do it."

Walter seemed to think about that before nodding in agreement. "No, my grandson does not have murder within him. If he loved this woman as you say, he would die before seeing her harmed."

"He did love her."

"Montana should not have to pay for another man's crime."

"I agree, but how do you suggest making Kale pay? He's a scary guy with a lot of equally scary people who jump when he tells them to."

Walter puffed on his pipe. Dakota watched his eyes. They were black, like Montana's, but Walter Willowcreek's eyes held within them the wisdom of their ancestors. Dakota hoped one of them might have a clue as to what to do, because he was flat out of ideas.

"We need to find out more about this Stone Kale. To defeat an enemy one must understand that enemy."

"I will never understand people like Kale," Dakota told his grandfather.

"Then you must talk to those who do."

"Those who do? You mean like other criminals? I don't think Kale's associates are going to help me. Kill me, maybe, but not help."

"Those who catch these men, they study them. I think in a sense they become like them, to understand how they think, how they live, so they can understand how they act and react. These are the people you have to talk to, I think."

"You mean like the police? From what Ito tells me, the police are not to be trusted."

Walter leaned forward, holding the pipe by the stem, his gaze intent on Dakota. "You have come to know very connected people, Dakota, very powerful people. Perhaps it would be possible for you to ask these people for help in exchange for what you have done for them."

Dakota creased his brow. "Maggie?" He shook his head, the possibilities occurring to him for the first time, then quickly dismissed. "I burned that bridge, Grandfather. I'm not sure if I want to try to rebuild it."

"Not even for your brother?" He handed Dakota his cellphone. When he gave Walter a confused look in return, his grandfather explained. "It was in the bag you had with you. I think it still works."

Dakota took the phone and held it. The only part of the story he had left out was his conversation with Maggie. Michael Ricco's death and the complications that brought to his life, he kept to himself. If he called Maggie, he was delivering himself right to her door. They would never let him go again. He'd had this choice once before. Ricco had told him he could walk away. The things done to Dakota at the hands of the man who kept Ricco, changed Dakota forever. Only a handful of people knew what really happened in that bunker two years ago. Most of them were now dead. The ones who weren't wanted him back—for his own good, they told him; for their research, his heart replied.

This was not the life he wanted, but it was the life he had been given. He tried to make the best of it. He tried to be a good man. Now he felt like he had no choices left to him. Despite every attempt on his part to prevent it, he had become exactly like Ricco. Just another lab rat, a curiosity, a freak demanding the attention of those staring back at him through the glass. He wondered what they saw when they looked at him.

His grandfather watched him, but Dakota didn't have the courage to return the gaze. He concentrated on the phone. For Montana, he told himself, for Montana. He closed his eyes, took a breath and wished he could think of another way. When he couldn't, he opened his eyes, punched in Maggie's number, and waited for the line to be picked up.

* * * *

About a half hour outside of Caliente existed nothing but desert, miles and miles of desert. On the surface it appeared lifeless, but the closer you looked, life exploded out of every crevice, even the sand seemed alive. The desert was beautiful, but it was a subtle beauty and one you had to look for.

De La Rosa's existed much like the desert. It looked like nothing on the outside. A small white restaurant off highway fifty-one with a neon sign announcing its name. Sometimes all the letters actually lit up, but most nights you might drive by De La Rosa's and never know what you missed.

The tiny Italian eatery was one of the best-kept secrets of the desert.

Mama La Rosa didn't speak English, but damn, the woman could cook a lasagna that would make you cry.

Stone Kale had a particular fondness for Italian food and made time to dine at La Rosa's at least once a week. It cost Ito all of fifty dollars to learn this information. That was loyalty for you. Kale drove a neon-blue Dodge Viper with white stripes running down the length of it. Flashy car, made it easy to locate.

Ito parked the Hummer next to the Viper and noticed they were the only two cars in the lot besides an ancient Chevy pickup that belonged to Mama La Rosa's son who also worked as the chef. That little tidbit cost Ito another bill, but he considered it money well spent. The Viper had a barely functional backseat, so Ito guessed Kale was either alone or he had one other person with him. The odds were in Ito's favor. He checked the Kimber, snapped a live one into the chamber, holstered it, and got out of the Hummer.

He took a minute to appreciate the sun setting over the buttes. The desert held a special place in Montana's heart and Ito swore his friend would see it again.

Candlelight lit the restaurant, bathing its occupants in a golden glow. Kale sat at a red-checked table near the back, a bottle of red wine open and poured into two glasses. A leggy blonde sat opposite him, leaning forward, exposing generous amounts of cleavage and smiling. Kale, preoccupied with the view, didn't notice Ito.

"I take it you are no longer in mourning." Ito took a chair from a nearby table, flipped it around, and straddled it. He rested his arms across the back and smiled at Kale.

"I don't know who the hell you think you are, but you're interrupting my dinner." Kale tried to give an indifferent attitude, but Ito could see the arrogance and annoyance simmering just beneath the surface. It wouldn't take much to turn annoyance into rage. It's what Ito counted on. The blonde gave Ito a disgusted look, then turned back to Kale.

"Harry, you promised me no business tonight." She clamped her lips together in a pretty pout.

Ito watched Kale's eyes glitter dangerously as he centered his attention back on the woman. "I told you it was *Stone*," he said.

The girl must have realized her mistake, but it was too late to do anything about it. "I'm sorry, honey. I meant Stone, you know I did." She reached across the table and stroked a red-tipped nail slowly up his forearm. "Tell the ape to take a walk and I promise I'll make it up to you."

"Get lost, Irene." Apparently Kale had lost his appetite.

"What do you mean, get lost? You drove me here!"

"Then wait for me in the car, or start walking, I really don't give a fuck either way."

Irene looked from Kale to Ito in open-mouthed disbelief. Anger and indignation apparent in the hard set of her mouth, she stood, threw her napkin on the table, and walked away as quickly as six-inch heels allowed. The tight, short dress swayed nicely across her ample backside.

When the door slammed behind her, Kale turned his full attention to Ito. He offered Ito the chair vacated by Irene. Ito stood, replaced the chair he had taken and sat down opposite Kale, who lifted his wine glass and swirled the contents. After taking a sip, he carefully put the glass back on the table and studied Ito.

"All right, you just ruined my evening. You better have one hell of a good reason for making me piss Irene off. She's a bitch in a good mood. I was looking forward to a little after dinner relaxation."

"Ah, so that's what she is."

"Who the hell are you? Do I know you?"

"No, but you know a friend of mine. I'm here on his account."

Taking another sip of wine, Kale looked at Ito over the rim and kept the glass in his hand. "A mutual friend? Who?"

"Montana Thomas."

Kale laughed. "Ito St. James. I should have guessed. Do you have a death wish, boy?"

The waiter came by the table, obviously upset that Irene had been replaced by another customer. "Will the lady be coming back?" he asked.

"No," Kale said. Ito could see the anger building in the man.

"Will the gentleman be wanting anything?"

"No," Kale answered with his eyes on Ito, then smiling he looked at the nervous waiter next to him. It was obvious to Ito that Mama De La Rosa's had seen Kale's rage in the past.

"I won't be staying long." Ito grinned at the waiter. The man gave Ito a nod and backpedaled away from the table as fast as he could. Ito had noticed the absence of other diners before entering the building and wondered for the first time if it was intentional on the part of the establishment to try and keep damage and casualties to a minimum.

Ito had carefully examined the layout of the room on entering. He was convinced that Kale truly had come here alone with the girl. He guessed even psychopaths didn't like to group date. The Viper might get a little cramped with an entourage in the back seat and Irene trying to straddle the gearshift in the front seat. The mental picture had Ito laughing.

"Something you want to share, boy?"

Ito pulled the Kimber free of its holster and almost casually laid it on the table between them.

"Is that supposed to impress me?" Kale asked.

Ito let the smile slip away. "It is what it is, but if you call me *boy* one more time, you might have a problem."

Anger flared to life in Kale's eyes. "I don't have problems, I *make* problems—*boy*."

Ito had no doubt that Kale was armed. He also had little to worry about. In one quick movement, Ito flipped the table between them, grabbed the Kimber and planted the barrel between Kale's legs.

"I am not in the mood for a pissing match—*boy*." Ito felt the staff staring in horror behind him, but ignored them and concentrated only on Kale. "Let me explain something to you, *Harry*. I'm going to talk real slow and use small words so even you can understand me."

Kale's eyes never left the weapon pushed against his crotch. He held his hands up and away from his body. "Easy, man, easy," he said, trying to smile. The smug self-confidence was gone. It's hard to be cocky when someone has a gun shoved between your balls.

"Do you know what this is, Harry?" When all he got was a headshake from Kale, Ito continued. "No? Well then, let me educate you. This is a Kimber forty-five semi-automatic pistol. In the right hands, it is dead accurate from about five hundred feet." Ito glanced at the five-inch barrel firmly pressed against Kale's boys and smiled. "I never finished college, but I have over a thousand hours of practice with this particular piece, so I can pretty much tell you from this distance, I ain't going to miss."

Reaching inside Kale's open jacket, Ito found the 9mm Beretta holstered under his left shoulder, and took it.

"This," he said, referring to the Beretta, "is a child's toy." Ito dropped the magazine from the Beretta and pocketed it. He placed Kale's now empty weapon back in the man's holster.

"What the hell do you want?" Kale asked.

"There, see, I knew you could be a reasonable man." Ito withdrew the weapon, pulled up a chair and sat opposite Kale, the gun still aimed at him. He knew with a man like Kale the threat of losing his manhood was far more intimidating than losing his life. "Okay, Harry, let me lay it out for you. My friend is in jail for something he didn't do. That just doesn't seem fair to me. What I *want*," Ito continued, "is several things, Harry."

"I didn't kill her," Kale told him. He seemed to have collected what little pride he had left to him and actually smiled at Ito. "No way you can prove I did."

"You know what, Harry, I actually believe you. Because I don't think you have the spine to do your own dirty work. You hire others to do it for you, but you were there, you were calling the shots. That's called accessory to the fact and that, my friend, buys you a whole lot of jail time."

"You have no idea how fucking wrong you are." Kale laughed. He went from being a whipped puppy back to his overconfident, cocky self in an instant.

Ito didn't show it but he knew he was missing something.

"Let me explain something to you." Kale leaned forward in the chair. "And I'll talk real slow and use small words so even you can understand. First, you need proof to even tie me in to Linney's murder. All you have right now is my so-called relationship with her. The jealous boyfriend thing is only going to get you motive, my friend. You have nothing to connect me to the crime scene."

At that moment Ito's cellphone vibrated. Still holding the Kimber on Kale, he looked at the caller ID and smiled. "Talk to me." Ito listened and then grinned. "Your timing could not be better. Very cool, my man." Ito flipped the phone closed. "That happened to be my proof, Harry. Damien Knight, Montana's attorney, has on a hunch acquired a warrant to search your premises from an appellate court judge you *don't* own."

"A warrant for what?" Kale didn't look worried yet, just confused.

"Tapes, Harry. Video tapes."

Now Kale looked worried. "That son-of-a-bitch Jefferies."

Ito laughed. "Yeah, Mr. Jefferies and I had a nice long chat. He was stuck on my every word. By the way, if anything happens to his daughter, I have your threat to him on record."

"You don't have anything. Like I told you, I didn't touch the bitch."

"Maybe not, but having the tapes in your possession makes you what they call a person of interest. I for one am very interested, Harry. Call your boys off Montana. If I find out he has so much as a splinter, you're mine."

"Jesus! You don't get it, do you, asswipe? I'm not the one calling the shots."

"What are you talking about?" It was Ito's turn to look confused.

"I told you, man, you don't know what the fuck you're talking about."

Ito brought the Kimber up once more. Kale shook his head as if he was tired of the theatrics. "You know what? You want to shoot me, go ahead. You go right ahead and shoot an unarmed man in front of all these nice witnesses because I would rather be shot by you than deal with what the man in charge would do to me if I talk to you. So you have the tapes. So fucking what? You know what you're going to see? A few dirty state cops having fun with Linney, and I do mean fun. Linney played her part well, hell, she enjoyed a good fuck. There was no rape. *That's* what you're going to see. Linney was in this right up to the end."

"What?" Ito let the gun waver a bit with the information. "But you killed her."

Kale shook his head. "Again, I never touched her, but yeah, she started getting a little pushy." Kale shrugged. "She outlived her usefulness. By getting herself killed, she gave me an opportunity to achieve my main goal."

"Which was what?"

Kale shook his head. "This was fun and all, but I'm not that stupid. You might get your boy out, but I'm not taking his place. That's a promise." Kale stood. "I'm going to do you a small favor because I appreciate the way you work. You want to live long enough to understand what I'm talking about? Then I would advise you to stay as far away from Dakota and Montana Thomas as humanly possible. Oh, and thanks for the armory lesson. I might have to look into replacing the Beretta." The cockiness was back in full force. Kale had given Ito more than he bargained for.

The man started walking out the door when Ito grabbed his arm and whipped him around to face him. Kale shrugged out of Ito's grip, his eyes blazing. If he could, it was clear he would kill Ito where he stood.

"Back off, man."

Ito held his hands out and smiled. Kale glared at him and smoothed down his jacket. Then just when he turned to leave, Ito grabbed him once more, this time he didn't let go. Drawing his right arm back and clenching his hand into a fist, Ito smashed Kale in the face. He put his entire weight behind the punch, and Kale dropped like a stone. Blood poured from his nose. He rolled on the floor, both hands clamped over his face.

Ito bent down. "That was for Montana," he said, then pulled his foot back and kicked Kale in the ribs. "*That* was for me—*boy*."

Ito turned to see the stunned faces of the restaurant staff behind him. He pulled a couple of bills from his wallet and placed the money on the bar. "Sorry about the mess."

Ito left the restaurant and headed for his Hummer. Irene sat waiting for Kale in the Viper. He walked over and rapped on the window. She gave him an irritated look and had to open the door to talk to him. Kale had the keys and she couldn't power down the window.

"If I were you, I'd think about calling a cab. Your boyfriend might be a while."

Irene's eyes went wide and her lips formed a bright red 'O'. She got out of the car, slammed the door shut, and ran back into La Rosa's.

"Harry, honey, what did he do to you?" Ito heard her yell as she ran through the door with short choppy steps.

Despite the hopefully broken nose Ito had given him, Kale had won this round, they both knew it. But Kale had also shown Ito enough of his hand that he thought he could figure out what the hell was going on. There was way more here than Ito thought. He'd been sure Kale was the one pulling the strings. Now he found out he was wrong. Being wrong could get him killed, or worse, get Montana or Dakota killed. That was not an option.

Ito might not have all the facts, but he was dead certain about one thing. One way or another Kale was going down.

CHAPTER 20

It was all falling apart. Stone Kale watched the media frenzy on the mid-morning news and paced in front of the sixty-inch plasma screen. The perfectly coiffed newswoman smiled brilliantly while the scene behind her blazed with dozens of police cars, their lights silently swirling, creating a patriotic kaleidoscope.

It wasn't supposed to happen this way!

Kale watched, transfixed by the images on the screen. It seemed almost like watching a movie.

"Early this morning, over two dozen Nevada State Police and FBI units converged on the Lincoln County Correctional Facility just outside of Caliente. You are watching a live feed of those proceedings. We are still trying to obtain information, but from what we have learned so far it appears as though Gabe Garrett, the warden of the local prison, has been placed under arrest, along with most of his staff, for accepting bribes and unlawful procedures occurring within the prison grounds. All of the inmates housed there are to be transported to other secured facilities until the extent of the infiltration into the prison system can be determined.

"WKYY news has also learned in an exclusive report that Montana Thomas, a life-long resident of Caliente and accused murderer in the death of his girlfriend Lindsay Keller, has been released and cleared of all charges. Evidence has been submitted by Mr. Thomas's lawyer,

Damien Knight, which has proved without a doubt Mr. Thomas's innocence in this matter. WKYY has not learned the nature of this evidence, but stay with us for breaking news on this ongoing story."

"That son-of-a-bitch!" Kale picked up the nearest object, a priceless crystal figurine of a horse, and hurled it at the screen. Kale's aim was exquisite. The anchor's smile shattered along with the screen, glass and sparks exploding from the impact. Kale couldn't have cared less, he had far more important matters on his mind, namely his way of life.

Irene cringed on the leather sofa behind him and let out a little squeal.

"Not one word," he warned her. If the bitch gave him any trouble, Kale swore he wouldn't stop at a black eye and split lip. She was becoming more work than she was worth. Hell, he missed Linney at times like these. At least she had a brain, but then again that was the problem with Linney, too smart for her own good. It was exactly why she ended up dead—she thought she was better than him.

Right now Kale could do with a little brainpower. There was no way he could avoid the fallout. If he ran, the man would find him and then Kale knew he was dead. Or worse. The psycho might use him in his *program*. No, thank you very much. Kale had seen firsthand what the man considered research. If he stayed to face him, there was a chance he could still be of use.

Kale knew he was screwed any way he looked at it. Maybe if he got to the brother first he would have a chance. The two cops who trashed Thomas's apartment were supposed to grab the brother and go, despite what they told St. James. They were still alive only because of that fact. They told St. James they were supposed to kill Dakota Thomas to throw him off the scent. From the encounter he had with St. James, Kale was convinced no one knew their true agenda. St. James still believed that Montana Thomas was the victim in all of this.

That fact and that fact alone was what would keep Kale alive—for now. That and finding Dakota Thomas and bringing him to the one man

Harry "Stone" Kale feared more than death. A man who perhaps Dakota Thomas did not know personally, but someone Kale was certain the younger Thomas brother knew by reputation.

A man known to Kale only as the General.

* * * *

Maggie Riley made the cross-country trip in relative silence. She only wished she could silence her thoughts as well, but control only went so far. She had messed up. She let her emotions rule her and because of that Dakota Thomas had slipped the net. Despite what Michael meant to her, she knew better. At the time she was willing to accept the fallout. She owed Michael and even Dakota that much. But now, in a bizarre twist, her promise to a dead husband might very well endanger the one person he was trying to protect.

The phone call from Dakota on her private line was just another unpredicted turn of events. *Grateful* could not begin to describe how she felt when she received the call. Dakota must have stumbled into something bad for him to even consider asking for her help. Maggie Riley always did her best to downplay her position and her connections. She wore her authority with dignity and respect. But the truth of the matter was that Maggie wielded a tremendous amount of power within the government. Because her department was not publicly prominent, her name was not synonymous with a position of power. But to those to whom it mattered, Maggie Riley's name opened some impressive doors.

She only hoped that those doors opened for Dakota in time. She had listened attentively while Dakota described his brother's situation and the man named Harry "Stone" Kale. The name sounded vaguely familiar to her, and she had her assistant do a search on the man. Maggie opened the folder containing Kale's life story and read it again for perhaps the tenth time.

The private plane landed on a small airfield in Alameda, Nevada, just outside of Caliente, where she and her team were met by a waiting car. Trying to be as inconspicuous as possible, the car was an unmarked blue sedan. It might as well have had a flashing neon light on top screaming *Look at me!*

The motel was off the main road, if there was such a thing as a main road out here. Maggie still had a hard time believing people could actually live out in the middle of nothing. Driving an hour one way for a quart of milk was not her idea of fun. Michael used to kid her about her urban appetites. She smiled at the memory.

He told her that once in her life she needed to taste milk straight from the source. When she made a face, putting a finger down her throat, making puking noises, he laughed and rolled on top of her, pinning her to the bed.

"I mean it, Maggs, there is nothing like it. All those years ago and I can still remember the taste. Warm and thick and almost sweet." His eyes had a faraway look to them as he remembered. "The barn cats used to fight us for it."

"What about pasteurizing and bacteria?" She made another face and shook her head. "No, thank you. I like my dairy in a box cold and fresh from the grocery store. You know you could get all sorts of diseases from cows."

"I turned out pretty healthy." He smiled down at her.

"That you did," she agreed. "Maybe there's something to this country living after all." She reached up and pulled him to her. He made every touch seem so precious, as if he knew it could be the last.

God, how she ached for him. Maggie shook her head, trying to rid herself of the memory, and lifted the file from her briefcase. She was surprised at the amount of information a preliminary search turned up. Harold "Stone" Kale had served in the military. Two years in Afghanistan with the army. Maggie read his profile and wondered how the hell the guy ever got into the military. The term *emotionally labile* came up more than once. It was no great surprise when she read he had been dishonorably discharged and served five years in a military prison for charges ranging from possessing and selling illegal drugs to aggravated assault and resisting arrest.

Kale did the time, and then simply fell off the face of the Earth before turning up in Nevada a few years later. On paper everything Kale did appeared perfectly legal. He owned several rental properties throughout the state, but most of his considerable income came from his import-export business. A handwritten side note on the report told her Kale was known to be a drug runner, but legally the police and FBI couldn't find a way to implicate him. He never got his hands dirty. His disposable people paid the price. What no one could ever figure out was why none of those who took the fall ever ratted him out. The Feds and the state police suspected Kale was only the tip of a very large iceberg.

Something was missing, Maggie could feel it. She read the press release about the mess at the local lock-up. Montana should be released by now. Technically Dakota didn't need her help anymore, but Montana's release didn't mean they were safe, not by a long shot. This whole thing smelled worse than a cat collector's house. She was *missing* something—she could feel it. Something happened between the time Kale got out of prison and his prosperous life in Nevada. Focusing on his army papers, Maggie went back and looked at the names carefully. Even though she had read the information many times, her heart still skipped several beats as she browsed Kale's contacts in the military.

Kale had walked out of prison on May the twenty-third, nineteen-ninety-nine. He took with him the belongings that were on him the day he was incarcerated and was met at the gate by his one and only visitor the entire five years he'd spent behind bars. Maggie looked at the name again. It seemed so innocent there in print. The name gave no indication whatsoever to the evil behind it.

When Harry Kale left prison that fine spring day he was met at the gate by John McKinley—a name that resurrected a ghost she thought long taken care of. Maybe she missed it the first time she read it because she never thought of the man by his given name. The only name she referred to him by was the one her husband, whenever he talked about his life back then, called him.

John McKinley was, to Maggie, nothing less than the devil incarnate. But to Michael and to Dakota he was and forever would be the man who called himself the General.

How had she missed that!

She knew John McKinley was safely locked away for the rest of his life with no chance of parole. She received annual reports on him, the last one less than two months ago. But what was it Michael told her? The man in charge changed from time to time, but he always went by the same name. Dakota told her the same thing. He rarely spoke of his brief visit with John McKinley after his arrest, but once after a particularly fine bottle of wine—or two—shared between the three of them in celebration of Michael's birthday, Dakota had told her that the General, AKA John McKinley, said his being in prison didn't change anything. He had laughed at Dakota and told him he would never be free, that the program owned him.

Maggie remembered Dakota vehemently proclaiming his freedom from the man, stating no one owned him. But Maggie had seen Dakota in the throes of his nightmares and she wondered if what she did to him wasn't the same thing. Personally, she liked Dakota. She felt for what he had gone through at the hands of a psychopath. It was almost as bad as what Michael went through. In a way it was worse. Michael adjusted to his experiences, but Dakota never got to that point. She thought with time he might get there. But time wasn't on their side.

Now she understood something that chilled her to the bottom of her soul.

The General was back, and he wanted Dakota.

CHAPTER 21

Dressed in clothes Ito salvaged from his trashed apartment, Montana walked out of Lincoln County Prison flanked by Cal Tremont and Damien Knight. Ito waited curbside in the Hummer. The distance from the door to the vehicle was fifty feet. Seemed a hell of a lot longer walking through the gauntlet of reporters thrusting cameras and microphones in his face. Montana paused for a moment to place the new pair of Ray-Bans over his still bruised and swollen eyes, then surveyed the mob in front of him through a veneer of neutrality.

"Mr. Thomas, is it true you can't remember anything that happened in regards to Ms. Keller's death?"

"Who do you think *did* kill Linney Keller?"

"Can you tell us what evidence set you free?"

Damien stepped in front of his client, shielding him from the verbal onslaught. "Mr. Thomas has no comment at this time."

Cal was less subtle in his approach. Towering over most of the paparazzi, he elbowed a path through the crowd. "Get out of the God damn way, you freaking vultures!"

The press backed off, marginally. Montana walked steadily toward the Hummer, ignoring the buzzing voices around him. Ito held the door open for him as he entered the rear passenger side. Damien sat beside him, Ito and Cal filled the front. As the Hummer powered away from the curb, Montana closed his eyes behind the glasses and relaxed for the first time in days.

"God damn parasites," Cal mumbled, still pissed off over the press.

"They're just doing their jobs," Damien said.

Cal grumbled something incoherent and stared out the window. Silence filled the vehicle, each absorbed in his own thoughts until Cal spoke once more. "Where are we going?"

"You are going home, Cal. For the sake of the town and your career, you can't be more involved in this than you already are," Damien said.

Cal shook his head. "Look, Gabe brought his own house crashing down around him. I'm the one who told him to make it right. I'm not leaving now."

Damien leaned forward, his hands on Cal's headrest. "That's exactly why you can't be here. You are too close to this, Cal. Your professional reputation is at risk, as is Montana's freedom. If there is even a *hint* that you had something to do with his release, the backlash could cost you your job, and could put Montana back behind bars until this is all sorted out."

"He was released because of what you found, not because of what I told Gabe," Cal said.

"He's out, Cal. Let's keep it that way."

Cal looked out the window once more. The expression on his face made it clear he didn't like being told what to do, even if it was the best thing for all concerned.

Montana leaned his head back and listened to them all discuss his life as if he had no say in the matter, as if he wasn't sitting right there. He stayed that way until Ito dropped Cal off at his home and they were on the road again.

"Where's Dakota?" Montana's posture didn't change, but it was clear from his tone he expected an answer.

"Don't know," Ito told him from the driver's seat.

"Not the answer I wanted to hear, Ito."

"He's safe."

"And you know this because…"

"He called me this morning. Wouldn't tell me where he was, just that he's safe and to tell you he's sorry."

Montana sat up and took the glasses off. "Sorry?"

"About your bike."

Concern turned to confusion, and then to sudden horrible clarity in an instant. Montana grabbed the back of Ito's seat. "My bike?"

Ito laughed.

"I'm going to kill him." Only then did Montana notice they were heading out of town. "Where are we going, Ito?"

"He wouldn't tell me what's going on, either," Damien said into the ensuing silence that was Ito's answer. "Said you would understand when we get there."

"Get where?"

Ito pulled into a nearly deserted Motel Six with a sign on its billboard proclaiming *last lodging for fifty miles*. He parked next to a dusty, dark-blue sedan in front of room thirty-six and shut the Hummer down.

"Here." Ito turned around in the seat and winked at Montana, then opened the door. "You coming?" he asked when Montana still sat unmoving.

"What's going on, Ito?"

"I think it's best we all hear this together." All traces of humor vanished from Ito's face with the words.

Damien exited the Hummer and walked to stand beside Ito. Montana opened the door. He tried for the stoic demeanor but it was getting increasingly difficult as confusion dominated the myriad of emotions playing out inside his head.

They followed Ito to room thirty-six where he knocked once on the dented metal door. It took Montana a moment to recognize the woman who opened it. It had been more than two years since they had last seen one another. She looked tired. Her black hair was longer than he remembered, and her blue eyes held a sadness he hadn't noticed before, but it was her. What he couldn't figure out was why she was here.

"Maggie?"

She took two quick steps toward him as if she wanted to hug him, and then stopped herself. "Montana." She seemed to settle for a smile instead. Montana closed the distance and wrapped her in his arms. Maggie hugged him back, hard. He pulled away and looked down at her.

"I heard about Michael. He was a good man."

Maggie averted her eyes, as if she didn't want to go where those memories took her, and nodded quickly. When she looked back at Montana her face was serious, her voice all business. "Michael is why we are all here right now."

"Somebody better start explaining," Montana said, his voice a quiet plea.

Maggie glanced quickly at Ito and then back to Montana. "Sit. Please," she added when he continued to stand.

Montana moved to the edge of one of the double beds in the cramped dingy room and sat, but he didn't relax. He wanted to shake somebody, break something. Instead he sat rigidly still on the bed and waited for Maggie to begin.

"I contacted Damien yesterday. I saw the tapes," she began.

"So far you're one step ahead of me," Montana told her.

"Montana, exactly what do you remember about the night the woman was killed?"

"Linney," he corrected. "Her name was Linney."

"I'm sorry, Linney. What do you remember?"

Montana gave Damien a brief sideways glance. "We've been

through this. Obviously, Damien's told you everything. What does this have to do with you? What's this have to do with why you're here?" Montana did some quick mental calisthenics. "Is Dakota okay?"

Maggie put a hand up, stopping his momentum. "One thing at a time."

He stood and towered over her. "Is Dakota all right?" The question demanded an answer.

Ito stepped between them and put a hand on his friend's shoulder. "I told you he was. I've never lied to you, and I'm not about to start now."

"Then let's cut to the chase," Montana said.

"All right," Maggie said, and Ito stepped back. "But hold on, it's going to be a bumpy ride."

Montana sat back down and Maggie began to talk. "You did not kill Lindsay Keller, but neither did Stone Kale."

Montana nodded in agreement. He knew this much already.

"She wasn't raped. I watched the tapes, the sex was consensual."

Montana shook his head. "You mean with me? The sex was consensual with me."

"This is the hard part. Linney worked for Kale. You were set up from the first time the two of you met."

Montana's face went blank. He shook his head, but said nothing.

Maggie continued. "You were used, Montana. You were nothing more than bait for the primary target."

"Listen to me." Ito knelt down next to his friend. "She used you, and then when she'd served her purpose, Kale had her killed. He didn't tell her that part of the plan. He told Linney she was supposed to set you up for rape, but Kale had other plans. If he pinned a murder rap on you, then Dakota would have to come."

"Dakota?" Montana's eyes went from Maggie to Ito and back again, waiting for an explanation.

Maggie took the story back from Ito. "This whole thing is all about

Dakota. Kale isn't the one at the top of the food chain, Montana. If you were in trouble he knew Dakota would come to be with you."

"And Michael and I played right into his plans. We practically brought Dakota to his freaking door, all I had to do was wrap him up and put a bow on him." Ito sounded disgusted by his actions in this.

"You couldn't have known," Maggie tried to reassure him. "We were all fooled by him."

"Wait." Montana tried to keep it together, but he was rapidly losing it.

Linney played him? No. He refused to believe that, despite what they thought. He would have known. He needed to watch those tapes for himself, but not now.

This whole thing was spinning out of control. Only half of what Maggie and Ito were saying was making it through to his brain, but the one thing that did was that somehow Dakota was involved. With more control than he thought he had, he put questions of Linney on the back burner. No matter what Linney did or did not do, the fact remained that she was dead and beyond any help Montana had to offer. Dakota was not. Right now Dakota had to take precedence.

Montana finally managed to articulate a question. "Who is *he*? What the hell does Linney have to do with Dakota?"

"Nothing," Maggie said. "You were deliberately set up to do one thing, get Dakota away from the protection of the government. He knew he couldn't touch him there, so he had to get him to leave. You were the one person he would do that for. If you were in trouble, he knew Dakota would stop at nothing to be with you."

"Who, Maggie? Stop dicking around and tell me who!" Montana stood and took a step toward her as he spoke.

"The General, Montana. This whole thing has been elaborately orchestrated for one purpose and one purpose only. The General wants Dakota back."

Montana's world tunneled. That name, that word took him back to a place that had changed all of their lives forever.

Two years ago, Michael Ricco had ended up in Dakota's emergency room with a bullet in his shoulder and dog tags implying he was born a century earlier. What Montana and Dakota found when they started looking into Michael's past was a nightmare.

A pseudo-governmentally run program that took young, healthy non-coms and listed them as "missing in action", the *Program* performed human medical and genetic experiments. There was nothing ethical or moral about it. Michael Ricco and others like him were literally tortured in the name of research.

Michael, however, was a special case. Something they had done to him slowed his aging process; his entire genetic blueprint had been altered. The program advanced medicine decades ahead of where it might have been otherwise, selling the results of their *research* to pharmaceutical companies, but the price had been countless human lives.

Michael Ricco escaped and the program had been shut down. The man who ran the thin excuse for a torture chamber had been caught and placed in a facility for the criminally insane. His true name was John McKinley. But before they had taken him, Dakota had become the last of his human test subjects. Not even Montana knew the full extent of the hell his brother had been through at the hands of the General. He told Dakota they would never shut the program down. Others would take his place. It had sinewy tentacles in every political and governmental department imaginable. Most of them had no idea where the new vaccines or antibiotics, even biological weapons, were really developed. They never asked.

Now that Michael Ricco was dead, Dakota was the closest thing they had to what Ricco was: a true medical miracle. Ricco's immune system was nearly irrepressible and Dakota had been transfused with a serum made from Ricco's blood. A nightmare Montana thought they had put behind them was now front and center. Another "General" was back and he wanted Dakota.

The one question foremost in Montana's mind: where was Dakota and did his brother know his own personal demon was back and looking for him?

The dirty motel room surfaced again for Montana. He found Maggie, Ito and Damien waiting for his response.

"We need to get to Dakota before he does."

"We do," Maggie agreed. "And we were hoping you could take us to him."

"You don't know where he is?"

Ito shook his head. "No, not exactly. Like I said, he called me this morning, knew I would be worried. He told me he was safe and gave me a message for you."

"A message? Other than he trashed my bike?"

Ito nodded. "He said to tell you he found the coyote."

Despite the roller coaster of emotions he had just been put through, Montana smiled. "He's right about one thing, he is safe."

"I hear a *but* in there somewhere," Ito said.

"*But* I have no idea where he might be."

Maggie sighed and ran a hand through her dark hair. "Do you know where we might start? He called me only to ask me to help get you out of jail. I couldn't trace his call, but he has to know I will be looking for him. I have the resources, Montana. You need it, I'll get it for you."

Montana paced the small room, then turned to Maggie. "Do you have a phone that can't be traced?"

She laughed. "You're kidding, right?" She walked over to the desk, opened a laptop computer, and as it was booting up, took a rather large looking cellphone from her bag and plugged it into one of the USB ports. After a minute or two, she handed Montana the phone still connected to the laptop. "The signal is encrypted, virtually impossible to trace."

Montana took the phone and punched in a number he'd long ago committed to memory.

"Hey, Dad, it's me," he said when the line picked up. "No, I'm good. Listen, I know you have questions, but I need to ask you one first. Do you have any idea where Walter is?" Montana smiled at his father's words. "Yeah, yeah, I remember. Listen, you didn't get this call, okay? I'll explain later. Yeah, I know—you too."

Montana ended the short call and looked back at Maggie. He was exhausted emotionally and physically, and he didn't have time to be either. "Do you know who this new General is, or where he might be?"

Maggie shook her head. "All we have right now is his connection with Kale."

"Then we follow Kale."

Ito and Maggie exchanged a knowing look. Maggie cleared her throat. "We lost him."

"You lost him." Montana repeated the words to see if they would correct him. They didn't.

"I should have watched him more carefully." Ito shook his head. "I took him for a small-time player, thought he was just talking big. When Damien told me he had the tapes, I didn't think he mattered anymore."

"Does he know where Dakota is?"

Maggie shook her head "I don't see how. *We* don't know where he is."

"You also didn't know Kale worked for someone else until recently either."

Maggie didn't have anything to say to that. Montana turned and headed out the door.

Maggie watched him for about two seconds before realizing he was leaving with or without her. "Hey! Wait! Do you know where Dakota is? Where are you going?" She followed him out to the parking lot.

Montana paused before getting back in the Hummer. "You coming?"

"You know where Dakota is?"

Montana nodded. "I'll take you to him, but I have a condition."

Maggie stopped in her tracks as if she couldn't make sense of the word. "A condition? Excuse me, but am I not the one helping *you*? Wouldn't your lovely little butt still be sitting in a jail cell, wondering how long it would be before someone slipped a shank between your ribs, if not for me?"

Montana looked at her over the rim of his Ray-Bans. "Brushing up on your jailhouse vocabulary?"

Maggie let out an exasperated sigh. "Look, Montana, I'm not sure I am in a position where I can bargain with you here. There are extenuating circumstances."

"There always are, Maggie."

"What?" she asked. "What is your condition?"

Montana pushed the dark glasses back in place. "When we find Dakota, it's his choice whether to go back with you or not."

"Would you say that if I told you his staying away could kill him?"

Montana's brow creased. "What are you talking about?"

"Extenuating circumstances."

He opened the door to the Hummer and put a foot up on the running board. "It's still his decision."

Maggie crossed her arms over her chest. "I'll do my best to make that happen, but I'm not top dog. At the end of the day I follow orders just like everyone else."

"But you have a say in how things are done."

She nodded. "Yes, I have a say."

"He needs someone in his corner, Maggie, someone besides me."

"I've always been in his corner, you know that."

Montana grinned and gave her a quick nod. "Yeah, I do, that's why if you tell me you'll try, I'll believe you."

"I swear to God, if it is within my power to do so, I'll make sure he has the choice."

"Fair enough." Montana tried to suppress a grin and failed. "Slip a shank between my ribs, huh?"

Maggie shook her head and sighed. "Just drive, Montana, we'll follow."

"We?"

"I didn't come alone."

"This is getting complicated, Maggie."

Maggie turned back to the motel room. "Welcome to my world. Give me a minute."

He gave her ten. The two government agents waiting in the car for her got out and introduced themselves. They told him their names—Kurtz and Casner. Montana shook their hands but said nothing. They looked liked hired muscle brought along to assure Dakota's return. He wasn't sure how he felt about them. But he knew one thing, there was no way he was leading the steroid brothers to Dakota.

CHAPTER 22

Stone Kale and the four surviving ex-Nevada State Troopers were in a new red Honda Pilot headed north out of town. The car had been paid for in cash, the paperwork listing a false name, address and references. Kale was pissed off, and someone was going to pay for that. He considered ignoring the cellphone when it vibrated on his hip, but picked it up before it went to voice mail.

"What?"

"You don't sound happy, Harry."

Kale sat up straighter and put his attitude on hold. He did some serious backpedaling as he recognized the General's voice. "Sorry. I mean, what do you need?"

"Just checking in, Harry. Is everything in order?"

"Yeah, we got the car, no problems, and the GPS is working fine."

"Glad to hear it. I will not accept failure, is that understood? The next time I hear from you I want you to tell me the package is in hand and you are on your way to deliver it."

The package, as if he were picking up something from UPS. "Yeah, I get it. Give me a day, maybe two at the most."

"The sooner the better, Harry, or I may have to use you as a replacement for the good doctor."

Stone heard the line disconnect, flipped the phone closed, and threw it on the dash. "In your fucking dreams!"

"Problems?" The driver kept his eyes on the road except for one sideways glance at Stone.

"I hate that guy."

The driver coughed out a laugh. "No shit, but the dude pays well. I'd rather work *for* him than be one of his projects, you know?"

Stone thought about that and kept any comments to himself. He stared out the window and noticed they had left the interstate.

"Exactly where are we going?" he asked the driver.

"Exactly? I haven't a clue. I'm just following the bouncing red ball." He pointed to the red marker on the GPS unit mounted to the dash. "Wherever this guy is, it makes nowhere look close by." He laughed at his own joke.

"Are you sure it's him? It's not just my ass on the line if this guy gets away from us."

"It's him. Relax. I personally put the GPS units on both the Jeep and the bike the night this all went down and the chick was killed. The General might be a little whacked but the guy knows what he's doing, I'll give him that. So far this has played out according to script."

"Except for the part about Thomas getting out. He was supposed to die behind bars."

"Yeah, well, that was your little screw-up, now wasn't it? Had to satisfy that inner voyeur, didn't you, *Harry*? You had to tape the whole fucking thing. *That* wasn't on the man's agenda."

"You didn't mind at the time."

"That was before you fucked up and lost the tapes, *Harry*. I keep waiting for them to show up on YouTube."

Kale pulled a switchblade from his jacket pocket and in less than a second flipped the blade open and had it against the driver's throat. The man didn't even flinch.

"Chill, Harry."

The two men in the backseat tensed, but the driver made eye contact with them through the rearview mirror and gave them a headshake. Kale was aware of the exchange but chose to ignore it.

"Let's get one thing straight. I am the one calling the shots here. *The man* isn't here, I am." Kale motioned to the men in the back with his head. "So unless you want to become collateral damage before even one round is fired, I suggest you tell your boys to give it a rest because I can drain you dry before one of them pulls the trigger, and with me dead and you bleeding out, who do you think is taking the fall for fucking up? You better believe your buddies here will become the General's new pet project if this whole thing goes to hell."

"Everyone relax." The driver strove to maintain a calm demeanor, but Kale saw the sweat trickle down his face. "You're right, Harry. You're the boss."

Kale withdrew the knife, but didn't relax. He whispered in the driver's ear. "It's Stone, asshole. *Stone!*"

The driver kept his tongue and most likely his life as he continued to follow the little red ball, moving deep into the Nevada wilderness.

* * * *

Walter Willowcreek left his grandson sleeping and walked out into the cool of the early Nevada morning. It was still another hour or two before sunrise, but the full moon splashed through the thin canopy of pines, giving him more than enough light to move with confidence. He didn't need to worry about waking Dakota. Two dissolved Percocet mixed in with the evening meal guaranteed him a few more hours before his youngest grandson woke. Walter had no guilt over drugging Dakota. The burn on his leg had to be extremely painful, not to mention the numerous cuts and scrapes he acquired during his less than graceful dismount from the Harley. Dakota refused to take anything for the pain, saying he couldn't afford to be groggy. Walter thought otherwise.

Dakota brought Walter up to speed concerning Montana and his own reasons for being here. The man responsible for the death of the girl was now after Dakota in an attempt to punish Montana. That was all Dakota knew of the situation.

Walter knew more than Dakota thought he did. Despite the fact that both his grandsons tried to conceal the ordeal they'd been through two years before, Walter knew about Michael Ricco. Not everything, but enough to understand that Dakota and this man nearly died at the hands of a lunatic. The details were hard to come by. Everything was very hush-hush and reeked of government cover-ups, but Walter understood that Dakota's move out East was one born of necessity.

Now he had one grandson framed for a murder he did not commit and another on the run. Walter sat on a boulder overlooking the valley below him and lit his pipe. He cocked his head and listened as the sounds of the single climber got progressively closer. He watched night grudgingly give way to a bone-colored dawn. Rain was in the air, he could smell it. Walter waited for it patiently.

Heavy breathing and equally heavy footsteps combined with swearing as Walter heard a misplaced foot on soft ground and then a hard fall. He slid off the boulder to gaze down the hill and offered a hand to help the man up the last few feet. "You used to be quieter."

David Willows looked up at his father smiling down at him. He took the offered hand and let the older man help him to the top of the ridge.

"I used to be younger." David was breathing heavily and sweating. He leaned against the boulder Walter had vacated, bracing his arms on his thighs, waiting to catch his breath.

"You didn't leave a vehicle at the access road, did you?"

David shook his head, wiping sweat and dirt from his forehead with the back of his arm. "Hitched a ride and got out about a mile from the turnoff." David straightened and grinned at his father. "Good to see you, Dad."

Walter puffed on his pipe and gave him a nod.

Wiping dirt from his hands, David asked, "Where's Dakota?"

"Sleeping." Walter searched through his pack, grabbed a bottle of water, and handed it to his son. David raised the bottle in thanks, twisted off the cap, and drained it dry.

"Better?" Walter asked.

"Yeah. Thanks."

"Good. Then maybe you can tell me why you are here."

"A few hours ago I got a call from Montana."

"From jail?"

David gave him a headshake. "Uh-uh, he's out. I had to find out from CNN that my son had been released from prison. Apparently some new evidence has exonerated him."

"And he called to tell you this?"

"No, he called to ask me if I knew where you were."

"Still not much into conversation, is he?"

"Yeah, I have no idea where he gets that from." When his sarcasm got no response, he continued. "I called you as soon as he hung up. Something isn't right."

Walter glanced at the sky. The sun should have made itself known by now, but heavy dark clouds dimmed the light and the warmth it offered to a dull imitation of dawn.

David followed his gaze. "Feels like rain."

Walter grunted in reply. "Better start back then. Busy day ahead of us."

Walter turned and headed back to the cabin, his pace slow and measured. His son didn't need to know it was as much to allow him time to navigate through the thick foliage as it was in deference to his arthritic knees. He was getting old, even if he didn't want to admit it, but he could still find his way through the woods without a compass better than any man, even if that man was thirty years younger. Walter heard David slip and swear rather creatively under his breath and stopped to allow him to catch up. Yes, it was going to be a busy day indeed.

* * * *

Dakota was seventeen in the dream, but at the same time a neutral observer. His adult self played voyeur. He was allowed to watch but unable to interact or alter the scene that played out before him.

Friday night freedom. He was squished comfortably in the back passenger section of Steve McCoy's Toyota Tundra with Danny Crossly. Danny, not Danielle, he remembered that. Steve and his steady, Lisa, were up front. Steve had liberated a fifth of Bacardi and a six-pack from his father's stash and they had already put a pretty good dent in it, everyone except Danny. She nursed the same beer all night long.

She was beautiful. Her long chestnut hair was pulled back into a ponytail, and her brown soulful eyes stole Dakota's heart. She wasn't shy, but not talkative either. Dakota thought he was in love with her, but he never had the nerve to ask her out—until Steve yelled at her from across the crowded gym.

"Danny! The D man wants to go out with you, that's cool, right?"

He'd held her hand at the movies, and they made eyes at each other in the back of Steve's truck. While Steve and Lisa fogged the windows of the truck, they sat in the dark of the desert night. He knew he'd had too much to drink, but he was seventeen, and the rum was liquid courage in a bottle.

"I've liked you since the first grade," he told her and looked away.

She caught his face and turned it back toward her. "Me too," she admitted, and then she leaned in and kissed him.

Working up the nerve, he moved closer and slid his hands up her back and into her hair, undoing the clip that held it up. She surprised him and opened her mouth. Their tongues touched and danced together. She tasted like beer and pizza. He wasn't sure if it was her or the alcohol, but his head buzzed. They lay entwined on their sides on the cooling desert floor, his leg over her hip, hers threaded through his. His erection pushed uncomfortably against the zipper of his jeans, and his hands somehow undid the buttons on her shirt, his thumb gliding over the thin material of her bra, teasing her nipple.

Steve called out to them and the moment was gone. Lisa, obviously drunk, smiled at them. Her shirt was on inside out, and she hadn't bothered to put her bra back on. Her full breasts swayed as she laughed and staggered while she asked Danny, "So, tell, is he as good as he looks?"

Steve pretended he was jealous and grabbed Lisa to keep her all to himself.

Danny smiled and whispered in Dakota's ear, "I don't know, but I plan on finding out." Her tongue darted in his ear and made it exquisitely uncomfortable to sit next to her without touching her.

Back inside the truck, headlights bounced off the road. Steve was way too drunk to drive, so was Dakota, but hell, they were immortal, they were seventeen. Dakota looked up as the truck swerved to avoid a coyote on the road, then watched the agonizing slow-motion pull of the utility pole as Steve tried to steer around it.

He watched from an angle he knew never existed in reality. The truck hit hard and fast on the driver's side. The engine was pushed into the front passenger section, the seats crumpling and folding into the back. No room to live.

No sound.

Was he dead?

When he found out he wasn't, he wished he was.

Danny sat half in his lap, a splintered three foot section of the pole impaling her through her chest. Her blood, warm and sticky, seemed to be everywhere. Her small body pinned him within the twisted metal.

No sound or movement.

In a moment three lives had been extinguished like blowing out the candles on a birthday cake. Dakota was the only survivor. He was alive because Danny had died, her body shielding him from certain death.

He waited.

Waited in the dark on a deserted road for…what?

Salvation?

Help?

He started to scream when he couldn't free himself from the death that enveloped him.

He screamed until his voice was gone.

Dakota the dreamer looked at the carnage from above it, beyond it. Lisa's bra was lying on the side of the road. And Steve's hand, just his hand, lay on the yellow line dividing the two lanes. The coyote they had swerved to miss crept down off the bluff to sniff at it, then grabbed it like a thief and ran away with his stolen meal.

Dakota the voyeur listened to his own screams echo in the desert night, answered only by the howls of coyotes, perhaps in thanks for the offering.

"They died instantly, you know."

"Yeah, I know." Dakota didn't need to look to know who sat beside him. Dressed in a bright orange jumpsuit, John McKinley sat with his arms around bent knees, as if they were the best of buds sitting down for a little heart-to-heart in the midst of death in the dark.

"Did you ever wonder why you survived and they didn't?"

"Every day."

"Ah, that's guilt talking. Did you ever come up with an answer?"

Dakota shook his head. He could see Danny's hair blow with the gentle night breeze out of the shattered back window.

"Stupid luck."

The General smiled his fatherly smile, the one that made Dakota's hair stand on end. "Not luck, fate. You were meant for great things, Dakota. Things they would never have accomplished. Tell me, would you have become a doctor if not for that moment in time? The feeling of helplessness, of being trapped in the dark with your friends' mangled bodies mere feet away from you? No, you know your life changed direction that day. If they hadn't been killed you might have ended up like all the rest of them. Pointless, mindless existences in a pointless, mindless life. If you'd never become a doctor you would never have met Ricco. If not for Ricco, we would never have crossed paths."

Dakota turned his head to look at the man for the first time. "Yeah, that would have been a freaking shame."

"Look down there. Are you in any way the same person you were then? Is there any resemblance?"

Dakota shook his head. "No. You made sure of that."

The General waved off his comment. "Always the negative with you. I made you strong, Dakota. I took the weakness from you and replaced it with a strength you would never have owned if not for me." He motioned to the smoking wreckage. "If not for their deaths. You understand that even if you won't admit it. The weak must die for the strong to live. It is the way of things. Even your Native heritage tells you much the same, as did Darwin, survival of the fittest. Those you listen to, but me? No. I am too repulsive for your delicate sensitivities." He laughed as he stood. "You are a survivor, Dakota. You always were. I just helped you put a name to it. Do you think what you do for the army is any different than what you did for me?"

"They don't torture me, they give me a choice."

"Oh, really? If not torture, then what would you call it?"

"Research."

"Semantics. They simply make you feel better about what they do to you. You are still wonderfully naive and unjaded, Doctor. We are not finished, you and I. We have much to accomplish."

Dakota looked ahead in the distance and saw the approaching headlights of the car that would call for help. It was over. He turned to tell the General as much. It was over, but he was gone.

It was over.

* * * *

Dakota woke. Not with a start, or covered in sweat, he simply opened his eyes. Not much scared him these days. He lay still, looking at the ceiling, the conversation playing over in his head. He hadn't thought about Danny in years. At least not consciously. Sometimes the subconscious sucked, and sometimes it only showed you things you already knew but were afraid to admit. But why his mental scrapbook chose now to replay that chapter of his life was beyond him.

John McKinley was another chapter he thought he'd closed. The General introduced him to a side of humanity he could not have imagined in the deepest recesses of his psyche.

It was over.

That was the one part of the dream he could argue with. It would never be over. It was always "one more test, one more set of data, one more time, Dak." Just one more piece of his soul he could never reclaim. One more piece of his sanity slipping away.

He'd had plans once. What happened to that person? What happened to that carefree seventeen-year-old who simply wanted to get a girl naked?

He grew up.

No, he told the voice in his head. He died along with his friends. The only difference was he kept breathing, they didn't.

Dakota tried to shake the dream off and sat on the edge of the bed, realizing for the first time he was alone. Walter was gone. His grandfather was often up before dawn, so his absence didn't concern him.

Dakota checked out the burn on his leg. In a little over ten hours the injury was barely noticeable. That was new. He ran a hand through his hair and discovered the gash on the back of his head all but gone too. Ricco had always called himself a quick healer, it seemed Dakota followed suit.

He stood in a t-shirt and boxers splashing cold water over his face and through his hair. He dressed in clothes left behind on his last visit—a faded pair of Levis and a long-sleeved black t-shirt—then pulled on his denim jacket to chase away the cold of morning. Or the dream. He wasn't sure which.

Hunger made his belly rumble, but he didn't feel like making anything, so settled on a breakfast bar he found in the pantry.

He ventured outside and added a few logs to the smoldering fire Walter must have started before he left. He stirred it back to life and glanced at the thick clouds above him. Embers brightened, giving birth to flames. Flames consumed the meal of dried twigs and small branches to become a crackling blaze. Dakota rubbed his arms and warmed himself at the fire.

It had been a long time since he could remember being this alone. Dakota realized that for the first time in over two years, no one on the face of the planet knew where he was or what he was doing. It felt strange and exhilarating at the same time, but it also left him feeling a little lost. He was used to the strict schedule that had been his life. Maggie's news of what had ended Michael's life came back to haunt him, as did his dream.

What was fate? Were there any choices left to him or was he and everyone else following some great cosmic blueprint written at the moment of conception? Were choices only an illusion to make people believe they had freedom? Wasn't freedom only a dissolvable concept? Or just another word for nothing left to lose?

If that was true, then Dakota figured he was as free as he could be. He shouldn't have come here. Maggie was looking for him as was Ito. He didn't want his grandfather involved in the mess he'd made out of his life, it wasn't fair to ask that of him. If he left now he could disappear for real. He hated leaving without knowing what was happening with Montana, but he would have to trust Damien and Ito with his brother's fate. Maybe he was feeling a little sorry for himself, didn't matter, he knew what he had to do.

He went back into the cabin to reclaim his bag and get what he came here for in the first place—cash. His father had come into a large sum of money when he and Montana were babies. Seems David had a penchant for gambling, but he made more than a fortune in the local casinos, he had made impressive enemies, the kind that wanted him dead. It was the reason his father had walked away from his family when Dakota was only a year old.

David Willows had been born Jacob Willowcreek, but after some muscle threatened to kill his wife and children if he didn't return the money that was rightfully his, he faked his death and hid his family under a new name and place. The ruse worked right up to the part where Montana went looking for a father he never knew. He found a secret their mother spent a lifetime trying to keep. He found David and nearly lost his life in the process.

In the time since, Montana and Dakota had tried to make up for a lost childhood. They found an entire family and heritage that had been denied them from nearly the moment of their births.

Prying up floorboards under the table with a utility tool he found on the counter, Dakota worried if David still kept the cash in the same place. He didn't have long to wonder. It looked as it did the first time his father showed it to him. *It's here if you ever need it. No questions asked.*

Hundreds of thousands of dollars in small bills neatly stacked and labeled. The money was legal and untraceable. Dakota knew his father would never deny him the money, but he still felt a twinge of guilt at taking it. He grabbed two packages, about twenty thousand dollars, slapped the floorboards back in place and covered it with the table once more.

He had no idea when Walter left or when he would be back, but time was ticking and he needed to go. He wondered if he would ever see this place again, then shook his head. No time for pointless wonderings. He shoved the money in his bag, checked to make sure Walter hadn't removed the Colt or the ammo, closed the door and walked away.

He headed toward whatever the cosmic architects had in mind for his future and decided fate could kiss his ass. He patted the comforting bulge of the Colt in his bag. He might go down, but damn if he was going alone.

CHAPTER 23

Eric Simmons, ex-Marine, ex-Nevada State Trooper, stifled a yawn and watched the red marker on the GPS. They had driven all day and into the night following the steady glow of the little red ball. The bleep stayed put, meaning their target was stationary. Kale and his two partners in the backseat slept through the night while he drove on. As dawn came with the promise of rain in the thick clouds that selfishly kept the sun from shining, Eric had a problem.

According to the tracking device he'd planted on the Harley-Davidson, he should be right on top of the sucker, but damned if he could find it. His third pass down the same stretch of road, however, showed him something he'd missed in the near darkness: a small overgrown dirt path leading up into the thicker woods above him.

He parked the Honda on the side of the road and walked the shoulder. When he reached the path, he bent down and shone a flashlight. Even though the day was beginning to lighten up, shadows still prevailed here. A smile crept across his face as he realized what he was looking at.

Kale got out of the Honda and rubbed sleep out of his eyes. "Why'd we stop?"

Eric walked up the trail a step or two before he answered. "End of the line," he said, coming back down.

Kowalski and Beck got out of the back, looking like bears coming out of hibernation. Eric didn't want them here, but he wasn't calling the shots. Hell, if he had things his way, Kale wouldn't even be here, but he knew that wasn't an option. Kowalski and Beck weren't much in the brain department; they were exactly what they looked liked—hired muscle. Army grunts who fell off the grid, stupid and mean, a dangerous combination in Eric's opinion, but they had their uses.

Kale turned in a small circle, looking around him. "What do you mean, end of the line? There's nothing here."

Eric went back to the Honda and unhooked the GPS from the dash. "We go on foot from here." He pointed to the tire tracks in the mud that disappeared up the trail. "This way. Doesn't look like he was too concerned about anyone following him."

"Who would follow him through that?" Kale asked.

"We would. Hope you brought another pair of shoes. Don't you own anything other than wingtips?" Eric gave Kale a disapproving look and went to the back of the SUV. He handed out two assault rifles and took one for himself.

The General had told him Dakota Thomas was to be taken alive, but that didn't mean they couldn't have a little fun. He slung the tranquilizer gun over his shoulder for just that reason. He took a duffle bag filled with supplies and threw it to Kale.

"Make yourself useful."

Eric slung another field bag filled with tranquilizer darts and extra ammo clips across his back. Kale laughed at the three of them.

"Jesus, you look like you're heading out to bag and tag Bin Laden."

Eric adjusted his pack and weapon until the weight was balanced and looked Kale over from the brown wingtip shoes to the tan Dockers and short-sleeved, navy blue polo shirt. He looked out of place compared to the camouflage khakis and hiking boots the rest of them wore.

"And you look like you're headed to the country club for lunch."

"Well, no one informed me we were going all commando. Is this really necessary?"

Instead of giving voice to the comment on the tip of his tongue, Eric shut the hatch of the Honda, locked it, pocketed the keys, and started up the trail. Kowalski and Beck exhibited predictable herd mentality and followed, with a disgruntled Kale bringing up the rear.

* * * *

Montana, Ito and Damien pulled onto the interstate. Maggie and her team were two car lengths behind them. Montana angled the side mirror so he could keep track of the dark blue sedan.

"Give them ten minutes, then lose them," he told Ito.

Ito smiled. "With pleasure."

"Lose them?" Damien looked confused. "What do you mean, lose them? They work for the government."

"That makes it all the easier." Ito laughed.

"I hate it when you guys do this to me. Fill me in."

Montana turned around to face Damien. "They won't keep their word. If they get their hooks into Dakota again, he'll never be free of them."

"But Maggie told you it would be his choice."

"You know, for an attorney, you are awfully trusting. Maggie would keep her word, it's the vermin above her I don't trust. They will never let Dakota walk."

"They can't just take him. I mean, this is still America, or did I miss something again?"

Ito and Montana locked eyes for a moment, an unspoken agreement passing between them. Montana turned back toward Damien. "All right, seeing how your ass is on the line too, I guess you need to know."

Damien narrowed his eyes at them. "Need to know what?"

"Make yourself comfortable, counselor, it's a long story."

Damien sat back, folded his arms across his chest and waited.

Montana took a minute trying to decide exactly where to begin.

"Let me tell you a story about a boy named Michael Ricco, he went to war in the summer of nineteen-seventeen and never came home," Montana began as the rain started to fall. Big fat drops sprinkled the windshield of the Hummer as Montana told Damien the story of Michael Ricco's life, his death, and how it had changed them forever.

As he spoke the skies opened and the rain came down in earnest, the wipers punctuating Montana's tale, slapping out the rhythm of a life that Montana would never forget.

By the time he was finished, Ito had lost Maggie, the rain helping considerably. He eased off the interstate and watched her drive by from the off ramp. Moments later his cellphone rang.

"Hey, we lost you," Maggie told Montana.

"Sorry, we got boxed in by a couple of semis. Just keep going, you should pick us up in a few minutes." Maggie signed off and Montana handed Ito back his phone.

"That's just scary how easily you lied to her," Damien said. "You're not kidding about this, are you?"

"I couldn't make it up if I wanted to."

"Damn. I had no idea what Maggie was talking about when she mentioned this General. How does Dakota do it? Why?"

"He thinks he's making a difference. It's the only way he has to live with it. I don't approve, but it's his life."

Ito pulled back onto the secondary road as Damien absorbed what Montana had told him.

"It's going to take a while for all this to sink in, but taking it on face value, I have a question."

"Only one?"

"Give me some time. Okay, if this General of yours is as connected as the government thinks he is, then how do you know who to trust? I mean, the person telling Maggie what to do could be one of his."

"Exactly," Montana agreed. "Which is why we need to get to Dakota first. He has no idea the rules of the game have changed."

"But Kale doesn't want him dead."

"No, worse. Kale wants to deliver him to his keeper."

Damien nodded, the only sounds the rain pelting the Hummer and wipers beating an almost hypnotic tune against the windshield.

"I'm in," Damien finally said.

"Damien, think about this, about your career."

"If you're right and the government is a front for this guy, then I want a part in taking him down."

"What if we don't take him down, what if we end up pissing off some important people and you pay the price? You could lose your job."

Damien thought about that. When he looked back at Montana, he leaned forward, his eyes hard and determined. "I realize I give off the impression that my job and all the things, the privileges that come with it are what matter to me." He shook his head. "I grew up dirt poor in the Bronx. Took me almost five years to lose the accent, still slips out sometimes when I drink." Damien grinned. "Yeah, I like the money, but I also love the job, man. I *love* it. I *believe* that what I do makes a difference and as laughable as it might sound, I believe in the system. Sure, I use it, but the day that system starts targeting innocent people is the day I want out. So yeah, I'm in. I never met Michael Ricco but I've met your brother and I know you. I'm not leaving."

Montana gave Damien a nod. He reached under his seat, withdrew a 9mm Glock and handed it to him. "Glad to have you on board. Know how to use one of these?"

Damien grinned as he took the weapon, popped the magazine out to check his ammo and clicked it back into place with the palm of his hand. "Hell, I practically teethed on one of these."

"Keep it close and don't hesitate to use it if you have to," Montana said.

Damien chambered a round as Ito looked to Montana for directions. Montana checked landmarks and realized he recognized the area.

"Slow down. There's a narrow access road up ahead on the left. You'll drive right by it if you aren't careful."

Ito drove by it anyway, turned around, and found it on the second pass. The road was barely wide enough to accommodate the vehicle. When the main road was no longer in sight, Montana pointed to a slight widening on the path. "You can park it here."

"Where exactly is here?" Damien asked as Ito positioned the Hummer as far off the path as he could.

"Just a back road."

"*This* is a back road?" Damien raised his eyebrows, peering out the rapidly fogging windows.

Montana started putting his pack together. "Technically. We are actually on property owned by my father. The path we want is about a half mile through the trees. We needed some place to park this," he said, referring to the huge SUV.

Damien sighed and pulled his own pack up over his shoulder as rain pelted the roof. "Something tells me we're going to get wet."

Ito pulled out a plastic rain poncho from the center console, the cheap kind in a square package, and flipped it over his shoulder to Damien. "See, it's that kind of deductive reasoning that makes you such an outstanding lawyer."

Damien opened the poncho and pulled it over his head, backpack and all. "Now I know why Montana hangs with you, you're a real funny guy." Damien looked at the dense trees around him and sighed. "This is the only way?"

"There's a trail off the main road, but either way it's a hike. The cabin isn't accessible by road."

"Interesting family you've got there, Montana."

Montana nodded. "You have no idea. Ready?"

Ito opened the door in reply. Damien pulled the hood of his poncho over his head. "Guess it's not going to get any drier."

"Follow me and stay close."

Rain fell hard and fast, the wind making it nearly horizontal. They were drenched before the Hummer was even out of sight. Montana picked his way through the thick undergrowth, his movements confident along an invisible trail. They reached the top of a rise and Montana crouched low, motioning for Ito and Damien to do the same. They flanked him on either side and looked where he pointed. The thick foliage almost hid it, but the bright red of a parked vehicle could be seen peeking out between the leaves below them.

Montana turned to Ito, his face mirroring frustration. "We have company."

Damien shielded his eyes from the rain that assaulted them without mercy. "Good guys or bad guys?"

Without answering, Montana headed back into the tree line. Ito turned back to Damien.

"We *are* the good guys," Ito said and followed Montana.

"Oh, great, that's just great," Damien said, wiping rain from his eyes.

Montana glanced over his shoulder to make sure Damien was close behind him, every step bringing them closer to what or who waited for them at the top. They didn't get far before the first shot echoed across the valley. They all froze as the single shot was answered by a volley of gunfire. Montana looked at Damien. His hair was plastered against his skull, rain running down his face like tears.

"Bad guys?" Damien yelled over the low rumble of thunder.

"Bad guys," Montana agreed. He headed up the hill directly into the line of fire, Ito on his heels. Their search mission had suddenly escalated into a rescue mission. The only problem was the good guys didn't know they had help on the way. If they were caught in the middle of a fire fight, they might have both sides firing at them.

"You know," Damien yelled as he ran, "there are only three of us."

Ito looked back over his shoulder and grinned. "What's your point, counselor?"

Damien struggled to keep up with the pace they set. "You've officially ceased being fun to hang with."

Ito slowed down and pushed Damien in front of him. "Move it, man. The real fun hasn't even started yet."

"Yeah," Damien gasped and tried to catch his breath. "That's exactly what I'm afraid of."

CHAPTER 24

Dakota knew the bike was trashed, but needed to see for himself. He also needed supplies in the saddlebags, extra clothes and personal items that weren't in the duffle bag. He remembered being airborne and that was about it. Walter said he hid the bike, so Dakota was reasonably certain it should still be near the trail or not far from it. Walter was in great shape for seventy, but the motorcycle was heavy, chances were he didn't push it far. Finding the trail, however, was proving to be more of a challenge than he bargained for.

Guess those tracking skills aren't genetic.

The rain didn't help. Dawn arrived, but the sun seemed to be having a difficult time punching through the clouds, making a dreary, gray start to the day. Dakota kept heading down where he thought the road should be. Cold, wet and hungry, all his altruistic notions about leaving suddenly didn't seem like such a good idea. He would rather be waiting for one of Walter's campfire breakfasts.

Dakota pulled the collar of his jacket up against the onslaught of rain, but the persistent torrent leaked down his neck and he was soaked to the skin in mere minutes. Head bent down against the driving rain, he kept up a steady pace and came across the top of the small trail by sheer happenstance. He turned sideways, using his arms for balance, and slid halfway down the slick, steep trail. He didn't see the bike, but stopped as he came up short against the trunk of a young tree.

Something was wrong. He strained his ears to listen beyond the steady drumming of rain on leaves and the wind whipping debris around him.

Voices.

The voices were coming directly below him, two, maybe three men. Not Walter, if Walter had been there, Dakota would never have heard him. Dakota peered around the trunk of the tree, but another blocked his view. The voices came to him on the wind making it difficult to determine how close or far away they were from him. He heard a branch break a few yards to his right, directly across from him. Dakota crouched next to his tree and listened. Silence but for the steady rain. Whoever waited down the hill had heard the noise as well.

A small movement off to his right, and this time Dakota saw a figure moving up the hill among the trees. Even with rain-plastered hair, Dakota recognized his father, but David had yet to see him. Dakota glanced from the men down the hill to his father. It was clear David had yet to realize the danger he was in.

Dakota watched David climb the hill. In another minute he would crest the slight rise and be out of sight from the men beneath him. It was a minute too long. The man closest to the top raised a weapon. Dakota didn't think, he reacted. He was too far away to have a clear shot, but at least he could draw the man's attention away from his father.

He brought the Colt up, sighted the weapon, and squeezed the trigger. His aim was off but the loud discharge had the desired effect; David hit the ground and searched for the source of the gunfire, as did the four men down the hill from Dakota. Four pairs of eyes swiveled and found Dakota standing on the ridge. Dakota fired off two more quick rounds as he moved to take cover. He should have had the advantage being uphill, but superior firepower had him pinned down and unable to move. He heard the spit of bullets as they hit the foliage around him. He couldn't see David, but the fact that he heard no return fire told him one thing—David wasn't armed.

Dakota had to hope his warning was enough. He didn't have time for anything else. The intruders advanced on his location. Even through the pounding rain he heard them move. David forgotten, one thing was perfectly clear, they were coming for him.

"To the right! Don't shoot if you can't get a clear shot. Pin him down, but he is not to be killed!"

Crap! Where had he heard that before? Not good—not good.

He was regretting his sudden heroism in the face of fire. Holding the Colt in front of him, Dakota sat on the rain-soaked ground, trying to figure a way out of this. If David was out there, he figured Walter was too. His grandfather did not carry a weapon and now he knew David was unarmed as well. If these men were Kale's his father and grandfather were as good as dead unless Dakota gave them the chance to get away. The one thing that didn't gel for him was the fact that these men wanted him alive. Kale wanted him dead. That made no sense, until another possibility came to him.

John McKinley's last words to Dakota came back to him. *You can't stop us. We are more powerful than you could ever realize.*

He had no time for this, the men below were rapidly closing in on his position. If this was some doing of the program, the hellhole Michael Ricco escaped from, Dakota was in more trouble than he'd realized. Suddenly Kale didn't seem so scary anymore.

Maybe they wanted him alive, but that didn't mean Dakota had to go nicely. In one smooth movement, he jumped and spun around, leading with the Colt. The men were a lot closer than he realized. Letting instinct take over, Dakota took a two-handed stance and opened fire. At this range he didn't miss. Two years ago, he wouldn't have known how to handle the weapon, but tired of being a victim, Dakota had made good use of his free time. One of the weapons masters had worked with him, and he'd become a respectable marksman.

Two rounds brought two of the four men down. Before he had time to aim for a third time, Dakota felt a sharp pain in his left thigh. The impact was hard enough to disturb his balance and his third shot went up and away from his intended target.

"Hold your fire! Hold your fire! Target down. Move in, move in!"

The Colt become too heavy to hold, and Dakota had no choice but to let it drop to the ground. Confused and disoriented, he fell to his knees in maddening slow motion. His hand found a dart with a bright red tassel on the end sticking out of his thigh. Voices came to him on the wind, making no sense. He wanted to move, but the connection between brain and body was no longer working. He felt wet moss tickling his cheek and realized he had fallen forward on his face. Rough hands pulled him onto his back. Looking up at blurred faces, blinking rainwater out of his eyes, he wondered, *if I open my mouth would I drown?*

No pain, no thought. Someone picked him up, his cheek smashed against a hard back, wet clothes. His last fading thoughts were of his father's face.

Let David be okay.

Then Dakota let the darkness win. He thought lately the dark always won.

CHAPTER 25

Dakota was awake. He lay on his back with his eyes still closed and took inventory. Nothing hurt, but he hadn't moved yet either. He was inside, he could smell the central air conditioning and the antiseptic clean that only comes from hospitals, but he knew he wasn't in a hospital.

Dim lighting greeted Dakota as he opened his eyes and blinked his vision clear. For the moment he was alone. He lay on a fairly comfortable bed, covered by crisp white sheets. To his right was a stainless steel sink and a commode, no curtain or doorway for privacy. That definitely ruled out a hospital, and it also ruled out his last hope that Maggie had somehow found him and taken him home.

Home. He laughed out loud at that. The fact he considered the army research facility home wasn't as much pitiful as it was laughable.

A wave of dizziness washed over him as he sat up on the bed, and he waited for it to pass before standing. The fact that he wasn't restrained surprised him. The room wasn't huge, but it wasn't a cell either. Three of the four walls were whitewashed cement blocks. The fourth wall dominated by a large glass window that ran nearly the width of the room and about half the height. Darkness on the other side of the glass denied him anything other than his own reflection. He spied a door on the far wall and knew it would be locked, but he had to try anyway. He jiggled the handle. No movement. No big surprise there.

Someone had dressed him in white scrubs and his hair was still damp, either from the rain or a bath. No mud, so his money was on the bath. He looked down at himself and noticed fresh puncture marks on the inside of each arm. Whether they had taken blood or given him something was up for grabs. Other than a little residual dizziness and a thirst that would kill a camel, he felt normal, so he gathered they had taken blood.

He walked the perimeter of the room and found a small table with a chilled pitcher of clear liquid. It didn't smell funky, and he decided he was too thirsty to be picky and poured himself a glass, and quickly followed it with another. He poured a third and then noticed the cameras. There were four of them, one in each corner, and they followed his every move. Dakota had the strong urge to drop his pants and bend over, giving whoever was watching an eyeful, but realizing they had probably already seen everything there was to see, he settled for saluting the camera nearest him with an upraised middle finger.

At some level he supposed he knew where he was the moment he became conscious. He'd dreaded this moment every day for the past two years now, but in an odd way he was almost grateful it had finally arrived. He was surprised at how calm he was. He didn't know how he got here, but he knew with a certainty that comes very few times in life that he was once again a guest of the General. Not *the General*, not John McKinley, but a colleague. John McKinley had told him the program would go on. Dakota always knew that at least that part of the man's ramblings was true.

Without any warning, the lights flared to life, and Dakota dropped the plastic cup to shield his eyes. Water splashed his bare feet as the cup hit the floor. Not only did his room lights dial up to near solar proportions, but floodlights from outside the glass window cut through to his optic nerves like a laser. Dakota squeezed his eyes shut against the assault, then heard a voice from the speakers hidden somewhere within the room.

"I am sorry about that, Doctor Thomas. I've lowered the lights a bit."

Dakota lowered his hands from his face and squinted one eye open to a narrow slit. The lights inside the room dimmed considerably, but the floods still shone in on him from behind the glass, leaving a solitary figure outlined in silhouette.

"Better?"

"Guess that depends on your definition of better."

"How are you feeling?"

Dakota ignored the question and asked one of his own. "So, are you him? Are you the General?"

Dakota heard laughter and thought it seemed out of place.

"God! I hate that antiquated title, but yes, I suppose I have to own up to it." The man's hand reached to his side and the floodlights shut off.

Dakota, still blinded, closed his eyes, trying to acclimate to the change. When he opened them again he had to stare. The man looking down at him was young, Dakota's age, maybe a little older. Short, light brown hair framed a tanned, unlined face. Dark, intelligent eyes observed him intently.

The man smiled. "Not quite what you expected?"

"You're no John McKinley," Dakota admitted.

"McKinley was a psychopath."

"As opposed to you?"

The General sighed. "You might not believe this, Doctor Thomas, but I am a physician like you. I believe in this research."

"I believe in it as well, but not like this." Dakota shook his head.

"Why? You don't like to see the results of your labor?"

"I've seen results."

The General laughed. "The army had you for two years. In all that time, they have managed to isolate one of the genomes for a vaccine against avian influenza, just one. How many genomes does it take to develop a vaccine? Twelve? By the time they manage to isolate them all, the virus will have mutated, making your research useless. If you had stayed with us, who knows what we could have accomplished in the same amount of time?"

"Who knows if I'd still be alive?"

"Now, see, there you go with those comparisons again. I think you'll find this facility a bit more humane than the Beaver Dam bunker where McKinley had you."

"You know about that?"

"I know everything there is to know about you, Dakota Rain Thomas. I know more about you than you, and I have waited a long time to make your acquaintance."

"Sorry, I can't say the same."

"You have no idea how extremely valuable you are, do you?"

"Well, with Ricco dead, yeah, I'm suddenly Mr. Popular."

The General took a step toward the glass. "Then he is dead. We heard rumors, but we were never really sure."

"What do you know, you're not omnipotent." Dakota paced in front of the window. The floor was chilly on his bare feet, but despite the air conditioning he was sweating.

"As far as you're concerned, I am."

"One question."

"Just one? Ask away."

"How? I don't understand what Kale has to do with any of this. It was Kale that took me in the woods, wasn't it?"

"Ah, yes, Mr. Kale. Yes, he was instrumental in bringing you here. The government might have their flaws as far as research is concerned, but they do have excellent security. We knew *where* you were, but we couldn't get to you there."

"You used Montana as bait." Dakota turned away from the glass as the reality of that sank in. He turned back, shaking his head, trying to understand the lengths this man had taken to get to him. "You had that girl killed just to frame Montana for her murder?"

"Well, that was a little freestyle on Kale's part. I just gave him the latitude to do what needed to be done. I knew the only way to shake you free of the grip the government had on you was to threaten your family. Your brother did quite nicely."

"This whole thing, sending Montana to jail—was about *me*?"

"One does what one has to."

"They'll be looking for me." He knew how useless the threat sounded.

"Let them. Enough niceties. We've wasted two years waiting for you, Doctor Thomas. It's time to get to work."

Dakota took a step away from the window and staggered. The door to his room opened and a man in a biohazard suit entered. Dakota took another step back. At six-two, Dakota didn't have to look up to a lot of people. The man walking toward him had a good foot on him. The face peering down through the plastic face shield was so black it looked like a shadow parting the light.

"This is Moses. He's not much of a conversationalist," the General's voice said through the intercom. "He had his tongue cut out by insurgents when he was captured in Fallujah. If it had been left to the army, he'd be dead now. We rescued him."

The dizziness Dakota had attributed to the side effects of the sedative hit him hard. This was more than residual drugs still in his system. Dakota wobbled and searched for something to steady him. Moses put a hand under his arm and led him back to the bed.

"You didn't just take blood, did you?"

The General smiled. "Perhaps we can work on finding those other eleven genomes. Don't worry, Doctor, Moses will take good care of you."

Dakota closed his eyes but found that only made the dizziness worse and opened them again. "I fucking hate you people."

Moses pushed Dakota down on the bed until he was lying flat and tied a tourniquet around his bicep, preparing to start an IV on him.

Dakota met the other man's eyes through the mask. "What, no monitors?"

The General answered for him. "As I alluded to earlier, Doctor, we are state of the art. When we took your blood, your DNA was initialized, the system now recognizes you. The room you are in has thousands of sensors all monitoring you. Your vital signs, all your blood levels, even your brain waves. This information is, even as we speak, being transmitted to monitors in our medical facility. It's a pity the information from when McKinley had you was lost. It would have been fascinating to compare the data. It may interest you to know that your body temperature has elevated three degrees in the short time we have been talking. That is most likely the cause of your dizziness. Not even Ricco responded as rapidly, and Ricco was amazing."

Dakota watched in morbid appreciation as Moses finished inserting the IV. The gloves of the bio-suit should have made it awkward, but the man completed the task with practiced ease. A sudden cramp had Dakota curling in a ball. His arms wrapped around his midsection as he grunted with the unbelievable pain. When he could speak again, he addressed the General once more.

"Do I get to know what the hell you did to me?" Another cramp had him gripping the sheet beneath him as he felt sweat running down his chest and back. "Or do I just get to be surprised?"

The General grinned. "I heard about your sense of humor, Dakota. May I call you Dakota? 'Doctor' seems so formal considering how intimately we will be working together." Without waiting for an answer, he continued. "As I suggested, we have decided to continue the work the army already started, just at an advanced level."

Moses managed to connect fluid to the IV and adjust the rate as

Dakota writhed on the bed. Non-stop abdominal cramps felt like he was being cut in half. "An…advanced…level?"

"The virus has been concentrated. Basically, we injected you with ten times the lethal dose, but don't worry, I have no intention of letting you die, you are far too valuable."

"Great." Dakota grunted. This was way worse than anything Maggie had put him through. His only comfort was the fact that his head was beginning to fuzz, taking the edge off the pain.

The General's voice came to him from what seemed very far away, but this time he was addressing Moses. "Keep the fluids running at a hundred cc's an hour, insert a Foley catheter so we can keep track of his urine output, and make sure you have the Valium ready. According to his records we downloaded from the army, he's prone to seizures once his core temp reaches a hundred and three. Let's not screw this up, people. We finally got the son-of-a-bitch back and I have no intention of letting him go again."

The cramps escalated and Dakota knew what came next. Apparently so did Moses. He rolled Dakota onto his side and held out an emesis basin just as Dakota let it fly.

Through shaking chills, Dakota wiped his mouth with the back of one hand. "God, I hate this part."

* * * *

The General turned off the intercom and the lights in the observation room. He couldn't take his eyes off the man in the room before him. *Two years!* He had waited two years for this moment.

"Satisfied?"

The General had almost forgotten about the man sitting just out of view from the window. He tore his gaze from Dakota Thomas and turned to address the man.

"Yes, Harry, I am very satisfied."

Stone Kale grinned. "Then I can expect the money to be wired to my account in the Caymans." He stood and straightened his shirt, getting ready to leave.

The General crossed his arms and gave Kale a disappointed look. "Well, we do have a problem there, Harry."

Kale dropped his hands and stood perfectly still. "Problem? What problem? Look, I did what you couldn't. I brought you your freak, I want my money!"

"True, you did that and I am more grateful than you can imagine, but I intend to keep *my freak*, Harry, and therein lies our problem. You left the brother alive. That was not part of the condition. He was instrumental in rescuing him last time."

"Fuck, man! Come on, the dude is not going to find him here!" Kale paced the small observation room, his face rapidly turning fuchsia with barely contained anger.

"He's a loose thread, Harry. Kill Montana Thomas and you will find your million dollars in your account."

"This is bullshit!"

The General pushed a button on the console in front of him. Two armed guards entered in less than two seconds. "If you insist on altering our agreement, Harry, I am certain I can find other uses for you. Perhaps as part of the control group in the experiment we are currently running."

Kale glanced through the glass at the man he had brought to the General. It was clear from the look on his face he thought the guy in the room below definitely was not having a good day. Kale shook his head and turned away from the scene. "No, uh, no. Okay, I'll take the dude out."

The General grinned and patted Kale on the shoulder. "Good man. Call when it is done and I'll wire you the money." Then turning to the guards, he said, "Please escort Mr. Kale out. Make sure he has whatever weapons and supplies he needs." The guards nodded and waited for Kale to start out the door. "Oh, and Harry?"

Kale turned back. "Yeah?"

"Do it soon. I run out of control groups very quickly."

Kale couldn't help but look down in the room again. He swallowed and nodded. "Yeah, soon."

The General smiled as Kale left the room. He settled back in the chair and flicked on the monitors, watching the live feed from Dakota Thomas. The record of his brain waves showed the start of seizure activity. He looked at the readout of the man's core temp, then down into the room where the doctor's body began jerking spasmodically on the bed. "One hundred and three, right on schedule."

The General grinned like a kid at Christmas.

"God, I love this part."

CHAPTER 26

Maggie Riley looked ahead of her into traffic. "What do you mean you lost him?" She hit the dash in frustration. "You can't lose him!"

Mark Kurtz, one of the two agents assigned to accompany Maggie and escort Dakota Thomas back to Maryland, gripped the steering wheel and sighed. He heard Tom Casner, his partner, grumble something in the backseat. Casner had little patience, and when it came to Maggie and her frequent rants, his hair-trigger temper simmered. Mark tried to diffuse the situation before it got out of control.

"I didn't lose him. He deliberately gave me the slip. I told you we should have split up. One of us should have went with them in the Hummer."

"God damnit!" Casner banged the window with a closed fist.

"Try calling him again," Mark suggested, trying to control his own temper. He knew Montana Thomas was long gone. Maggie punched in Ito's cellphone number and snapped it shut, indicating voice mail had picked up.

"Shit." Mark positioned the car in the far right lane and took the next exit off the interstate.

Maggie looked at him, her face scrunched up in confusion. "What are you doing?"

Mark pulled into a Dunkin' Donuts and parked, then turned halfway around in his seat so he could talk to both Maggie and Casner. He didn't usually play the voice of reason, but Maggie was too involved in this personally and Casner simply didn't know how to be reasonable. His part was to strongarm the doctor if he proved difficult. Mark and Casner had been given strict directives that Maggie was not privileged to. Dakota Thomas was to be brought back to the institution at any and all costs. Failure was not an option. Casner and he had been given the green light to use as much force as necessary to get the job done. The only restriction was the man needed to be alive. That left a lot of leeway.

But with the brother purposely losing them, he had no choice but to call it in. He failed and that was something he was not used to. Montana Thomas just seriously pissed him off.

"Why are we stopping?" Maggie asked. "You're letting him get away!"

"He already got away, Maggie. Look, I don't like this any better than you do, but the guy is gone. We need to call Geoffrey."

Maggie rolled her eyes. "I am *not* calling Geoffrey. He never treated Dakota like a human being. Dak was never anything more than an experiment to him."

"But he is also the guy who calls the shots. We need to call him." Mark picked up his own cellphone and punched in a few numbers before Maggie stopped him.

"Let's see if we can find them a little further up the road, maybe they're in a dead zone and the call isn't picking up."

"He's not answering because they want us gone, Maggs. Accept it."

Maggie opened her mouth to say something, and then seemed to rethink it and turned to look out the window at the rain that had started. Mark finished punching in the rest of the number and waited. The number was a direct line to the creator of the program. Maggie was the director, but Geoffrey signed the checks and told Maggie what to do. As the line picked up, Mark took a deep breath. This was a conversation he dreaded.

"You have him." The voice on the other end of the line didn't ask, he assumed.

"The brother played us. He gave us the slip on the interstate."

"You lost him." Mark recognized the impatience and anger in the voice.

"Yes, sir."

Silence, long and nerve-racking.

"Put Maggie on the line."

* * * *

Maggie had been looking out the window only half listening to the conversation. She still couldn't comprehend that Montana had intentionally ditched her. He knew she would never do anything to compromise Dakota's safety, didn't he? Mark interrupted her silent debate and handed her the phone.

"He wants to talk to you."

Maggie gave Mark a questioning look and took the phone.

"Look, Geoff, I know what you're going to say, but I don't think Montana lost us on purpose. I think—"

Geoffrey cut her off mid-sentence. "Maggie, listen. Montana has never liked Dakota doing what he does, you know that. You also know the guy never does anything by accident or by the rules. If you can't find him it's because he wants it that way."

Maggie sighed. "Yeah, I know. I was just hoping. Maybe Dakota will come in on his own."

Now it was Geoffrey's turn to sigh. "Look, I know you're close to Dakota. I never wanted you to deal with him on this project, but you promised me you could be objective when it came to him."

"And I have."

"Yes, up until now."

"What are you trying to tell me, Geoff?"

"Lose Mark and Casner. I need to talk to you confidentially."

"Give me a minute," she said to Geoff, then taking the phone from her ear, she looked at Mark. "Why don't you guys go get a cup of coffee and a donut?"

Mark growled under his breath and unbuckled his seatbelt. "Sure, that's just what Tom needs, caffeine." He opened his door and motioned for Casner to follow him.

"Man, this is *such* bullshit!" Casner complained, but he followed Mark out into the rain, slamming the car door behind him.

"Okay, you just made me piss off two very big guys with guns. Mind telling me why before they start pointing them at me?"

"Is your computer on?"

"Geoff, what does this have to do with anything?"

"Just do it."

Maggie shook her head in confusion and booted up her computer. "It's a good thing Dunkin' Donuts has a wireless connection," she mumbled. "All right, I'm on."

"I'm going to secure this frequency. Do you have the code to access Dakota's files?"

"Sure." She held the phone between her ear and shoulder and plugged in the data. The government homepage came up and she entered her access code to get into Dakota's files.

"Okay, what's the mystery, Geoff?" She couldn't see anything amiss. The files looked exactly how she left them. Dakota's last project listed as *in progress.*

"You have a level five security clearance, right?"

"Yeah?" Maggie's brow crinkled in confusion. Level five was as high as the security levels went, but she had a bad feeling about where this conversation was headed. "Geoff, what's going on?"

"Maggie, you need to listen very carefully to what I'm about to tell you. I have just cleared you for level six security and signed you in."

"Level six? There is no level six." Maggie watched as the screen in front of her disappeared to be replaced with a government seal. Geoffrey had control of her computer, she sat back and watched and listened as he explained what she was watching.

"What you are about to hear is known only to six other people in the world. Not even the president knows this information."

"Geoff?"

"Just listen and watch the screen. When Dakota Thomas and Michael Ricco were brought to the center two years ago, a decision was made. It was not made lightly, and it was made with the protection of this country in mind."

A picture of Michael giving blood flashed on the screen. He was smiling. Maggie remembered the picture being taken, he had been smiling at her.

"We promised Michael's days of experiments were done. So we took only his blood. But my God, Maggie! You have no idea the properties we found in his serum. It was like nothing, and I mean nothing, medical science has ever seen before."

Maggie made a huge leap and hoped to God she was wrong in her assumption. "What did you do to Dakota?"

"Dakota's abilities were not nearly as astounding as Michael's. He had an increased reaction to pathogens, but hell, they nearly killed him before his immune system kicked in. You remember how violently he reacted in the beginning?"

"Yeah, we almost scrubbed the program, but then he started having better response times."

"Yes, but it wasn't his immune system that was responsible, at least not at first. We decided if one infusion of Michael's serum could produce even the small reaction it created in Dakota, then maybe we could increase the reaction."

Maggie felt nauseous. "Oh my God."

"We spun down Michael's blood until we had an extremely

concentrated version of the serum that was originally given to Dakota. *That* is what we have been working on for the last two years, Maggie. We did it. Dakota's immune reaction times are off the scale. He has five times the immune reaction that Michael ever did."

"You weren't trying to find a vaccine for avian flu? All this time— What the hell did you do, Geoff?"

"This is why you were never involved in the decision, Maggie. I knew you would react emotionally."

"What about Dakota? Did you happen to let him in on what you were doing to him?" Maggie couldn't believe what she was hearing, then her attention was drawn to the webpage in front of her. Geoffrey had brought up the insignia for Homeland Security.

"No, we figured if it worked, we would develop the vaccine quicker anyway, and everyone would be happy."

Maggie wasn't listening anymore, she was reading. Dakota's file was filled with suggestions for using what they had learned as a biological weapon in conjunction with homeland security and national defense. Maggie's breath caught painfully in her chest. Dakota Rain Thomas was being used by the government, just as Michael had been.

"Geoffrey, tell me what you did to Dakota." Her voice was quiet and filled with barely contained anger.

"Maggie, you have been made aware of this project because it is vital we get Dakota back. A lot of people are going to die if we do not have him back under controlled conditions in a little over forty-eight hours."

"Tell me!"

Maggie heard Geoffrey take a deep breath. "The last project Dakota was involved in, the one he left in the middle of... Maggie, Dakota was injected with an inert form of the Ebola virus. It was why he reacted so violently to the infusion."

"Dakota has Ebola? My God, you killed him!"

"No. No, listen carefully. The virus will lie in a dormant form until it's activated. Then Dakota will act as a carrier. He won't be affected by the virus, but he will spread it. Ideally we could send him to a secured area, activate it, and all he would have to do is infect one person in a densely populated area. The virus would do the work for us. Think about it, Maggie. He's the perfect assassin. Who would suspect a doctor sent to, say, Nasriye, Tikrit, or Baghdad on a humanitarian mission?"

"I can't believe what I'm hearing. Have you ever considered that the virus doesn't care who it kills? It doesn't know the difference between a ten-year-old child and an insurgent! Dear God, Geoff, you're talking about genocide. Dakota would never have agreed to be used like this."

"Which is precisely why we chose not to inform him."

"You *chose* not to inform him?" Maggie laughed at the absurdity of it all. "You turned the man into a walking biological time bomb and you *chose* not to tell him?"

Geoffrey continued, unfazed by Maggie's accusations. "Maybe you missed the part about the virus being activated. That's where I need your help. Remember I said the virus lies dormant until it is activated inside Dakota?"

"Yes?"

"Well, see, that's the thing we haven't perfected yet. The virus is designed to go active at high body temperatures."

"High body temperatures? As in a fever?"

"Yes, to activate the virus, Dakota needs to get very, very sick."

"Just how high does his fever need to get, Geoff?" Maggie felt lightheaded.

There was a pause on the other end of the line. "We're not sure."

"We need to find him."

"Yeah, the sooner the better. There's more, Maggie. We needed to find out if we were successful, so we also infected Dakota with the flu."

"The flu?"

"Yeah, your average variety flu, but in a concentrated form. It was designed to hit him in a little over forty-eight hours."

"Dakota's going to get sick."

"Very sick. And anyone around him at the time is going to die. We are looking at mass deaths in pandemic proportions, unless we can contain him."

"Can you fix this, Geoff? Can you take it back?"

"No, Maggie, we can't."

"So Dakota spends the rest of his life isolated? You're a son-of-a-bitch, Geoffrey! I hope you burn in hell."

"Get in line, Maggs. Will you help me get him back?"

"What other choice do I have?"

"None. You have the entire homeland security team at your disposal. Let me know what you need and where, and you'll have it."

"I promised Michael I would cut him loose."

"You didn't know about this when you made that promise. Get Dakota back before a lot of innocent people die. I know you don't believe me, but I am sorry."

Maggie shut down her computer, she didn't want to look at what they'd done anymore. She was ashamed to be a part of it, however uninformed she may have been. "You're right, I don't believe you. I know what I have to do. I'll let you know when I have a line on him."

"Make it soon, Maggs. Make it soon." She heard Geoff sign off and sat with her head full of what he had told her. She thought she was doing the right thing, she convinced Dakota of that, now she had to tell him that she had delivered him into the hands of someone worse than the General.

She closed her eyes and leaned her head back on the car seat. "I'm so sorry, Michael. I didn't know."

I have to make this right!

Casner and Mark left the donut shop and headed back toward the car. Maggie knew exactly what she had to do. She slid over to the driver's seat and locked the doors just as Mark and Casner reached the sedan. She saw Mark say something to Casner as she turned the engine over and put the car in gear. Peeling out of the parking lot, she left the two men covered in the mud from her spinout. Maggie never bothered to look back.

She had made her choice and now she had to do something she'd promised her husband. She had to find a way to make this right. When she was far enough away, she pulled to the side of the road, took her phone off the seat next to her and sent a text message to Ito. It was a message she knew he would have to answer.

Dakota in trouble. I am alone. Call me ASAP. Maggie.

CHAPTER 27

Montana ran up the slight incline toward the cabin with Ito and Damien on his heels. His feet slipped on mud and rain-wet grass, but his pace never slowed. He had heard gunfire, two, maybe three shots. It was difficult to tell echoes from the real thing with the wind and rain. The only thing he knew for sure was Dakota was in trouble—again. Maybe Walter too.

That fear was put to rest quickly as the footfalls he heard coming toward them proved to be his father with his grandfather just behind him. He turned to Ito and Damien before any mistaken identities could cause a fatal mistake. He lowered his own weapon and motioned for Ito to do the same. "My family," he yelled to be heard over the storm.

Ito nodded in understanding and put a hand on Damien's weapon just to make certain he heard Montana as well. The three of them stood in the downpour waiting for David and Walter to clear the rise and meet them. Montana looked for Dakota, but his brother was not bringing up the rear.

With no time for introductions, Montana ran to David and grabbed his arm. Wiping rain out of his eyes, he took his father by the shoulders and shook him, yelling in his face. "Where's Dakota?"

"Let's go inside." David freed himself from his son's grasp and headed toward the cabin, but Montana stepped in front of him.

"Where is he, Dad?"

"They took him. I don't know who, four men down at the access road. I had no idea they were there. They took him!" he repeated.

Walter put a hand on David's shoulder and spoke to his grandson. His voice was soft, but still carried over the fury of the storm. "Inside." He turned and walked back to the cabin. It was clear he expected to be obeyed.

Once everyone was in with the door shut behind them, Montana wasted no time in asking his questions. "I heard gunfire. What happened? Who has Dakota? Where did they take him? How long ago?"

Walter shrugged out of his rain-soaked coat and shook water off his clothes like a dog after a bath, then tended to the dying fire. Without turning to look at the men behind him, he told Montana what had happened.

"I found my grandson here yesterday. He was not doing a very good job of riding your motorcycle. While he slept, my son decided it would be a good time to pay me a visit."

Montana and David exchanged glances. "I didn't want you to get involved," Montana said.

"You involved me the minute you called. What did you think I would do? I get a frantic call from you asking for Walter's whereabouts. I know you, Montana. I knew something was wrong."

Montana closed his eyes for a moment, trying to calm the storm that raged within him. When he opened them again, he spoke quietly. "This is not important, just tell me what you know about Dakota."

"I left him sleeping and went to meet my son," Walter said. Pleased with the fire now burning in the hearth, he turned to face the men behind him.

"I went to retrieve the motorcycle from where Walter hid it," David explained. He pulled his soaked shirt off over his head and shook water from his hair. "Thought maybe I could fix it, save Dakota a little grief from you." He shook his head. "He saved my life. I never even knew they were there until Dakota fired at them."

"It was Dakota's shot?" Montana asked, confused at the information.

David nodded as he wrapped his naked shoulders in a blanket from the bed. "The first one, yes. They had to be looking for him. How did they know where he was? Why did they take him?"

Montana's brow creased. "They shot him?"

"I don't think so. It all happened so fast. I didn't have a weapon, and I knew Walter wasn't far behind me." David looked miserable, and Montana wasn't sure what he could do to change that. "I didn't know who was shooting at who, but I think they just hit him with a tranquilizer dart. I saw a red tassel sticking out of his thigh just before I hit the dirt. You have to understand, they would have killed me, there was nothing I could do to help him. One man came up the hill, he picked Dak up, and two others had his back. They were well armed and organized," David said.

Montana laced his fingers at the back of his neck and turned in a small circle, feeling as if he was about to come undone. "We're too late." His voice was quiet and in direct contrast to the frustration he felt.

"Fill me in, Montana," David said.

"Some very bad people have my grandson, don't they?" Walter asked. "The same ones who took him two years ago, the ones who forced his life on a different path."

Without asking how he knew the information, Montana simply met his grandfather's gaze. "Yes, Walter. Very bad men."

"Then we must go and bring him home."

Montana let his hands fall back down to his sides. He looked up to meet Ito's and Damien's eyes. "My thoughts exactly. The only problem is I have no idea where they took him."

Ito's cellphone broke the ensuing silence. "Probably Maggie again.

I should let her know what happened." He pulled the phone from his pocket and read for a minute, then met Montana's frustration with his own. "It would seem Maggie is one up on us."

He handed the phone with the text message still on the screen to Montana.

Damien looked over his shoulder to read the message. "Wait a minute, I was under the impression that Maggie still thought she lost us. How does she know Dakota is in trouble?"

Montana shook his head. "She doesn't, at least not the trouble we know he's in."

Damien wiped a hand over his face to clear it of water. "What other kind of trouble is there?"

Ito and Montana exchanged looks. "Not the good kind." Ito stood in a puddle of water dripping from his clothing. The hardwood of the cabin floor was more wet now than dry and nobody seemed to care.

Montana nodded in agreement. "Maggie asking us for help can't be a good thing." He scrolled through Ito's contacts until he came to Maggie's number and pushed *send*.

* * * *

Maggie was too wired to drive. The sedan might as well have a beacon on it and as soon as Casner and Mark called Geoffrey she would be wanted property. Which meant she needed to ditch the car. The only problem, Maggie had no experience with this sort of thing. She didn't run from things.

Her hands were shaking as she pulled into the parking lot of an abandoned gas station. The place had been shut down long enough for weeds to be sprouting out of the cracks in the concrete.

God! What had she done to Dakota?

Guilt ate at her until she thought she might be sick. They used her and her relationship with Michael to get Dakota to trust them. She felt dirty at the thought as she gripped the steering wheel and forced her hands to be still. She stared at the phone thrown on the seat next to her and willed it to ring.

"Come on, Ito. *Call me!*"

She picked up the phone, intending to try him again, when it rang in her hand. Maggie held it and stared for the first two rings, then snapped it open. Before she had a chance to speak, Montana's voice came to her, insistent and demanding.

"Start talking to me, Maggie, and don't stop until I know what the hell is going on."

"Montana?"

"Now, Maggie. Dakota is gone. Kale took him, and Kale works for the General. I don't want to hear government bullshit, and I sure as hell don't want to ask this, but I need your help, Dakota needs your help."

"Wait a minute, *the General* has Dakota?"

Now it was Montana's turn to be confused. "You know that, you told Ito he was in trouble. What were you talking about if not that?"

"You're right about one thing, we don't have time for a verbal sparring match. I need to see you. I am, for the moment, unattached to the government. Where are you, Montana? We need to talk. A lot of people are going to die if we don't find Dakota and find him soon."

If Maggie expected the usual argument from Montana, she didn't get one. She got directions.

CHAPTER 28

Stone Kale couldn't have been more pissed off. He'd done what the General asked. Not only did he get the doctor dude to leave the army research facility, he actually delivered him right to the man's doorstep. In the process he received a black eye, a split lip, some seriously bruised ribs, had his evening with Irene disrupted, not to mention ruined a two-hundred-dollar pair of Italian leather loafers. Oh yeah, two of his team had been killed too. That fucking doctor was starting to be more trouble than he was worth.

Now, here he was back on the road on the pain-in-the-ass Ranger's trail once again. He swore to God when he found the guy, he was going to make him suffer before he finally offed him. Maybe cut him up a little at a time, slice a finger or two off, make him beg for mercy. *That* would be vindication. Just the thought of giving it to that prick gave Kale a hard-on. He'd had enough of Montana Thomas to last him a lifetime.

He wanted to take Kowalski and Beck along with Simmons, but both had been shot. Beck was out of commission and Kowalski might not make it. He and Simmons alone now had the dubious task of hunting down and killing Montana Thomas. Simmons wasn't much of a conversationalist, which would normally piss Kale off even more than he was, but the quiet suited his mood.

He was watching the dreary scenery flash by when Simmons

surprised him by starting a conversation. "If you would have told me the brother needed taken out, we could have done it the first time around. I don't like not having all the information." He turned to look in Kale's direction. "Consider this a warning, if you make it look like I fucked up again, I will kill you."

Kale met the man's eyes and smiled. "Well, you can try. Don't threaten me, Simmons."

"I don't make threats. I make promises." Simmons looked back at the road.

Kale shook his head. He was in no mood for a pissing match. "Remind me to kick your ass after this is all over, okay? Look, do you even know where to go?"

Simmons glared at Kale, his knuckles turning white on the wheel. He settled his eyes forward once more and took a breath before answering. "Our sources traced him back to the same place we took the doctor from." He pulled a manila envelope from the seat between them and handed it to Kale. "Recon obtained these from satellite images a little over an hour ago."

Kale opened the package and looked at grainy black and white photographs. If not for the blurred image circled in the left-hand corner, he would have missed it.

"It's the black guy's Hummer. Big-ass white thing stuck out enough for us to get a picture through the gaps in the trees. They blew up the license plate—it's his. The Ranger was last seen with him in that vehicle. There is also evidence of a structure deeper in the mountains."

"How can you tell? Satellite images can't see through the trees."

"No, but gas analyzers picked up CO-two emissions concentrated in this one area. That indicates a permanent structure. The emissions are caused by either campfires or exhaust from a heat source—maybe both."

Kale looked closer at the pictures and made a face. "You've got to be kidding me."

Simmons took one hand off the wheel and let it hang out the open window. "The General is one very connected man. If I were you, I wouldn't screw up with him again."

Kale nodded in absent in agreement. "So we have the dude with the Hummer, the Ranger. Who was the other guy? The one on the ridge with the doc?"

Simmons shrugged. "Doesn't matter. Whoever it is, if he's still there when we find them, he's dead along with the rest of them."

"Fine with me. I don't care what you do to the rest of them. The only thing I want you to understand—Montana Thomas is mine."

Simmons seemed to consider the demand. Just when Kale thought he had lapsed back into silence, he spoke again, his tone quiet and tight with frustration. "Don't fuck this up, Harry."

Something in Simmons's voice made Kale ignore the intentional use of the name he hated. He knew the General hired men who fell off the grid. Men who had no problems with following orders—any orders. Simmons was no exception. But unlike most of the General's men, Simmons was smart. Kale hated to admit that even to himself, but he couldn't deny it. Simmons was big, strong, smart, and had very little conscience to speak of. For perhaps the first time in his life Kale listened to the little voice in the back of his head that told him to shut up.

He held the satellite images in his lap and tried to picture Montana Thomas begging for mercy right before he killed him. The mental image brought a small smile to his lips as Simmons brought him closer to their target.

* * * *

Montana met Maggie at the access road and brought her to the cabin. He said nothing to her as he hid her car with cut tree branches and made the twenty minute walk in silence. Maggie did her best to keep up with him, but he refused to alter his pace to accommodate hers. Even after she fell the second time, he never looked back until she cried out in pain.

"Montana!"

He walked two more steps before she got to her feet and fell once more.

"Would you stop!"

Montana whirled around and advanced on her. He grabbed her by an upper arm and yanked her to her feet. She grunted and fell into him when she tried to regain her balance.

"It's my ankle, I think it's sprained."

The scowl he gave her was less than sympathetic. She pushed away from him and balanced precariously on one leg while giving him a little attitude right back.

"Look, I'm here for one reason and one reason only—to help Dakota. I'm not asking you to like it." She hopped to a nearby tree to lean against it, but misjudged the distance and lost her balance again. Instinctively she tried to keep from falling by placing her weight on her injured ankle and collapsed with a small cry.

Montana caught her before she hit the ground and helped lower her to the grass. His gentleness in handling her this time belied the anger he showed her on the outside. He settled her on the ground and paced a few feet in front of her before stopping. "Tell me what you know, Maggie. I am not in the mood to dance around this thing with you."

"You know, I'm the one who should be pissed here. You ditched me, remember?"

"Not you directly. The people you work for. I trust you to keep your word, I don't trust the government."

"Can't say I blame you." Maggie pushed the hair off her face with both hands and held it there for a moment before speaking again. "I spent the entire trip here trying to figure out exactly what to tell you and what not to."

Montana didn't like what he was hearing; his face told Maggie as much. If she happened to miss the non-verbal cues, the verbal ones were blatant. "Let me make it easy for you. Tell me everything. I can't help Dakota if you decide to pick and choose what to tell me."

Maggie met Montana's eyes and chewed the inside of one cheek. "Understand something first—I knew nothing about what they did. You have to believe me on that."

Montana stared back, his voice low and even, but demanding. "Just start talking."

"Are you sure the General has Dakota?" She scooted back and leaned against a huge Pinion tree.

"Yeah, I'm sure."

"Then Geoff doesn't know that, so we're one up on him there, but probably not for long. I'm not even supposed to know what Geoffrey told me, but he's desperate." Maggie took a deep breath and locked eyes with Montana. "They screwed with Dakota big-time. All this time we thought we were doing a good thing, developing a vaccine that would save people's lives. It's the only reason Dak agreed to be part of the experiments in the first place. The only reason Michael agreed as well." Despite her best efforts, Maggie's eyes welled. She didn't bother to wipe the tears away, she let them fall.

"What did they do?" Montana asked. Maggie could see the struggle it took for him to keep his own emotions in check. She knew what Montana thought about the research she and Dakota did. To his way of thinking, the government was little better than the psycho that had nearly killed his brother two years ago.

"They turned him into a weapon. A biological weapon."

Montana's face screwed up with confusion, concern, fury. "Explain."

"Without my knowledge, or Dakota's for that matter, Geoffrey decided to play God. Dak was infected with the Ebola virus. Do you understand what that is?"

Maggie watched his face and for once the black eyes were not veiled. They told her he understood, but perhaps could not yet believe what she was trying to tell him.

"That's the virus that wiped out some remote village in Africa, it has no cure, highly contagious—tell me I'm wrong here, Maggie, please."

Maggie shook her head. "I wish I could. The virus is not the basic Ebola, though. According to Geoffrey it was designed to go active when Dakota's body reaches high temperatures. Dakota won't get the virus, he's the carrier. They intended to use him as a genocidal weapon."

Montana closed his eyes briefly at the information. He opened them again as he spoke to Maggie. "Dak doesn't know?"

"Not a clue. But they also infected him with a designer flu virus. That's the key to start the process. The flu makes him sick, increases his body temperature, and activates the virus."

"Who the hell were they planning on killing?"

"Nobody—yet—that's the problem. Dakota was still supposed to be under observation. They wanted to make sure it worked."

"So, we have no idea how this thing will affect him?"

Maggie shook her head. "It could remain dormant, it could activate just as they planned, or…" She let the sentence hang between them until Montana finished it.

"Or it could kill him."

"Yeah, and everyone around him. Montana, anyone around Dakota could be infected. Ebola doesn't kill right away and is transmitted via airborne properties."

"Meaning what, exactly?"

Maggie licked her lips and prepared herself for Montana's reaction to what she needed to say next. "Meaning that if we cannot get Dakota back under controlled conditions in the next thirty-six hours—the time we have left before the flu virus in his system goes active..."

"No." Montana shook his head. The single word conveyed to Maggie exactly what he thought of her plan.

"Montana—"

"No! Maggie, no, I can't do that. He's my brother."

"And he's my friend. Montana, think about this. What would Dakota want us to do if he knew? He would not want to be responsible for anyone's death. We aren't talking about one person dying—we are talking about mass deaths, pandemically. You know I'm right."

"You're asking me to kill my own brother."

"I'm also asking you to save countless lives."

Montana laced his hands behind his head and paced almost manically. He stopped in front of Maggie. "What happens if we get to him before the thirty-six hours are up?"

Maggie raised her eyebrows as if she thought the deed would be next to impossible. "*If* we can find him and *if* we can get him back to a secured, contained facility before the virus goes active, yeah, maybe he has a chance."

Montana thought about that and nodded. "Then that's what we will do."

Maggie shook her head again and struggled to get to her feet. Leaning against the massive trunk, she reached out and put a hand on Montana's arm. "You are taking a hell of a chance. What if you're wrong?"

"What if I'm right? He deserves the chance. I *will not* count him out. Understand that, Maggie. Don't fight me on this—you won't win."

If Maggie didn't know the man as well as she did, she might have feared for her life. "Wasn't planning on fighting you, I was planning on helping you. Michael would never forgive me if I did anything else. I just wanted you to have all the facts."

"I appreciate that. Right now we need to combine all our facts and get moving—fast."

Maggie looked a little dubiously at her injured ankle. "Fast is something I don't think I can do at the moment."

Montana took a step toward her and in one quick move, scooped her up and unceremoniously plopped her over his shoulder and started walking.

"Hey!" Maggie protested, but Montana cut her off.

"Clock's ticking, Maggie."

"Okay, okay, just don't drop me."

"Wasn't planning on it," Montana said.

As Maggie bounced against Montana's back he hiked the quarter-mile back up the ridge, and Maggie made Michael a silent promise. Dakota *would* be coming home. She didn't care anymore what it might cost her personally. Whatever it took, however she could help, she would see to it that Montana brought his brother home.

CHAPTER 29

Stone Kale and Eric Simmons hiked the small access trail up into the woods above them. The white Hummer was exactly where it should have been, so they were confident Montana Thomas was nearby. They parked the Honda at the end of the trail in front of the Hummer. Not only would it block the vehicle from leaving, it was in position to aid in a quick retreat if one was called for.

Kale sweated and his breath came in short gasps after only five minutes into their climb. He stopped, bending over with his hands on his thighs, trying to catch his breath. "Hang on," he managed to yell at the other man.

Simmons turned and gave Kale a look of supreme annoyance. "Jesus! Stay here, I'll take care of Thomas myself."

Kale narrowed his eyes at Simmons and stood up. "The hell you will."

"Face it, Harry, you're not up to this. Why the General put you in charge has always been a mystery to me. You give orders, you don't do the dirty work."

Kale felt his breathing ease up and his temper flare. "Shut up, Simmons."

Simmons stopped and turned on Kale. "Fuck this! Dealing with the General doesn't worry me half as much as you're pissing me off! You have no business here—although at least you dressed for the role this time." Simmons approached Kale and indicated his more appropriate boots and green military fatigues.

"Look, asshole, I don't care what you think. But the man put *me* in charge, not you. Deal with it. I call the shots—*not you!*"

Simmons brought his rifle up and advanced on Kale. "I had men like you under my command, and you know what? Not one of them made it out of combat. You want to know what the only difference is between them and you?"

Kale couldn't help himself. He took the bait. "What?"

"They were smart."

Kale brought his weapon up just as Simmons chambered a round. They were both snapped out of their own thoughts of killing the other by a voice above them.

"As much as I would like for you to save me the trouble and shoot each other, my grandson tells me we need you."

Kale and Simmons looked up the hill. Leaning against a tree, smoking a pipe was an old Indian in faded jeans and a red flannel shirt, his long silver hair pulled back in a braid.

"What the hell?" Kale didn't lower his weapon, he simply swung it toward the old man.

"Who are you supposed to be?" Simmons asked. He sounded mildly amused at the unexpected visitor. It was clear neither Kale nor Simmons considered the man a threat.

"I'm Walter."

Kale did laugh then. "Walter, is it? Well, Walter, you picked a hell of a time for a stroll. Now unless you can tell me where to find Montana Thomas, I suggest you bend over and kiss whatever you got left goodbye."

Before Kale could chamber a round, he was stopped by the sight of Simmons on the ground, an arrow through his throat. "What the f—" A soft click just behind his left ear caused him to leave the sentence unfinished.

"Drop it."

Kale could feel the cold steel of a gun barrel push against his skull. He removed his finger from the trigger housing and let his gun dangle for a moment before letting it fall with a soft *thud* to the ground. His eyes followed its descent and locked on the blood forming a growing puddle around Simmons's head. The other man's eyes were open, he wasn't dead yet. But it wouldn't be long. His eyes were unfocused, roving from side to side. His mouth gulped air that no longer traveled to his lungs. The arrow had pierced his trachea.

Another man came from the cover of the forest and picked up Kale's fallen weapon. He had a compound bow in his hand and a quiver of arrows slung across his back. It was becoming clear to Kale that they had been ambushed.

"Hands up," the voice behind him instructed.

Kale obeyed as the man with the bow searched and relieved him of a handgun and a knife sheathed at his hip. He had no doubt as to the identity of the man holding the gun on him.

"What, you had to enlist an old Indian and a guy with a bow to do your dirty work for you, Thomas? Not man enough to take me on your own?"

The gun at Kale's head was removed. "Turn around."

Kale did, with a cocky smile on his face. The smile faltered a little as he came face to face with Montana Thomas. The bruises on the man's face were faded but still evident. His natural dusky complexion hid most of the damage, but ugly, thick, black sutures curved up the line of his jaw, making him look like he was perpetually grinning on that side. Kale had to look up to meet the man's eyes, then wished he hadn't bothered. Nothing friendly about those eyes.

Kale tried to maintain the cocky attitude. "Figured you'd be here."

"Where's my son?" The man with the bow came up beside him.

Kale raised his eyes at the question. Maybe he could still salvage something here. He looked at the old Indian, then back at Montana.

"All in the family, Thomas?" Kale turned in a small circle, indicating the two men surrounding him.

"My father asked you a question."

Kale shrugged. As long as he had information they wanted, he figured he was safe. "No clue what you're talking about."

One of the biggest black men Kale had ever seen, except maybe for Moses, parted the brush above him and stepped out. Behind him was a blond man. Kale recognized them both. Ito St. James and Thomas's lawyer. They were armed, their weapons trained on him.

"Perhaps we could refresh your memory," Ito offered. Sweat glistened off his bald head and bare arms. He looked as if he were carved out of solid rock. Nerves started to jangle down Kale's spine. The odds were not with him getting out of this alive.

Montana pulled the slide back on his weapon and put a live round in the chamber. "Where did you take my brother, Harry?"

Kale looked around him and weighed his options. "Or what? You kill me? That doesn't get you what you want, now does it?"

Montana handed his father his weapon. "Wasn't planning on killing you just yet."

Kale took a hesitant step away from Montana.

"What's the matter, Harry?" Montana walked around Kale. The other men formed a loose circle around him, denying him any opportunity of escape. "Having to face me not shackled to a chair too much for you? Or maybe it's the fact that I'm not a defenseless, innocent woman."

That got a laugh out of Kale. "Linney might have been a lot of things, but innocent wasn't one of them."

Kale saw the veins cord up the side of Montana's throat. He didn't think he was walking away from this but maybe if he pushed the man, he might be able to get a few hits in of his own. A man acting out of anger wasn't nearly as dangerous as a calm one. He thought he would be able to dodge the first couple of blows at the very least.

Not even close.

Montana lunged. The first blow knocked Kale flat on his back and left him breathless. If he was thinking Thomas was going to play by any rules, he was wrong. The second blow came in fast and hard, bare knuckles connecting with the soft underside of Kale's chin and making his head spin. The only thought that made it through his dazed brain was a simple one.

I'm a dead man.

* * * *

Montana knew Dakota's life might very well lie in this man's hands, but he had waited for this moment and he would not be denied. Montana started with Kale's face. He had wanted to destroy that cocky grin from the first moment he saw it. The satisfying crunch of cartilage as Kale's nose broke almost made him smile. Blood, warm and sticky, flowed between his fingers. One more slam to the man's mouth, and then a hand on his arm pulled him off. Montana's instinct was to whirl on the owner of the hand, but realized it belonged to Ito. Montana shrugged his friend off and walked away from the bleeding mess writhing on the ground at his feet.

Montana advanced once more but stopped just short of making contact. "You worthless piece of shit! You couldn't stand the fact that she chose me! She chose me!"

Kale rolled to his side and propped himself up on one elbow. He spat out blood and shook his head. "You fucking broke my nose!"

"Be happy you're still breathing." Montana circled the man. Rage bubbled through him. He wanted nothing more than to pummel the man into a bloody bag of pulp, but he knew he couldn't. He would have to settle for a verbal assault.

"Man, you are some kind of delusional psychopath! When are you going to get it through that thick, brainless skull of yours that Linney *used* you?"

Montana squatted down next to Kale and grabbed the front of his shirt. He was breathing heavily, covered in Kale's blood, and suddenly realized he was no closer to finding Dakota than he was before. He let Kale go and watched him fall back to the ground.

He nodded at Kale. "Yeah, maybe. Maybe at first that's how it was. But not in the end. I refuse to believe that and *that's* why you killed her—because she *did* love me."

Kale sat up, carefully guarding his nose, looking at the blood on his hands. "Whatever gets you through the night."

Montana couldn't control the beast that escaped this time. He pulled back his booted foot and caught Kale under the chin, sending him flying backward in the wake of an impressive arch of blood flowing from the gash ripped through his lower lip down to his chin. The next kick broke several of his ribs. Kale curled in a ball and cried out in agony.

Montana grabbed Kale's hair and lifted his head off the ground. His voice was deadly quiet when he spoke. "Say it. Say she loved me."

Kale surprised him by spitting blood in his direction.

Montana kicked him squarely between the legs. "Say it," he repeated.

When he could, with his hands cupping his balls, Kale nodded. "Yeah, fuck, yeah! Okay, man, she did, she loved you—the bitch. I offered her double the pay, but she wanted out. Christ! That hurts!"

Montana stood and turned away.

Ito came to Kale and pulled him to his feet. "Smart man, Harry. Now I suggest you tell the man where we can find his brother, or I'm not pulling him off you next time."

Kale wiped at the blood still pouring from his ruined nose and smiled. "Won't do you any good, man."

Montana still had his back to Kale and heard Ito speak to him. "Just start talking, Harry. Just start talking."

CHAPTER 30

He was cold. His head ached as if someone had used it for a punching bag, and he hurt—*everywhere*. Dakota heard distant murmurs of conversation and couldn't decide if he was still asleep, but the rude intrusion of someone's thumb opening his eyelid and a bright light shining into his field of vision brought him acutely aware that he was awake.

Dakota turned his head away from the painful light and tried to shield his face with his hands only to find he couldn't. His wrists were tied to the bed frame by soft restraints. He tugged on them lightly, then gave up, saving his energy. The voices became more focused, and he realized he was surrounded.

"He's awake, sir."

"Vitals?"

"All at base line. No seizure activity for the last ninety minutes. Pupils equal and reactive."

"What does his recent blood work show?"

"Slightly elevated white count, but significantly decreased from the last check. A few aberrant findings in his T-Cell markers, but we think that may be normal for him. It hasn't changed from his initial labs."

Dakota tried to ignore it all and crawl back inside himself, but he started shivering. God, he was cold.

"Dakota."

A small touch on his cheek. He turned his head away, still not ready to confront whoever wanted him. The touch became a slap. His hands pulled against the restraints once more in automatic defensive posture. All he could do was open his eyes.

"Dakota?"

He turned and looked in the direction of the voice. A man looked down at him through the clear face shield of a biohazard suit. The face looked vaguely familiar, then it clicked. Everything fast-forwarded and he remembered.

Kale. The General. Crap!

The face behind the mask belonged to the man himself. All Dakota could manage was to stare.

"Talk to me," the General told him.

Dakota waited for the worst of the shivering to subside and locked eyes with the ones behind the mask.

"Fuck you." It didn't come out as forceful as he intended, nor did it elicit the response he wanted.

The General smiled. "Glad to have you back with us, Doctor. What a remarkable experience. Tell me, how are you feeling?"

How was he feeling? How many times had he asked the same question of his own patients? How he despised those few words. Dakota tore his gaze away from the General and looked down the length of his body. He lay naked on his bed, spread eagle and in four-point restraints. No dignities left to him, not that he expected any.

"Is freezing me to death part of this remarkable experience?" he asked through chattering teeth.

The General looked to one of the other white-suited people in the room. "What's his core temp now?"

"Ninety-seven degrees Fahrenheit."

The General seemed to consider the information and walked to a stainless steel cabinet that Dakota didn't remember being there before.

He withdrew something, and when he turned around, Dakota saw it was a blanket. The General approached Dakota again and began unbuckling the restraints.

"Your seizures were quite violent. These were only for your protection."

Moses came to Dakota's other side and helped the General release him.

Dakota rubbed his wrists to restore the circulation. "I'm sure my clothes were endangering me as well." He took the offered blanket and sighed in relief when he found it heated. He let Moses wrap it around him and curled inside its warmth.

"It was the best way to try to bring down your body temperature. It peaked at a hundred and three. Considering the concentration of the virus we infected you with, I'm surprised it didn't go higher. It's almost as if you've never been exposed to it before."

"Well, you're the omnipotent one. If you had access to my records, you know I have been." Dakota closed his eyes. He felt battered and bruised and now that he was beginning to warm up, his eyes wouldn't stay open. All he wanted to do was go back to sleep.

"It's very curious, Doctor. I was hoping you could elaborate on the experiments the army conducted on you."

"I have a better idea. Why don't you go to hell and leave me the fuck alone."

The General smiled inside his plastic shield. "Well, we can always find out for ourselves. I thought I would offer you a chance to avoid unnecessary pain."

Dakota opened his eyes. If this General was anything like McKinley, he knew he would have no problems living up to that promise. Pain was something Dakota could live without. But the question confused him.

"Look, I don't know what you want from me that you can't just take. I can't stop you. I get that! I *fucking* hate that! I *fucking* hate you—but I get that." Little black dots started to swim in front of his eyes at the outburst, but Dakota chose to ignore them. "You already hacked into my files, so you probably know more than I do. I only know they were working on creating a vaccine for avian influenza. Your bud, McKinley, already exposed me to it two years ago." Dakota's voice lost a little of its venom and he had to close his eyes once more as the room started to swim around him. "Jesus, can't you people just leave me alone?" There was a tone of begging in his voice that Dakota hated, but one he couldn't take back.

His mind played back to the one moment of freedom he could remember in the last two years. Straddling Montana's Harley with the throttle pulled back. No one knowing who he was, where he was.

In the wind.

He would have given anything to get that moment back. As he slipped into sleep once more, despite the General's nagging questions and thinly veiled threats of torture, one thought kept repeating itself. If he ever had the chance at freedom again, no one was ever going to take it from him.

* * * *

The General looked at one of the physicians in the room. "Is he unconscious?" He put a hand on Dakota's face and lifted an eyelid. Dakota turned away from the contact but did not open his eyes.

"No, sir. Just sleeping. My advice would be to let him. Seizures exhaust the body and as you pointed out, his were nasty. We'll monitor him."

The General nodded in understanding and then made a decision. "Doctor Fitzpatrick, you are familiar with Private Ricco's records?"

The physician finished adjusting the IV flowing into Dakota's veins and looked up. "Yes, sir. It's practically required reading."

The General digested that and continued. "You have also read Dakota's files."

"Every word."

The General moved to the foot of the bed and looked down at the sleeping man. "Let me ask you something. In your professional opinion has Doctor Thomas been exposed to increasing doses of the virus we infected him with today?"

Without hesitation Fitzpatrick shook his head. "No, sir. In fact that really concerned me."

"How so?"

"Well, according to his files, over the last two years the army has been infecting him with gradually increasing doses of the virus. They were getting nowhere fast. I mean the dose we gave him was toxic, no doubt about it, but according to the results they achieved, he should have handled it better than he did."

"Better how?"

"If his body had been systematically exposed to this virus he should have had a better handle on it. He should never have spiked a temp like that, let alone gone into seizures."

The General nodded. "I agree, Doctor. I have another question for you. If the army was not trying to develop a vaccine for avian flu for the last two years, what exactly did they do to Dakota Thomas?"

"Yeah," Fitzpatrick said. "That's what I want to know too."

The General took another look at Dakota and walked to the door. "Let me know if there are any changes. If this man dies, I will hold you personally responsible."

"Of course you will."

The General smiled. "It's good to be understood, Doctor."

The General left the sealed room and entered an anteroom, a small area between the two main rooms where any contamination could be caught and eradicated before spreading any further. There he stripped, showered and changed.

In his office, he read over Dakota Thomas's file once more. He shook his head at the inconsistencies he now found. And they called him evil. The government obviously had a hidden agenda where Dakota Thomas was concerned. Now all he had to do was figure out what that might be. No reason he couldn't profit from what the government had already started for him. He always did love a challenge and Doctor Thomas was proving to be just that.

CHAPTER 31

Montana left Walter and David behind, much to their displeasure.

"I don't like this, Montana. You can use all the help you can get," David argued.

"Look, Dad, I know you're worried about Dak, but right now the less people I have to keep track of the better."

"You wouldn't have to *keep track* of me." David paced in front of the red Honda down at the access road. Walter watched him without comment.

Ito and Damien made sure Kale's hands were secured behind his back, and then pushed him into the front passenger seat. His nose was still bleeding, and he had to breathe through his mouth.

"You know, I could choke to death here." He tried to wipe at the blood dripping off his chin, but with his hands behind him he had to settle for using his shoulder, and then yelled when the pressure pushed against his already smashed nose.

"Do we really need him?" Damien looked in the car, making a face. "I'm sure I could come up with a case for justifiable homicide if you just killed him."

Kale looked at him as if trying to decide if he was serious or not.

Montana ignored them all and took his father by the shoulders. "I need you here. Please, Dad. Dakota needs you here. I have no idea what kind of shape he might be in when I find him."

David looked away from Montana. It was clear he didn't like his options. "How do you expect to do this alone? I know you're good, Montana, but nobody's *that* good."

Montana looked at Maggie waiting near the car, then to his father again. "I have help."

David followed Montana's gaze and shook his head. "They're the ones responsible for all of this. *Now* they tell you they'll help! How can you believe them?"

"I don't, but I don't have any other way around this. If you do, this is not the time to keep it to yourself."

Maggie came to stand just behind Montana. "I don't blame you for being angry, but trust me, Geoffrey doesn't want Dakota in the General's hands any more than you do. He's an asshole, I admit that. But he's an asshole with an extraordinary amount of power. If anyone can get Dak out of there alive it's him."

David glared at her, then turned and walked a few steps away.

Maggie followed him, staying a foot or two behind him as she spoke. "You have every reason not to trust me. I understand that. All I can tell you is I love your son, Mr. Willows. He was the best friend my husband had. I promise you with everything I hold dear, I promise on my life, I won't let Geoffrey touch him again. I swear that one thing to you."

"We will be here when you bring my grandson back home." Walter's voice was quiet but demanded the attention of everyone in the small clearing.

Emotions played across David's face. He took a deep breath and looked out into the trees. Maggie put a tentative hand on his shoulder.

"I feel responsible for all of this." She shook her head, cutting off anything he might have to say. "But Montana is right. The fewer people getting involved the better. I don't know how yet, but I swear to you on a promise I made to my husband, I will bring Dakota home to you."

David looked unhinged at the words. He turned and touched Maggie's face, gave her a nod, then walked over to stand next to Walter. He kept his back to Montana and Maggie as if watching them leave would take what little control he had left and shred it to pieces.

"I have moved the camp," Walter told Montana. "But I know you will find us. Bring my grandson home."

Montana gave his family one last look. Without another word, he got into the driver's side of the Honda and waited for Maggie, Ito and Damien to join him. They pulled out of the small access road and onto the larger paved two-lane blacktop.

What he was doing went against everything he knew was right. He was relying on information from a man sent to kill him and enlisted the help of another man who had no honor. If Montana had his way, Dakota would never have been working for the government to begin with. Hindsight was as useless as a gun devoid of bullets.

Bring my grandson home.

Montana wanted nothing more than that. The problem was he wasn't sure he could do that one thing. He wondered what his father would think if he knew Montana might have to do the unthinkable. Would his father forgive him if he killed his own brother?

Would he forgive himself?

It was a question that ate away at the very soul of him. The General and all the atrocities he had performed on Michael Ricco and Dakota suddenly seemed like the lesser of the two evils.

"You're never going to get him back, you know." Kale interrupted his internal debate. "The man, this General, he'll kill you. All of you, you're all dead."

Montana gave Kale a sideways glance. "Shut up, Harry." Montana turned his attention back to the road.

Something in the way Montana looked at him must have made it through the false bravado. For the rest of the trip back to the main highway, Harry became an obedient puppy with tail appropriately tucked between his legs.

* * * *

According to Kale, the General used one of his export warehouses as a front. On the outside, everything appeared legitimate. Kale used it for importing drugs, all with the General's assistance. The man's connections kept Kale out of jail and kept what local as well as federal law enforcement agencies that weren't already loyal to the General looking in other directions. Hiding in plain view, the General operated three floors beneath the ground of Kale's warehouse. Who would suspect a low-life drug lord of running subversive medical experiments on human subjects? Kale wasn't that smart. He was the perfect cover.

"What kind of security are we looking at?" Ito asked from the back seat.

"Fuck you, I'm already dead. He finds out I helped you, he'll use me in one of his control groups. I don't have a clue what that is, but I don't want to find out, you know what I mean? The couple times I had to go down there—man, you can hear the screams." He looked back at Ito. "You guys don't scare me. You want to kill me? Go ahead. The General—he'll do far worse. He'll keep me alive."

Ito reached around the seat and almost casually wrapped his arm around Kale's throat, lifting the man half out of the seat. He squeezed until Kale gasped and panted, his face turning crimson and then blue as the last of his oxygen depleted. Just before the man's eyes rolled back, Ito released him. "You might want to rethink that, Harry. Because, you see, we're here and the General isn't. I have become rather fond of the good doctor, and I would take it very personally if any harm were to come to him." Ito placed his hand around Kale's throat once more, but just let it sit there. "Very personally. Understand?"

"You're all fucking psychos, you know that?" Kale coughed and choked, gasping for air.

"Security?" Ito repeated the original question.

Kale rolled his eyes as he realized his precarious position between certain death and certain death. "Fuck. Okay, the perimeter is surrounded with motion detectors that activate heat sensors. Anyone who works for him has had bio-scans, the fuckers don't even know it, but their DNA has been scanned and when the bio-sensors recognize them they don't set off the alarms, but they are identified and that information is sent to a central database which tells the system if they should be where they are at that particular time. If they are, nothing goes down."

"And if they're not where they should be?"

Kale stretched his bruised throat and looked back at Ito. "Then they get to play with the General. He goes through control groups pretty quick." Kale managed to smile, his teeth stained red with the blood now starting to clot in his nose. "Bet he'd love to get his hands on you." He waggled his eyebrows at Ito and turned his eyes on Maggie. "And you." He stuck his tongue out at her and wiggled it up and down. "Oh, baby, Ricco's widow? I might get off easy if I deliver you to his door. The guy practically gets a hard-on every time the dude's name is mentioned."

Montana flicked his hand out and slapped Kale across the ear. "Shut up, Harry."

Kale yelped, edged closer to the window, and decided to take Montana's advice.

"It's all right, Montana," Maggie said. "We need him to get us past security. Geoffrey has a Special Forces team on the way now. But he wants us to get inside and secure Dakota before he makes a move."

"How much time is left?"

Maggie glanced at her watch. "Less than thirty-six hours until the flu virus activates. After that?" Maggie hitched her shoulders. "I don't think anyone knows. Geoffrey has a plane on standby to transport Dakota back to Maryland."

Montana gripped the steering wheel until his knuckles whitened. "I don't want him going back there."

"It's better than the alternative."

Montana caught Maggie's eye in the rearview mirror. "I hate this."

Maggie nodded. Montana knew she hated it too. They were both caught in a net and running out of time. There were no good endings in sight that Montana could see. The best he could do was to deliver his brother back to the bastard who treated him as nothing more than a possession to be used and studied. The alternative Maggie spoke of, Montana didn't want to think about. That alternative consisted of him putting a bullet in Dakota's brain. He would rather put one in his own.

CHAPTER 32

A division of Army Special Forces and Homeland Security sat in the cramped confines of the Military Air Transport unit. In addition to the armed military presence, the plane also carried a full medical team familiar with Dakota Thomas. A sealed bio-chamber was on board as well, a small coffin-sized container that would safely transport a sedated Dakota Thomas back into the waiting and anxious hands of the government research center in Maryland.

Geoffrey Banks personally instructed his staff and the military escort. They had one objective—to secure Doctor Dakota Thomas before the deadly virus inside him became active. Thirty-four hours. Every member of the team, medical or military, was aware of the ticking clock. Their watches were all in synch, and they knew if they failed it could mean their own deaths. If the thirty-four hours went by and Dakota was not in their hands and safely secured within the bio-chamber, the mission objective would radically change. Dakota Thomas would then have to be eliminated.

Geoffrey had a headache, right behind his left eye. He tried to ignore it, but the pressurized cabin made it impossible. A few days ago he'd been accepting congratulations on his success from his superiors. Dakota Thomas, with a little help from Michael Ricco, was the military's best kept secret. If the Ebola proved to be nonfatal to Dakota, and he in turn became a carrier for the deadliest known virus on the face of the Earth, Geoffrey would be hailed as a hero.

But his *experiment* went to ground. It was a risk not telling Dakota what they were doing, but one Geoff thought was worth the outcome. He knew Dakota would never agree to be a part of killing possibly thousands of lives. He would never understand he was saving thousands more as a result.

Maggie was another unexpected complication. Dakota would be a lot harder to manage without Maggie and Ricco around. He had to find a way to bring Maggie back in. At least she had enough sense to call him.

In five hours they would be landing at a secure airstrip in Alamo, Nevada. They'd already contacted the National Guard. The area around the warehouse was being evacuated even now. A story about some chemical leak was all it took. The warehouse would be surrounded quietly.

If all went according to plan, Maggie and her unofficial team consisting of Montana Thomas, his partner, and some lawyer should have Dakota in hand. If not, the team on board would have a go at it. Geoffrey would rather not deal with a hostage situation involving this new General. But Geoffrey knew Montana Thomas. He didn't think it would come down to that. Montana would do the dirty work for him and if the man happened to get a little dead in the process, Geoffrey would try to act upset over that. All Geoffrey wanted was Dakota Thomas back where he belonged, under his thumb, with a needle in his arm.

* * * *

Dakota paced the dimly lit confines of his room. He was dressed in the pair of scrubs that had been left at the foot of his bed. They were clean and smelled slightly of antiseptic. He felt good, strong and edgy. There was no clock, and he didn't have a watch. He hated that, not knowing what time, or even what day it was for that matter. There were no windows and no way to gauge if it was day or night. Not that it mattered.

He was stiff, his body covered in bruises. His wrists and ankles were encircled in purple, tender flesh. That part at least he understood, he had pulled against the restraints while his body was in the throes of unrelenting seizures. But he wasn't seizing now. He couldn't remember bouncing back so quickly before.

Dakota paced in front of the dark glass window and really wanted to go for a run. Muscles too long at rest begged for release. Energy coursed through him almost as strongly as anger. He wanted *out*. Claustrophobia bit down hard and the room seemed to shrink around him. Stopping, he placed both hands on the smooth, cool glass and tried to see through it, but couldn't get past his own reflection, and what he saw there made him turn away. He circled the room a dozen times or more. Every time he passed the door, he jiggled the handle, even though he knew it was locked. Even if it wasn't, he had nowhere to go.

When walking around in circles wasn't good enough, he started running. Slowly at first, then building up as much speed as the small room allowed. It wasn't enough, he couldn't go fast enough. Ten laps, fifty, one hundred. Even when sweat rolled off him despite the air conditioning, he ran. On the last lap he abruptly stopped in front of the dark glass and threw himself at it.

He screamed his frustration as he slammed into the barrier again and again. "Let me out! I am not your freaking pet!"

He grunted as his body pounded the glass wall. It shook and vibrated from the abuse, but it held firm. He started taking running leaps, hitting the glass with his outstretched palms. The pain felt good. He didn't even stop when he left bloody handprints sliding down the once spotless surface.

"Enough!" *Slam.* "Enough!" *Slam, slide.*

Dakota had backed up for another assault when the floodlights cut through the gloom, stopping his headlong plunge into the glass.

"Yes, Dakota. I would say that is quite enough."

Shielding his eyes from the glaring light, Dakota recognized the voice. The General had come to see what havoc his prized subject was causing.

Dakota rested bloodied hands on his knees, sucking in air. Bright red palm prints marred the previous white of his scrub pants. Fat drops of sweat falling from his hair and face joined the blood, diluting it and causing pink drops to dirty the pristine concrete floor of his cell.

"What do you think you are doing?" the General wanted to know.

Dakota squinted up through the blinding lights. He couldn't see the man, but he knew he was there, staring down at him through the glass. In one sudden movement, Dakota charged the glass once more. He landed with all his weight on his shoulder causing the glass to shudder. He smiled when he saw a shadow jump away, startled by the sudden attack.

Despite the pain registering through his shoulder and down his arm, he laughed. "What's the matter? Can't handle it when your pets aren't docile and compliant?"

The floodlights switched off, leaving Dakota temporarily blinded. He heard the door to his room open and as his eyes adjusted, he recognized Moses's now familiar bulk cross the threshold.

"I'm glad to see you're feeling better, but you need to control yourself, Doctor," the General told him, his voice enhanced by the speakers.

Dakota backed away from Moses. He didn't know what the man intended to do, but he didn't want to find out. "Or what? You'll punish me?"

"More like control you. I can't have you injuring yourself."

"Why? Want to save all that fun for yourself?"

Moses circled and Dakota put the bed between them. The light flashed off something in the big man's hand. Dakota thought it might be a syringe, but realized that wasn't what Moses held.

"We're running a controlled experiment, Doctor. I'm sure you can appreciate that. Any injuries you sustain must be factored in."

Dakota glanced at Moses on the other side of the bed and rubbed his injured shoulder. "Yeah, well, factor in this, asshole!" Dakota went for the window again. He didn't know what he wanted to prove, he only knew he was tired of going down without a fight.

Moses simply reached out one massive arm and reined him back in. Dakota kicked and clawed, but Moses picked him up with one hand around his throat as if he weighed no more than a child, then turned and pinned him to the bed. Dakota wrapped both hands around Moses's forearm and fought him with everything he had. He looked up to the room above him and locked eyes with the General looking down on him.

"You want to study me? Do an autopsy. That's the only way you're ever touching me again."

The General smiled and shook his head. "I've been lenient with you, Dakota, because I'd prefer that we work together. But I do have limits to my tolerance. As you yourself said, you have no choices. You are mine. It's time you learned that."

Dakota watched him give a nod to Moses. The man released Dakota and aimed the object in his hand at Dakota's chest.

Dakota scooted back on the bed, resting on his elbows, his eyes never leaving the thing. He was gulping air, sweat soaking his clothes, running down to settle in the small of his back.

"It is a Taser," the General informed him. "Very effective in controlling unwanted behavior."

"I hate you."

"So you've said. Moses."

Dakota never saw Moses move. But he felt the jolt as electricity coursed through his body. His muscles contracted violently, painfully. Pain like Dakota never felt before. Sharp, stabbing, burning pain. It stole his breath and left him momentarily dazed but conscious. He lay on the bed with Moses standing over him, involuntary tears streaming down his face as the General looked down at him.

"That was the lowest setting. Would you care to try for the next level up?"

The muscles and tendons in Dakota's neck corded as he struggled to get past the worst of the pain.

"Will you behave yourself, or does Moses need to be more convincing?"

Dakota tried to slow his breathing as his muscles relaxed. His eyes shifted from the man casually observing him to the one standing over him. Moses gave him a confused look, the only expression Dakota had ever seen on his face. He flicked a lever on the Taser and shook his head. Dakota couldn't read the expression but if he had to guess, he would say Moses was asking him to back down. Dakota also saw a thin trickle of blood drip down from the big man's left eye.

"Gotcha', didn't I?" He smiled and jumped at Moses. Maybe if he could get the Taser, he could at least try to disable the weapon, break it, throw it—something!

Moses brought up his free arm and backhanded Dakota as if he were waving off an annoying bug. Dakota flew back and tumbled over the bed, landing hard against the far wall. He tasted blood, but didn't have time to investigate as Moses came toward him. The big man flipped the bed out of the way and bent down next to Dakota. He couldn't be sure, but as Dakota tried to back away, he thought he might have broken a rib or two.

There was nowhere to go. The wall was firmly behind him and Moses directly in front of him. Moses looked at him like a disappointed parent right before he pushed the Taser in his side and discharged the weapon.

If Dakota could have screamed, he would have. The pain he experienced the first time was nothing compared to this. It was as if someone put him in a red-hot vise and turned the screws. No breath, no screams, only contorted open-mouthed agony as his body writhed, his muscles constricted with the electricity that flowed through his body. Moses held the probes against him longer this time. Even when the weapon was removed his body remembered the pain. He felt tears running down his face, then collapsed in a senseless heap, trying to remember how to breathe.

"I will ask you once more, Dakota." The General's voice came to him again. It seemed much closer this time without the enhanced tinny echo from the speakers. Dakota opened his eyes and saw the General squatted down next to where he huddled on the floor. He hadn't heard the man enter the room. "Will you behave?"

Dakota watched Moses as he flicked the lever on the Taser to the next highest setting. "It won't kill you," the General told him. "But there are two higher settings."

Dakota brought a shaky hand up and wiped blood from his mouth.

"The choice is yours. All you have to do is say one word and the pain stops. Say 'yes' and I can make it all go away. Moses will tend to your injuries, give you something to eat, clean you up. Wouldn't that be so much better than discovering how much more pain your body can take? I will ask you one more time, will you behave?"

Dakota tried not to look at Moses and the weapon he held. He stared directly into the General's eyes and nodded as if he were considering the request. With one hand bracing his tender ribs, he pushed himself to a sitting position against the wall. He took a deep breath and winced with the pain it caused him, then spat a glob of blood and mucus in the General's face.

"Screw you, you fucking psychopath." Dakota smiled at the look of disgust and maybe disappointment he saw on the General's face.

The man stood and withdrew a white handkerchief from his back pocket and wiped the mess from his face. He walked back toward the door and gave Dakota a small sigh before turning his attention to

Moses.

"You know what to do." He looked back at Dakota. "I was hoping you would be a bit more cooperative, but no matter, you will be. All you have to do is say 'yes' and Moses will stop. Anytime, just the one word. You will say it. The only question is how much pain will you force on yourself before you do." The General turned his back on Dakota and walked out.

Dakota returned his attention to Moses and the Taser. "Don't suppose you want to talk about this?" he asked, trying to stand. His legs refused to listen and he ended up just pushing himself along the wall. "Ah, fuck." Dakota closed his eyes as Moses advanced on him and he felt the Taser probes pushed against his thigh.

CHAPTER 33

The warehouse looked innocent enough. It was a four-story brick façade, well maintained and humming with the noise of a normal workday. Eighteen-wheelers sat idling at the docks while cargo was loaded into their empty holds. People walked purposefully from one place to another, clipboards in hand, hard hats and name badges firmly in place. They had no idea their daily bread was bought with proceeds from Kale's drug trade which in turn was funded by the program and the work accomplished by the General.

Montana parked the Honda Pilot in the employee lot and turned the engine off. He took a small pocketknife from his pants and leaned over to free Kale's hands.

"Don't be stupid, Harry. I would rather take you down a little at a time, but I don't have a problem with putting a bullet or two in select places."

Kale rubbed his wrists and said nothing, but the look on his face told Montana everything. The man was not to be trusted. Kale would betray them at the first available moment. Harry lived by one rule: love the one you're with. As they were preparing to enter the devil's lair, Montana knew Harry's loyalties were about as firm as his spine.

Ito went around to the back of the car and began to unload. Montana had asked him to make one quick trip to an old barn outside of town and access a door to an underground storage shed. It wasn't a root cellar, though. Ito was the only person besides Montana who knew what was really stored there. Weapons, all kinds of weapons. It had taken Montana a while to stockpile the stores. The FBI had confiscated his previous weapons store over two years ago and while the stash he had hidden in the abandoned barn was nowhere near as elaborate as the one taken from him, it was a start. Ito handed flak vests to everyone save Harry.

Maggie was a little dubious as she slipped hers on. "Don't you think the people are going to be a little concerned if they see us waltzing in dressed to kill? And I mean that literally."

Damien covered Kale with the Glock Montana had given him while Montana helped Ito.

Maggie accepted one of the weapons with noticeable appreciation and obvious skepticism. "Jesus, where the hell did you get these?"

Montana turned to Maggie with an incredibly straight face. "Found them."

"Yeah, right. So, what, we just walk in fully loaded and expect no one to care?"

Montana secured his vest and slung the weapon over his shoulder. He took the Ray-Bans from his shirt pocket, carefully put them on, then turned his attention to Maggie. "That's pretty much the plan."

"No surprises," Ito warned Kale as he prodded the man. Ito didn't need to make it clear that if he made one wrong move, he would drop Kale on the spot.

Kale led the way into the front of the building and with a few nods to his startled employees, walked to the back hallway and up the flight of stairs leading to his office. They made it inside with the door closed firmly behind them.

"What about all this security?" Damien asked. "No one seemed to care who we were."

Kale barely gave him a glance. He opened his top desk drawer with

Montana and Ito watching his every move. "That's because we haven't entered a secured area yet." He took a single key. "Now the real fun begins."

Kale walked back around the desk and to an elevator door on the opposite side of the room. There was only one button—*down*. Kale put the key into the lock at the control panel and turned it while pushing the button. Alarms sounded a few seconds later.

Kale jumped at the unexpected sound. "What the hell is that?" he asked.

"Company," Montana said.

"That's the evacuation alert." Kale looked from one face to the next trying to figure it out.

"No shit, Harry." Ito smiled.

Hurried footsteps and voices could be heard outside the office. The elevator swung open with a quiet *swoosh*, looking about as inviting as an open grave. Before anyone had a chance to enter, a knock on the closed door had Montana and Ito cocking their weapons and pointing them in Kale's direction.

"Play this very carefully, Harry," Montana warned.

"Mr. Kale?" a muffled voice asked from the hallway. "Are you in there, sir?"

Montana watched the handle turn and pulled himself up against the wall behind the door. Ito and Damien ducked behind the desk. The door opened, leaving Maggie in plain view. Thinking quickly, she jumped at Kale and locked lips with him. Kale winced a little at first with the pain from his split lip, but then ignored it and took advantage of the situation just offered to him.

A three-hundred-pound Hispanic linebacker entered the room. Montana could see him through the crack between the door and the frame. His head sloped straight down to his shoulders like a lampshade. His features were so flat they almost blurred together.

Maggie tried to pull away in mock embarrassment, but Kale had circled his arm around her waist and held her close.

"Harry, honey!" Maggie pulled her face away from Kale's. "You promised me we would have some *privacy*."

The linebacker grinned as Kale got into his impromptu role and snaked his free hand under Maggie's shirt. Montana saw Maggie flinch as Kale took a handful of her breast.

"Sorry to interrupt, sir, but they are evacuating the plant and everyone in a three block radius. Something about a derailed train, some chemical spill—thought you should know."

"I appreciate it, Freddy, but as you can see I am in very safe hands."

"*Harry!*" Maggie kept the smile on her face as she tried to squirm away from Kale's embrace.

"Yes, sir," Freddy said. "I just thought you should know is all."

"Message received. Make sure everyone gets out, including you. I'll shut it down."

Freddy gave Kale a wink and a nod and shut the door.

Montana moved from behind the door with every intention of rescuing Maggie. He needn't have wasted the energy. The second it was closed, Maggie grabbed the hand on her breast and pushed Kale's thumb back toward his wrist while twisting his arm.

Kale let go and dropped to his knees. "Fuck! Let go!"

Maggie did, then put her foot on Kale's chest and pushed him until he fell on his back, holding his damaged wrist in one hand.

"You ever touch me again, I'll kill you." Maggie bent over and grabbed Kale by the shirt to make sure he completely understood the threat. "Got it?"

Kale composed himself. "Hey, you started it. What's the matter, babe? After two years of fucking a farm boy, you can't handle a real man?"

Maggie pulled her foot back and kicked Kale in the face. Montana could have stopped her, but didn't see the point. Kale wiped blood from a split lip and just smiled.

Montana stepped between the two and helped Kale to his feet. "You done?" he asked Maggie.

Maggie's blue eyes glared at Kale. "For now."

"Good, then might I suggest we go get Dakota?"

Kale kept the smile on his face as he stood. "You have no fucking clue what you are in for."

"Get in the elevator, Harry." Ito motioned with the Kimber.

Kale shrugged and entered the small waiting cubical. When everyone was in, Kale shook his head. "You realize the General knows something is up. He can hear the sirens."

"And he'll see the corresponding news story about a chemical leak."

"He'll kill you."

"So you've said."

"Screw this, man. When he finds out I helped you—fuck it. You want to kill me, go ahead. I'm not going any further."

Montana came up beside Kale and looked at the control panel in front of him. No buttons, just a smooth rectangular panel.

"Now, I'm guessing here, Harry, but that looks suspiciously like a biometric palm analyzer. Since this is your office, I am inclined to think that your palm print operates this elevator."

Kale looked back at Montana, and then at the weapon he carried.

"You know what the great thing about palm prints are, Harry? You don't need to be alive to use them."

"You start shooting, the sensors are going to pick it up, and the General will know for sure your chemical spill is bogus."

Ito came to Kale's other side. "I don't think the man was thinking of shooting you, Harry."

Kale glanced at Montana, and Montana smiled. Whatever he might have had in mind never got a chance to play out. Maggie stepped in front of Montana and reached down between Kale's legs—and squeezed.

"I learned a lot fucking a farm boy. One thing I remember is bulls are a lot easier to handle after they're castrated." She twisted Kale's scrotum, and the man dropped to his knees in a silent scream.

Montana and Ito exchanged startled looks of appreciation. Damien laughed. "Damn! Remind me never to get you pissed at me."

"This is nothing. Second-degree black belt—jujitsu. But the direct approach does have its merits." She looked up at the three men behind her. "Well, is someone going to put his hand on the plate? Mine are a little full—with great emphasis on *little*."

Damien pulled Kale's hand away from his crotch and placed it, palm down, on the sensor. A blue light came on and scanned Kale's hand.

"*Lower level access granted,*" a computer-generated female voice informed them. The elevator started a smooth descent into the bowels of the warehouse. The klaxons and hurried sounds of people leaving the building were quickly replaced by relative silence. The mechanical hum of the elevator and Kale's gasps for air were the only intrusions.

Montana studied Kale's face and thought the man was on the verge of passing out. Maggie appeared to be enjoying herself. "Maggs, we might still need him."

Maggie looked up at him with a mixture of disappointment and mirth. "Yeah? Do me a favor, let me know when we don't." She gave one final twist and let Kale go.

"Stand in line." Montana watched Kale grab his crotch and roll on the floor.

"You bitch! You freaking, psycho bitch!"

"Shut up, Harry, or next time I won't pull her off you."

Kale found his feet, but still couldn't stand fully straight. "There isn't going to be a next time. You're all dead."

Montana and Ito ignored him and checked their ammo. Damien wiped sweat off his face despite the cooler temperatures.

"Relax," Montana told him. "According to Mr. Kale, they only have ten, twelve armed men at any given time. The remainder of his staff is strictly medical."

"Yeah, sorry, but I choose to remain nervous. Four to one odds do not relax me."

Ito laughed. "You got to get out with us more often, man."

"I'll pass. So what do we do? We shoot anything that moves?"

"You keep talking like that and I'm taking your gun away."

Montana put an extra magazine in his jacket pocket and pushed a live round into the chamber of the Colt. "Just keep a low profile. Trust me, you'll know when to start shooting."

"Thank you, I feel so much better. You do realize we have broken about two dozen laws already, don't you?"

Montana put a hand on Damien's shoulder as the elevator came to a gentle stop. "Damien?"

"Yeah?"

"Stop talking now." Montana looked over Damien's shoulder to Maggie. "How much time?"

Maggie glanced at her watch. "Officially? Twenty-nine hours. But we aren't talking about a fuse being lit here, Montana. This is biological, nothing is for certain. We could be way off on our timeline in either direction."

Montana nodded but kept his thoughts to himself. He pushed Kale out of the elevator into the deserted hallway.

"Take me to my brother, Harry."

CHAPTER 34

Kale led them down the empty corridor. Maggie and Montana followed directly behind, weapons at the ready, nerves primed and on edge. Ito and Damien brought up the rear.

"Is anyone besides me noticing the complete absence of bad guys?" Damien asked.

Ito gave him a glance over his shoulder and a quick nod.

Damien stopped as the rest of the team continued their slow jog up the hallway. He opened his mouth in disbelief, his arms held out, the weapon in his right hand waving through the air. "Am I the only one who's bothered by this?"

Ito turned and quietly walked back to Damien. He put a hand on the barrel of his rifle and pushed the muzzle down until it pointed to the ground. "Only point it at what you intend to kill."

Damien pulled the rifle in and kept the barrel down against his thigh. He held his tongue and his place and stood there. The only sound, their soft footfalls.

"Unless you want to face all those hidden bad guys by yourself, I suggest you keep moving, counselor," Ito told him, turning to walk back up the hallway.

The words unglued Damien's feet. He jogged up the hallway until he was next to Ito once more. "So, you think this is weird too?" Damien asked.

Ito and Montana exchanged knowing glances but kept their thoughts to themselves. Kale stopped at two electronic doors at the end of the long hallway. A large red sign across both doors made it perfectly clear who was and was not allowed through.

Authorized personnel only beyond this point.

A biometric print analyzer was in the wall by the door. Montana turned to Kale. "My brother is through there?"

"Last time I saw him he was. Dude didn't look like he was having a very good day." Kale smiled.

Montana stepped in quickly and punched Kale in the kidney, dropping the man to the floor. "Save the commentary, or I'll let Maggie have another go at you, and when she's done, I get what's left over." Montana stood over Kale, his presence enough of a threat. "Open the doors, Harry."

Kale scooted away from Montana. "Sorry, but I'm not *authorized personnel*. You are so fucked. You think the General doesn't know you're here? Do you think he doesn't know who you are?" Kale rubbed his side. "Fucking amateurs."

Montana stepped in fast and threw Kale hard against the wall. Before Kale had a chance to respond, Montana grabbed him by the throat and pinned him there. He pulled the .45 out of its holster at his shoulder and pushed it against Kale's cheek.

"Guess that means we don't need you anymore." Montana clicked the safety off with his thumb. "Do we, Harry?"

Kale's eyes widened at the sound and he stopped struggling. "No, wait… I, uh…"

Montana let Kale go and withdrew the weapon. He turned halfway around and then in the last moment pulled his arm back and hit Kale in the side of the head with the butt of the weapon. Blood sprayed in an arch above Kale's head. He did a small turn, following the momentum of Montana's strike, and dropped to the floor.

Damien ducked and stepped back at the sudden attack. "Holy shit. Is he dead?"

Maggie spared the man sprawled on the floor a disgusted look. "God, I hope so."

Montana ignored them both, knelt on one knee next to the doors, and swung the backpack off his shoulders. He withdrew a small gray-green ribbon and molded it around the locking mechanism and doorknob in the shape of a 'C'.

Maggie watched over his shoulder. "C-four?"

Montana gave her a grin as an answer.

"What's he doing?" Damien asked Ito as he watched Montana.

With his back to Montana, his eyes peeled for trouble, Ito didn't need to turn around to answer Damien. "He just wrapped a ribbon of plastique around the lock."

"Time's up," Maggie said, touching her own earpiece.

Damien stepped up next to Maggie. "What's that mean? What are they doing?"

"My boss is outside, he and all of Homeland Security have this entire complex surrounded. The National Guard cordoned off everything in a six-block area."

Damien turned to Ito as Montana still worked on the door. "And just when were you planning on letting *me* in on this secret?" When he got no answer he focused on Maggie again.

"We have ten minutes to get Dakota out of here before they open fire," she told him.

"Wait a minute. Open fire? Did I miss the part where they negotiate?"

Maggie shook her head. "I thought you were a lawyer. There are no negotiations where Geoffrey is concerned. Do you remember Waco? It was no accident, trust me."

Before Damien had a chance to reply, Montana and Ito handed

them earplugs. "Put them in tight," Ito suggested.

"You might want to step behind me. Fire in the hole!" Montana slammed his hand down on the detonator.

Kale lay where he fell on the ground as the locking mechanism on the door blew apart. The resulting explosion made their ears ring. A strong chemical smell filled the air.

Damien shook his head as the pressure in his head returned to normal. "Well, so much for being quiet."

Montana pushed past Ito and booted the door open. He entered quickly and dropped to one knee, his rifle muzzle sweeping from side to side. "Hallway clear—dead end with multiple closed doors." He turned back to Damien. "For once, Harry is right. They already know we're here."

Damien rubbed the back of his neck, trying to ease the tense muscles there. "And that's supposed to make me feel better?"

Montana returned his attention to the open space in front of him.

"No." He stopped briefly to bend down next to Kale's body. He felt for a pulse at the base of the man's neck, when he found one he pulled a pair of zip-cuffs from a small supply bag strapped to his thigh and bound Kale's wrists. Without further explanation he stepped over him and continued down the hallway with Ito, Maggie and Damien following. The closed doors to either side didn't interest him, but the one directly at the end of the short hallway did.

Subject 234 procedures in progress.

The door was frosted glass as were the walls around it. It was obvious it was not a secured door. The one they had just entered was supposed to keep out anyone who didn't belong.

"What about him?" Damien asked, referring to the still unconscious Kale.

Montana didn't spare Kale a second glance. "What about him? He served his purpose."

Damien stepped over Kale's body. He couldn't argue with facts. He also couldn't help but notice that Maggie stepped *on* Kale instead of over him. She glared at Damien when she saw him look at her.

"You have a problem with something, counselor?"

Damien readjusted his weapon and backpedaled as fast as he could. "Nope, no problem here." He stepped aside and let Maggie pass in front of him.

Damien and Maggie stopped outside the door. Ito motioned for them to stay put on either side tight against the walls.

Montana entered the unlocked room first, peeling right with Ito on his heels moving in the opposite direction. Montana immediately swept his sights over the first corner of the room. There was a sealed glass door in the far right corner and a wall-sized window closing off a darkened room below them. Two rows of computer terminals faced the glass wall, bisecting the room along its length, blocking the view of whatever might lay at the far end of the room.

The monitors on the desk displayed various readouts recognizable to all as heart rate, blood pressure and respiration. Above the numbers was a name: *Subject 234 Thomas, Dakota.*

Montana whispered to Ito on the other side of the doorway. "Got two red zones."

"Red zones clear!" Ito swung the muzzle over the remaining expanse of the room again to be sure it was empty of any threat.

Montana turned toward the door behind him. "Maggie, room clear."

Ito emerged from the shadows.

"Can you give me security on the door, my friend?" Montana asked.

Ito grinned and almost looked as if he were having fun. "Consider it done. Just like old times, eh?"

Montana couldn't help but return the smile. "Old times. I suppose this makes up for the lame Fourth of July party last year."

Keeping his eyes ahead of him, Ito gave a quiet chuckle. "*That* was not my fault—it rained." Ito went down on one knee just inside the doorway. From this vantage point, he could secure the only way in or out.

"Uh huh. Sure, you keep sticking to that story." Montana searched for the lights among the many buttons and pads among the monitors. He pushed a recessed pad accidentally. A room hidden behind the darkened glass became illuminated. The first thing he noticed was the blood. Dried bloody handprints slid down the inside surface of the glass. Montana placed his own hand over the print on the other side.

A small movement in the room below him grabbed his attention. As his eyes adjusted to the low overhead lighting, he recognized the figure huddled in the far left corner of the room. Behind the overturned bed, Dakota curled into himself, his head between upraised knees, his arms wrapped around his legs. He didn't move, not even when Montana pounded on the glass and screamed his name.

"I'm coming, Dak," he said looking for a way to release the door to his right.

Maggie came to Montana's side and grabbed his arm, demanding his attention. "That might not be a good idea. You don't know what they did to him. *The virus*, Montana, what about the virus?"

"Found it." Montana jerked his arm free of Maggie and pushed a button. With a soft metallic click the door near the console unlocked. "It's an anteroom. There should be another release to get inside."

Maggie stepped in front of the door, blocking him. "Think about what you are doing, Montana."

"Time's not up yet, Maggie. I can still get him out."

"What if they already activated the virus? What if that's the reason no one is here?"

Montana and Maggie faced each other down, neither willing to give way. Before it came to a confrontation, the staccato echo of gunfire could be heard above them, followed by a room-shaking explosion and heavy footsteps running down the hallway on *their* level.

"What we got?" Montana moved quickly to stand above Ito, who leveled his weapon and methodically began to place rounds through the door—one round every other second. He searched for exposed limbs, heads, or at least sought to keep the enemy from engaging them. Montana desperately needed more time. They had ammunition, but it wouldn't last forever.

"We got incoming," Ito warned as he opened fire on the four-man squad advancing down the hallway toward their position. The lead two men dropped with Ito's rounds in their heads as the remaining two hugged the walls and laid down heavy fire.

Montana reloaded as Ito continued to fire. Two more squads made their way toward them, taking cover in offices and alcoves along the way. Damien stood behind Montana, opening fire when Montana provided him with cover.

Maggie stood by the unlocked anteroom and made a decision. She could stay and fight or she could go to Dakota. Maggie put her hand on the door—and quietly closed it behind her.

With their backs to the wall and no room for retreat, the three men opened fire as more troops advanced on their position. The bulletproof glass wall behind Ito and Montana took its share of hits, small holes absorbed the rounds, but the glass didn't break.

Montana aimed at anything moving beyond the door. "How many?" he yelled over at Ito.

"Haven't had time to count." Ito ducked as another bullet hit just behind his head.

Montana saw a narrow, squat, dark tube thrown blindly from one of the rooms down the hall. He recognized it immediately.

"Flash bang!" He ducked away and closed his eyes. The thunderclap centered inside his skull and gave him an instant headache. He looked back, bringing his carbine up as Ito laid down a burst of suppressive fire. "My eyes got dazzled, man—can't see!"

"I gotcha'! Check fire." Ito got to his feet and helped move

Montana back along the opposite glass wall out of the direct line of fire. "I gotcha', man. Damien! Cover us. Shoot anything that moves down that hallway!"

"Yeah, sure." Damien shouldered his rifle, looking scared but determined not to let them down.

Ito helped Montana sit next to a row of terminals. He pulled a fresh magazine from his front vest and shoved it into the carbine. Ito knelt down and lifted Montana's face to him. "How ya doing, my man?"

Montana blinked furiously, his eyes tearing uncontrollably and pulled another pod of ammunition from his vest. "I think I'm okay." To prove it he locked the fresh pod into place, slapped the cover closed, then lifted a hand to wipe at his eyes. "Let's rock and freaking roll, baby!" He stood and shouldered the machine gun and sighted in.

A pause in the firing had Damien dropping his clip to the ground as the guards just outside the door reloaded.

"I'm out!"

Montana threw him another clip as Ito kicked the door closed and wedged a chair under the handle. All three men stood with newly loaded weapons pointed at the door and waited.

Damien started laughing. Ito and Montana turned to him and saw him holding out a hand covered in blood. Damien had a weird smile on his face as his eyes went from the blood on his hand to Montana.

"I thought it was sweat." He laughed again as he stumbled against the sidewall he used for cover and slid to the floor, landing heavily on his backside.

Montana knelt next to him. "Where are you hit?"

Damien laughed again. "I'm hit?"

Ito stayed where he was, prepared to cover the two men beside him. "How bad?"

Montana lifted Damien's arm and saw his vest had taken a hit. The low-impact body armor no match for rounds fired at such close range.

Montana ripped the vest open and Damien grunted with the pain. A large inverted V formed as blood from the wound continued to pour out down his jeans. Montana tore off Damien's shirt, ignoring the hiss of pain from Damien. The bullet had entered low on the left just above the waist of Damien's pants. Montana slid a hand around to Damien's back; it came back clean. He balled the shirt up and held it against the bleeding wound in an attempt to staunch the flow of blood. Montana looked up at Ito and shook his head.

Ito frowned at the news and looked back at the door. "Why are they waiting?"

Montana pushed harder on the still bleeding wound on Damien's side. "I don't like this."

Ito gave him half a grin. "Which part?" He then noticed Maggie was missing at the same time Montana did. "Down with Dakota?" Ito gave voice to the question they both wanted an answer to.

Montana, with his hand still pressed to Damien's side, craned his neck to look into the room where he had last seen Dakota. "Can't tell."

Damien grunted with pain as Montana pushed. "She's there… God! That hurts… I saw her go down."

Gunfire rippled through the complex, the sound distant and above them. Ito relaxed his stance and readjusted his grip on his weapon. "Geoffrey?"

An explosion rocked the foundation and dust sifted down from above. Montana shielded Damien, then turned to Ito. "Yeah, that would be my guess. We have to get Dakota out of here."

Ito bent over, one hand still on his weapon, and moved to take Montana's place at Damien's side. "Go. I'll cover you."

Before Montana had a chance to move, another explosion shook the building. This one closer and the effects more devastating. Besides the dust and now pieces of the ceiling falling on them, smoke starting filtering through the ventilation system above them. Another explosion reverberated through the walls. A horrible rumbling, like a semi barreling down on them, got louder.

Montana shielded his head as pieces of plaster fell on him. "What the hell is Geoffrey doing?" The smoke grew thick and black as it poured through the slats of the ventilation shafts.

Damien went slack against Ito's hands. "Montana, we need to get the counselor out of here."

Montana bent and lifted one of Damien's eyelids. The man didn't respond. "I can't leave Dak."

"I can't get Damien out on my own. If I carry him, I have no cover."

Another explosion made the decision all the easier. This time the damage centered over the room below them. The room Montana had seen his brother in. He turned to the wall in a panic. Both hands pressed against the glass, he strained to see past the smoke that now filled the small area.

"Dak!"

Montana tried the door leading into the anteroom only to find it jammed with debris falling from the ceiling.

"We're three floors down. What the hell did Geoffrey do—nuke the place?" The ceiling in the room below them cracked. Dust rose like a dirty cloud to mix with the poisonous smoke. Plaster, steel and internal wiring dangled from above, obscuring anything and everything. Montana pounded on the door, trying to break loose whatever wedged it closed.

Ito's voice broke through the panic. "Montana, we have to go— now."

"Dak!" Montana turned to the glass once more, trying to see his brother somewhere below in the ruined room.

"He's beyond our help, Maggie too if she's with him."

"No!"

"Look at me, Montana." Ito waited until Montana turned to him.

"We might still be able to get Damien out of this. If we stay, no one gets out. Not you, not me, not Damien." Ito spared the unconscious man in his arms a brief look. "He didn't know what he was getting into and he still signed on. His job was done when he got you out of prison. His wife expects him home."

Montana shook his head. "I can't leave Dak, Ito. I can't."

Ito considered that and nodded. "Then we all die here, my friend. Simple as that."

Montana closed his eyes and turned back to the devastated room below him. He pounded his fists on the bullet-riddled glass once. He turned back to Ito, then bent down to retrieve both his and Ito's weapons. "Move, I'll cover you."

Ito kicked the chair that barricaded the door out of the way and stepped to the side. When he was convinced no threat other than fire and smoke greeted them, he stepped into the hallway, and shifted Damien over one shoulder so he could have one hand free for the assault rifle.

Montana took a last look over his shoulder, then followed Ito into the eerily abandoned hallway lit only by the red glow of emergency lights now hazed with smoke.

CHAPTER 35

Dodging a barrage of gunfire, Maggie opened the door to the anteroom and slipped through the door into the room where they'd seen Dakota. The lighting was dim, and she squinted against the shadows until her eyes adjusted.

She whispered into the gloom. "Dakota?" When she received no answer, she crept further into the room. "Dak, are you all right?"

A slight movement to her left had her turning in that direction. Sitting in a corner behind the toppled bed was Dakota. He sat much as Maggie had seen him from the room above, head bowed between upraised knees, arms wrapped protectively around his legs.

She approached him slowly, not sure what to make of his condition, then reached out and touched his arm. "Dak?"

That got a reaction. Dakota snapped his head up and pushed her hand as he tried to move away from the contact. "No!" he yelled. His footing slipped as he stood too quickly and settled on scooting backward along the wall.

Maggie, startled by the sudden outburst, backed away. Dakota sat again, his eyes looking in her direction.

"Dak, it's me. It's Maggie."

The name or the voice made it through to him. Dakota brought his hand down from the defensive posture in front of him and stared at her.

"Maggs?" He leaned forward and made it to one knee.

Maggie's eyes quickly traveled over the bloodied scrubs to the dazed expression on his face. "What the hell did they do to you, Dak?"

Before he could answer, an explosion shook the foundation of the building. It finally seemed to bring Dakota out of his stupor. Maggie shielded her head from the dust and small debris raining down from the ceiling.

Dakota grabbed her wrist and pulled her next to him, trying to keep her safe with his own body. "Maggs, what are you doing here? How did you get in?" He looked past her, all around the room. "It's not safe here."

"Dak, I need you to listen to me very carefully." Another explosion caused Maggie to duck under Dakota's protective embrace.

Dakota looked above him to the source of the noise. "What the hell is going on up there?"

"That's what I need to talk to you about. *That…*" Maggie pointed to the sounds of gunfire and firefighting above them. "Is Geoffrey."

Dakota moved back from Maggie, his face creased in confusion. "What? Why?'"

"Why do you think? He's come to take his prize back."

"And why are you here, Maggie? To make sure I come quietly?" He walked a few steps toward the overturned bed.

Maggie shook her head. "No! There's no time for this. Just listen, if you want to hate me after that, fine. I came to make sure Geoffrey never lays one slimy finger on you ever again. He lied to you, he lied to me. God! He even lied to Michael."

"Lied? About what?"

"They weren't trying to find a cure for avian flu. They turned you into a walking biological time bomb. Geoffrey infected you with an inert form of Ebola, and then he lit the fuse by adding a designer flu virus to kick it off. When your body temperature reaches a certain degree, that will initiate the Ebola. You won't get sick, but you'll infect anyone you come in contact with."

"Oh my God." Dakota's arms dropped to his side as the information sank in. "Maggie, they already messed with me. This new General— makes McKinley look like a pussycat, by the way—told me my temp maxed at one-hundred-and-three degrees. I went into seizures and they brought me out of it. What if they already initiated the Ebola?"

Maggie considered the information and shook her head. "I don't think so, they would all be sick by now—or dead. Ebola isn't subtle. Your temp must need to go higher to kick things into gear."

Another explosion sent them both stumbling back into the wall behind them. Black acrid smoke started making it hard to breathe.

"You have to leave now, Maggs. Get yourself out of here."

"I'm not leaving without you." Maggie held her ground, her arms folded across her chest.

"Maggs, Michael would understand. Please, just go!"

"I'm doing this *for* Michael. Dakota, you aren't the only one Geoffrey will want."

"What do you mean?"

"I'm pregnant with Michael's child. What do you think Geoff would do with that information if he ever found out?"

Dakota's eyes went wide with the revelation. He took a breath and nodded in understanding. "The kid wouldn't stand a chance."

Maggie coughed and wiped her tearing eyes as the smoke thickened. "We have to get out of here without Geoffrey knowing about it." Maggie paused. "Without Montana knowing about it."

"Montana's here?"

"Who do you think got me this far?"

"Oh, that's just great. Any suggestions as to how we might get out of wherever the hell we are without the good guys *or* the bad guys finding out?"

Maggie smiled. "Not a clue."

Dakota grinned back at her, and then his expression changed as he looked behind her. Dakota put an arm around Maggie's shoulder and pushed her behind him.

Maggie turned and looked up, and then looked up some more until she got to the top of one of the tallest men she'd ever seen. "Holy shit."

"Don't even think about touching her." Dakota took a step toward the other man.

A violent explosion shook the complex. The ceiling above their heads cracked. The support beam running the width of the cell broke under the stress and gave way, taking half the ceiling with it. The man dove forward and pushed Dakota and Maggie out of the way and most likely saved both their lives. When the worst of the debris stopped falling, he rolled off Dakota and wiped blood from an open wound on his scalp.

"Why?" Dakota asked, helping Maggie to her feet. "Why'd you save us?"

"Dak?" Maggie didn't know what to make of the man in front of them. He made Ito look small in comparison.

"This is Moses," Dakota told her.

"A friend?" Maggie asked hopefully.

"Not lately."

Moses walked past them to the wall in front of him where the sink and toilet were connected. He pushed on the two screws holding the polished piece of chrome that served as a mirror to the wall. The wall about halfway up separated and swung out on quiet, hidden hinges. Moses reached inside the dusty entrance, withdrew two windup flashlights, and threw one to Dakota. He stepped inside, having to bend nearly in half at the waist to do so, and motioned for Dakota and Maggie to follow.

Maggie moved to follow when Dakota grabbed her hand, stopping her. "Maggs, we can't trust him. For all we know he's leading us right back to the General."

What was left of the ceiling above them creaked and groaned and threatened.

"What choice do we have?" Without another word she turned and followed Moses into the dark.

* * * *

Dakota turned the handle on his flashlight and illuminated the gaping hole before him, just making out Maggie's disappearing backside as she climbed a twisting stairway up into the unknown.

He had no idea where Moses might be leading them, but unless they had a death wish, Maggie was right, they had no choice. The building was coming down around them. He could only hope the hidden stairwell held up until they made it to wherever Moses led them.

The air was stale with the taste of smoke and sweat. The smoke, Dakota assumed from the fire that now fully engulfed the complex and he hoped to hell the General. The sweat was his own. The blood-spattered scrubs clung to him. His hands slipped on the metal rails, with his blood or sweat, he couldn't tell which. His bare feet became shredded and bloody by the sharp, raised metal surface of the steps. Every muscle in his body felt the after-effects of the abuse he had recently endured at the hands of Moses and his Taser.

Dakota ignored the complaints of his body and kept putting one foot in front of the other. To stop was to die, and for reasons he didn't have time to contemplate, he didn't want to die, not now. Not like this.

He'd climbed the Statue of Liberty when he lived in New York. Three hundred and fifty-four steps to the crown. He knew, he counted. Dakota thought he'd long passed that number, but then he hadn't been climbing for his life in New York. His feet throbbed with every step. He slipped on his own blood and rapidly fell behind.

Maggie moved out of his narrow beam of light. He could still hear their footsteps as they echoed off the metal rungs, but the darkness swallowed them and left him alone.

He pushed himself, every step an accomplishment. He thought the higher they climbed the clearer the air should become. He also thought that good conquered evil. He'd been proved wrong on both counts.

Dakota didn't realize he'd stopped moving until he felt hands lift him. His arm was slung around a thick neck. He opened eyes he didn't know were closed and found Moses at his side. The huge man tried to help Dakota walk, but as he tripped and missed half the steps he aimed for, Moses simply ended up placing Dakota in a fireman's carry over his shoulders, the extra weight barely slowing him down. The air felt solid in Dakota's lungs, his eyes burned, and the narrow stairwell was so hot it seemed about to burst into flame at any given moment.

Searing bright light accosted his eyes and clear, cold air flooded his lungs. He was flung unceremoniously onto the cool grass. Dakota coughed and gagged, vomiting soot. He rolled to his side, then pushed to his knees. Moses and Maggie lay beside him, looking no better.

Sirens cut through the air between the explosions that now came at regular intervals. Dakota saw they'd exited a small door cut into the bank at the back of the building. They were completely concealed and out of view from everyone. Ahead of them was a hedgerow of trees. Moses recovered first, helped Maggie to her feet, and gestured for Dakota to follow as he took off toward the concealment of the trees.

From the safety of the hedgerow, the three of them watched flames and smoke consume the warehouse.

"Montana…" Dakota couldn't see how his brother could have made it out of the inferno.

Maggie understood his distress. "Dak, it's Montana. If anyone could get out of there, you know he could. We did."

Dakota narrowed his eyes at Moses. "We had help. Why? Why did you help us?"

Moses seemed to consider Dakota's question for a moment, and started making rapid hand movements. It took Dakota a minute to realize Moses was communicating to him in sign. He might have recognized the hand signals, but it didn't mean he understood them.

"Is he deaf?" Maggie watched Moses with keen interest.

"No, his tongue was cut out—he's mute. The General said he saved Moses from insurgents."

Moses signed frantically, his face twisted with emotions. Dakota shook his head in frustration. "I don't understand, I'm sorry."

"He says the General didn't save him. The General is the one who did this to him."

Dakota wiped soot out of his eyes and coughed as he looked at Maggie in amazement. "You understand him?"

With her eyes still on the rapidly signing Moses, she nodded to Dakota. "My Gram was deaf most of her life. I don't remember *not* knowing how to sign." She held her hand up to get Moses's attention. When she got it she began signing back to him as she spoke. "Slow down, I'm a bit out of practice."

Moses looked impatient but slowed down the almost beautiful fluid movement of his hands and fingers. Maggie nodded as she watched him. "The bastard!"

"A little translation, if you please," Dakota reminded her.

"Yeah, sorry. Your friend Moses here tells me the General and his boys kidnapped him. He was on active duty in Iraq and became separated from his squad. The General took him. *He's* the one who cut his tongue out."

Dakota glanced at the Taser still in Moses's possession. "Then why? Why do his bidding?"

Maggie watched Moses answer. "His family. The General threatened him with the life of his family. God, it's Michael all over again."

An explosion had them all ducking for cover. "We have to get out of here." Dakota looked at the flames that reached far into the sky and the smoke that provided perfect camouflage, for a little while at least.

Maggie smoothed her hair out of a sweaty face. "No argument there. We can't go back and we can't go forward—the good guys are just as bad as the bad guys. If either one of you have any idea of where to go or who to trust, now is not the time to keep it to yourself."

"We need to disappear. I think I know how. You don't happen to have a cellphone, do you?"

Maggie pulled her phone from her pocket and handed it to him. "Cellphones can be traced, Dak."

Dakota flipped open the phone and punched in a number very few people had access to. "True, but seeing as I'm fresh out of quarters and there doesn't seem to be a pay phone nearby, I'm willing to risk it. Besides, who's going to try to trace calls from someone they think is dead?"

Maggie nodded in understanding. "Who are you calling?"

Dakota smiled as the line on the other end started to ring. "The coyote, Maggs. I'm counting on the clever coyote to get us out of this."

CHAPTER 36

The flames licked at the window like hungry tongues desperate for a feast. The heat seared him, scorching eyebrows, hair and skin alike. The glass was hot like the inside of an oven. Montana didn't care. He placed his palms on the boiling surface, desperately looking for some sign of life, some sign of Dakota in the inferno below him. Blisters formed on his palms, then his skin turned black. He stayed in the room even when he could have left, the flames roaring all around him, feasting on him, burning him alive as it had done to his brother.

Montana opened his eyes, fighting for breath, the imagined heat still very real. The nightmares never changed. Dakota trapped in a fiery tomb and Montana not able to get to him in time. It wouldn't be so bad if it wasn't so close to the truth.

He wished it were all true, his nightmares. He wished he had died in that warehouse trying to get Dak out. Because the truth was something he didn't want to live with. The truth was what he woke up to every morning.

He swung his legs over the side of the bed and rested his head in his hands for a moment before facing the inevitable day. Sometimes he wondered why he bothered. Six months had passed since he had failed at the warehouse, and failure never tasted as bitter as it did now. Dakota was dead. Nothing would change that. Montana had picked through what was left of the building himself and found nothing but ashes. The fire that claimed his brother's life burned so fiercely it didn't even leave him a body to bury.

Just as well. Geoffrey would only have laid claim to Dak's remains. Maggie's too—she'd died alongside Dakota. Maybe Maggie found peace. Montana hoped she found Michael in her afterlife. Maybe Dak finally found what he'd looked for all his life. Something Montana now knew didn't exist—justice.

Montana knew justice was a mirage, a concept meant to seduce people like his brother. People who used to believe in things like truth. Montana believed only one thing—his brother died for a cause that never existed. They used him, like they used everything, to accomplish an agenda of their own making.

A knock on the door brought reality back into focus. *Virginia. A motel.*

"Montana, you up?"

He recognized Ito's voice and glanced at his watch. Ten in the morning. He'd slept right through his alarm.

"Montana?" Another knock put him in motion.

"Yeah, okay, hang on a second." He stepped to the sink outside the small bathroom and splashed cold water on his face. When he caught his reflection as he dried his face, he saw dark smudges under his eyes. The scar on the left side of his face stood out bright pink and puckered where stubble refused to grow. He knew he could do no more about the way he looked than he could about the way he felt.

Since he fell asleep with his clothes on, he opted to change his shirt only. He pulled the wrinkled t-shirt over his head and took an equally wrinkled denim shirt out of his bag and buttoned it up. Six months ago it would have bothered him to be seen like this—disheveled, wrinkled, bruised and wounded. But then again, six months ago his brother was still alive.

Dakota's body had been reduced to nothing more than ashes in the sub-basement of Kale's warehouse. Neither Harry Kale nor any of the

General's team made it out. It was assumed Maggie went down to help Dakota. She died as Montana wished he'd died...by Dakota's side.

No matter how often Ito told him Damien was alive because Montana chose to leave his brother behind, it did little to soothe his pain. Dak's ashes couldn't even be identified among the debris. Fueled by a meth lab and other caustic material Kale stored in secret parts of the warehouse, the fire had burned violent and hot. It took almost a week for it to cool enough to begin excavating the ruins.

The body of the General was found in a stairwell. The last Montana heard, a positive identification as to his true name had yet to be determined. It made little difference to Montana. Nothing made much of a difference to him these days.

Dakota was dead.

That was the one fact Montana could not refute. The one fact he lived with everyday and wished to hell he didn't have to.

He opened the door and reached for his Ray-Bans in defense against the brilliant Virginia sunshine and Ito's searching appraisal. His friend meant well, but Montana could not begin to put into words exactly what the loss of Dakota meant to him. Ito had no way of knowing that without his brother, Montana was nothing more than a shadow, a wraith existing on the outer fringes of life.

His heart beat. Blood pumped through his veins. His body went through the everyday things it needed to do to survive, but its owner received no pleasure or had any interest in living.

Ito pushed off the hood of the rental car and lowered his glasses down his nose with one finger as he did exactly what Montana expected him to do—looked him over. "You look like shit."

Montana walked to the driver's door, ignoring the comment. "I'm driving."

Ito shrugged his indifference and tossed him the keys. He pushed his glasses back in place and opened the passenger door. Before Montana got in, Ito caught his attention. "Dakota would want this, you know that."

Montana held the car door open and looked over at Ito. He tried to convey nothing, but was aware his friend knew him too well for that.

"Yes, I do know that." He held Ito's gaze a moment longer, then ducked beneath the roof and turned the engine over.

The only other time Montana had been to the small cemetery was two years ago. He could never have guessed that fate would call him back so soon. They walked slowly, side by side, looking at the stones marking the passing of so many lives.

"Here." Ito pointed, but it was hardly necessary. In a row devoid of the weeds that dominated most of the plots, a line of polished granite markers stood with one name in common—*Ricco*.

The one they came to see was the newest. Gleaming black granite rose from the plot, the grave still so new the grass had only just begun to grow over the dirt. The name brought emotions to the surface, emotions Montana thought were behind him.

Michael John Ricco

Soldier, Husband, Son, Brother, Friend

April 24, 1898 - August 21, 2010

May you rest in peace at long last

Montana read the name on the marker next to Michael's. "They laid him next to his father. He would have liked that."

Ito and he knelt down at the grave. He didn't know what thoughts occupied Ito's mind, but Montana could only think of the small ceremony they'd held for his brother. In the hills of the Black Mountains, Montana, his father and grandfather had released Dakota's spirit. There would be no marker, no grave. Dak wanted it that way. Montana thought he'd cried all the tears he would ever cry, but surprised himself as he felt his face wet with the thought of Michael Ricco somewhere beneath him in the cold ground.

Ito disturbed his thoughts when he spoke. "What is that?" He picked up a sealed envelope nearly concealed by the growing grass at the base of the memorial. "It's addressed to you."

Montana's head came up. "What? Let me see that."

Ito handed him the small package. On the front, in what looked like a woman's handwriting, was Montana's name. Nothing else. Just his name. He felt the lumpy contents and looked over his sunglasses at Ito. "This hasn't been here long."

"You going to open it? Or are we just going to guess as to what's in it?"

Montana looked at the package once more, then ripped it open and tipped it on end. A pair of dog tags slid into his hand. Montana cocked his head at the discovery and picked the tags up to read them. He couldn't help the smile he found on his lips.

"These are Michael Ricco's."

Ito raised his eyes at the news and stood. "Interesting. Now tell me, what would Ricco's one prized possession be doing sitting next to his grave?"

Montana took a breath at the next thought slamming into his head. "A possession I clearly remember hanging around his wife's lovely neck—*after* his death. A possession she had with her the last time I saw her." Montana felt as if he were taking a breath, the first breath he had taken since learning of Dakota's death.

"Someone's trying to tell you something, my friend." Ito took the dog tags from Montana and examined them.

Montana stared at Michael's Ricco's grave and nodded. "Yeah, but what if I'm not interested in listening anymore?"

"No one is asking more from you than you've already given."

"I just want the truth, Ito. Something no one has seen fit to give me. The government won't even admit Dakota was in that warehouse. Their official view is so far from the truth it's not even laughable. Kale's hidden meth lab blew up in a failed raid, only the quick thinking of local and state officials saved untold lives." Montana shook his head in disgust. "Dakota deserves so much more than that. Maggie too. The bastards have swept the whole thing under the rug and sanitized it to make it palatable to the general public!"

"We know the truth," Ito reminded him.

Montana took the dog tags back from him and nodded with certainty. "Dak's dead, Ito. Nothing is going to change that. Let someone else worry about mysteries for a while, I'm tired."

"They could mean Maggie is still alive. If Maggie survived maybe—"

"No!"

Montana stopped him before he could finish. Before he could say the words he wished were real—*maybe Dakota is still alive.*

*What if...*the two most dangerous words. Montana played that game once. He didn't have the heart to play it again, because *what if* he played it one more time only to find someone playing a sadistic trick on him? If Dakota was alive he would have made himself known to Montana by now—*wouldn't he?*

Despite his protests, the *what ifs* still played themselves out inside his head.

"I can't. I can't do this. Dak is dead."

Ito gave him an understanding nod. "We paid our respects to a friend. What do you say we go home."

"Wherever that is," Montana said quietly.

He had an urge to leave Ricco's dog tags where he'd found them, but at the last moment hung them around his own neck. Maybe out of respect. Maybe out of remembrance. He didn't know for sure.

All Montana did know was they felt right there.

EPILOGUE

Dawn was still hours away as Montana struggled up the steep cliff. He stopped at the top to catch his breath and appreciate the view. The last man-made intrusion, a power line he passed about two weeks ago. He sat on the edge of the world and lifted his head toward the sky. More stars than he could count spilled light down from the heavens above. The moon had long ago dipped below the horizon, but the stars refused to give way to day so easily. They sparkled through the velvety blackness, illuminating the valley below him almost as brightly as the sun. Montana preferred to travel at night. It was cooler and he covered more ground with the confidence that he would not be followed.

He took great care to eliminate any traces of his presence. Nothing that could be tracked was left behind. He'd forgotten how good it felt just to be out in the wild again. Two years. Nearly two years now since he'd felt the old Montana surface. His brother's death hit him hard, but after the initial grief passed, he found a numbness that nearly suffocated him.

Montana settled himself against an ancient Pinion tree and watch as the night grudgingly gave way to dawn. Subtle shades of blue replaced the black, and the brilliance of the stars dimmed as morning clouds marched across the distant hills. He leaned forward, his arms wrapped around his knees. The dog tags he wore slipped from beneath his shirt and dangled against his arms. He hadn't taken them off since the day he'd found them at Ricco's grave. They hung around his neck along with the coyote fetish his father had given him years ago. The fetish he would wear until the day he died, the dog tags he would keep safe until he could return them to their rightful owner.

He knew the day he'd found them what they meant. Maggie was alive, and if Maggie survived then maybe, somehow, so did Dakota. He did not have the strength to believe it could be possible until nearly a year ago. That's when the search began in earnest. A search that couldn't look like a search.

Not even his father could help him. David told him Dakota was dead, to accept the fact and get on with his life. But when Montana asked about his grandfather, that was when the pieces started falling into place.

His father told him a story. "After Dakota was taken in the woods, Walter decided the camp was too close to civilization. He moved them deep within the Playas—the sacred Black Hills. Someplace safe, someplace hidden. He wouldn't even tell me where, Montana."

Montana understood. *The camp* consisted of fifty to sixty mostly full-blooded Lakota Indians. His grandfather, Walter, led the little tribe in an attempt to remember where it was they came from. An entire culture had nearly been wiped off the face of the earth. Sanitized and Christianized, Walter fought to preserve a way of life that few even remembered. The way of a once proud people—the way of the Lakota. They lived liked their ancestors lived, off the land. No electricity, no running water, no groceries. Most of the people chose to be with Walter because civilized life was slowly killing them. They forgot who they were and who they were supposed to be. Walter opened their eyes and reminded them.

If Dakota could hide away from the rest of the world, it would be there. Wherever *there* might be. Montana had searched for the last eight months and couldn't even find the remains of a cold fire. He lived off the land, hunted when he could. With only his bedroll and meager supplies to sustain him, he did not relish another winter out here in these unforgiving lands.

But October had arrived and despite the still summer-like weather, he knew time was running out. The four month deadline he'd given himself had come and gone. But he convinced himself that he would find them just over the next ridge, in the next valley, behind the next bluff. Montana lost track of time, his cellphone had died long ago. He wouldn't be able to get a signal out here anyway. *Can you hear me now?*

He smiled and thought it would be something Dakota would say. Maybe he was crazy, chasing dreams in the dark. He shrugged at the thought and stood to move out because that's what he did these days. He walked until exhaustion or hunger forced him to stop, then he would keep moving. Always moving, always searching.

He looked out over the valley as the first meager traces of dawn emerged. Weak sunlight filtered from behind the distant buttes. Something below him caught his eye and he turned to look. There was no sense in getting excited. Often he thought he finally saw something only to find he'd chased fingers of morning fog.

A thin ribbon of gray cut through the pristine air. The morning held promise of being clear, no mists. It took Montana nearly twenty seconds for his brain to accept what he was looking at—smoke! A campfire. As he stared, more ribbons joined the first. The trees below him blocked his view, and he desperately looked for some landmark he would recognize when he came down off the mountain.

To his left he saw a large outcropping of rocks with a jagged, almost wolf-looking nose jutting out. That would do. Hope surged for the first time in so long he almost didn't recognize it. Adrenaline zinged through him as he nearly ran off the mountain and into the valley. It took him longer than he thought to find the wolf rock, but once he did, he also saw the smoke rising above the tree line.

It had been ages since he'd moved with a purpose. Agile and

confident, he came across the hidden valley suddenly. Breaking through the tree line, Montana skidded to a stop as the valley opened up before him. He had to remind himself to breathe as his eyes took in the sight.

Tepees and more traditional tents spread out over nearly fifty acres. He crouched down and watched the camp come to life with the dawn. Wood pulled from neatly stacked piles started morning fires. Women with infants on their hips and toddlers in tow stoked the flames and heated water in kettles. A mixture of dress ranging from jeans to buckskin adorned the people. He laughed and sat down, unwilling or unable to go any further.

"I found them. I found them."

The words still made the realization difficult to believe. After nearly eight months of searching, he had found his grandfather's camp. Now the question remained: was Dakota with them? Was Maggie?

When he felt his legs wouldn't betray him, he stood and started to make for the camp. The cold barrel of a rifle pushed into the small of his back made him stop. He never heard a thing, the gun just appeared in his back. He couldn't remember the last time anyone snuck up on him like that.

He tried to turn around but the barrel only dug deeper.

"Easy, I'm a friend." He held his arms out to his side to prove he carried no weapon. The pressure in his back eased up and Montana turned around. Before him stood a black giant. Easily seven feet tall, the man wore buckskin and carried a semi-automatic Ruger. The contrast was startling. The man motioned for Montana to pick up his belongings and move out in front of him. He never lowered the weapon.

"Look, it's okay. This is Walter Willowcreek's camp, right? I mean Running Wolf, Chief Running Wolf. I'm his grandson Montana. Maybe he's mentioned me?"

When he received silence as an answer, Montana shrugged and kept walking.

"Or maybe not," he said, more to himself than the man behind him.

They were a few feet from the edge of the camp when a familiar voice stopped both men.

"So, my grandson has finally found us. Moses, you can put away the weapon. Montana is what he says—family."

Montana turned and found his grandfather looking back at him in that complacent way of his. Montana always felt ill at ease under that stare. But not today. Today the emotions he felt on seeing his grandfather could not be expressed in words.

"How long have you known I was here?" Montana asked, referring to the hills around them.

Walter seemed to consider this and turned to the black man he called Moses. "What has it been, a week now, or two?"

Moses played the game and brought his hand up and tapped his chin in thought. Then showed Walter three fingers.

"Three? Really?" He nodded and turned back to Montana. "City living has dulled your senses. You should have known you were being tracked."

Montana raised his eyes. "City living? I'm not sure Caliente ranks as a city. It's barely on the map."

"Compared to this, it's a city."

"I can't argue with that." A smile could no longer be suppressed as Montana wrapped his arms around his grandfather.

He was met with a warm hug and a whisper in his ear. "We have worried over you, grandson."

Montana pulled away, but held Walter by the shoulders. "David knew, didn't he? He knew where you were."

Walter shook his head. "I wouldn't have him lie to you. He told you the truth when he said he didn't know where we were."

"Grandfather, I need to know. Is he here? Is Dakota here?"

Walter ignored the question. "Come and meet my family, Montana."

Montana knew he would get no more answers just yet, so he followed the old man into the heart of the camp. He tried to see Dakota in every man he passed. But there was no one who even vaguely resembled his brother. Maybe it was too much to ask, but to come this far, this long, and still not have answers to his questions—Montana didn't think he could take it.

They were in the approximate middle of the camp when a small boy no more than two, maybe less, ran to him and tugged on his jeans.

"Da-da!" the toddler exclaimed and opened his arms, asking to be picked up. In a camp full of dark-haired people with the dusky complexions of their forefathers, the tow-head, fair-skinned little boy stood out like a candle in the dark. Sparkling blue eyes laughed as Montana bent to pick him up.

"Well, who do you belong to?"

"Da-da," the toddler exclaimed once more.

Walter opened his arms, and the boy slid over to the old man. "His name is Michael, my great-grandson."

Montana screwed his face up in confusion. "Your great-grandson?"

"By marriage."

Montana watched as a young woman stepped around one of the fires. Her waist-length black hair lay in a braid down her back. She wore jeans and a sweatshirt too big for her slender frame, but it was the eyes Montana recognized. They were the same color blue as the child in Walter's arms. The boy saw the woman as well and squirmed to be released. Walter let him down, he squealed and ran to the woman, who scooped him up in her arms.

"Mommy!"

She kissed him and put him back down where he immediately ran off in another direction.

Montana looked at her with a little less certainty now. It had been over two years since he had last seen her. "Maggie?"

She put her hands in her pockets and gave Montana a delicate shrug. "Surprise, surprise."

He closed the distance between them in two steps and enveloped her in a fierce embrace. "Maggie." When the tears came this time, he did nothing to stop them. He pulled back and saw her face wet as well. "I have so many questions."

She nodded and smiled as she wiped her face. "I know. I'm so sorry it had to be this way."

"I have something I think belongs to you." Montana reached around his neck, lifted the dog tags he had worn so reverently for the last two years, and handed them to her.

She let out a little "oh", took them, and held them next to her heart. "I was never sure if you got them, or if you did, if you understood. I guess you did."

Montana looked at the little boy throwing sticks into the nearest fire. "He looks just like his father."

Maggie smiled that secret smile all mothers have when they look at their children. "Yes, he does. It breaks my heart that he will never know Michael, but his daddy is the best I could ever have hoped for."

"His daddy?"

"My husband. I remarried. Somehow I think Michael would have approved of my choice."

Montana's heart skipped a beat. He watched Michael Ricco's son laugh at sparks disappearing into the morning air. "He called me Da-da when he first saw me. He thought I was his father."

Maggie took a breath and wiped fresh tears from her cheeks. "You two always did look more alike than you realized."

"Where is he, Maggs?"

She pointed beyond a row of trees where the bank sloped gently to a small stream. "Just on the other side of the bank, fishing. Montana?" She waited until he faced her. "It nearly killed him, letting you believe…"

Montana could only nod as he walked beyond the little growth of trees.

He was exactly where she said he would be. His back was to Montana. The first thing Montana noticed was how long his hair was. It hung below his shoulders and moved in the slight breeze. Unlike Maggie, he wore tan buckskins. Fringes on the arms and down both legs made him look like someone from a century gone by. He squatted down next to the small stream and pulled a good-sized trout out of the water with a net. He placed the still wiggling fish next to the others he'd already caught.

"I used to hate fishing, do you remember? I couldn't stand putting a hook through the bait." He laughed as Montana came next to him and sat down on the bank.

"I remember." Montana wrapped his arms around his knees and looked at his brother. "You used to make me skin and gut them too, but as I recall, you had no problem eating them."

Dakota laughed, a gentle sound floating away on the early morning breeze. He finally turned his head to look at Montana.

"There wasn't any other choice. You know that, don't you? They would've never left us alone. Especially if they found out about the baby."

"You married Maggie?"

Montana thought Dakota looked good, he was tanned and healthier than Montana could ever remember him.

"I love her."

Montana thought about that and gave him a nod. Focusing somewhere ahead of him, Montana suddenly felt very tired.

"I thought you were dead. I mean, I really thought you were gone.

We had a ceremony in the Paha Sapa. Released your spirit to be with Mom's."

"I know. I was there."

That got Montana's attention. "You watched? You were there?" Dakota grinned and hooked his fish together on a line. "Yeah, it was kind of a Huck Finn moment."

Montana stared at him in open-mouthed amazement. "You know, I can believe Walter played me and even you, but Dad? Please tell me David was not in on this whole thing."

"It had to be convincing. I'm sorry to put you through the last two years, Montana. But you could never have pretended not to know—we couldn't risk it."

"You couldn't trust me?"

Dakota closed his eyes for a moment and looked like he was trying to find a way to explain himself. "Trust was not the issue, Montana, and you know it." He motioned toward the camp. "You look at my son, you look at Michael and you tell me if you would have risked his life just to spare you some grief."

"He's not your son."

"Maybe not biologically, but in every other way that matters, yes he is. I am the only father he will ever know. He'll know all about Ricco when he's old enough, Maggie and I will both make sure of that, but right now I just want him to be a kid. That would never happen if they knew he existed."

Montana bowed his head, the anger diffused. "You're right. As much as I hate to admit it, you're right."

"Wow, I wasn't expecting this to be so easy."

"Oh, it isn't. I'm tired and haven't eaten in two days. Wait until I regain my strength." Dakota laughed and Montana truly felt like he had his brother back. "God, I missed you, Dak."

"Right back atcha', man."

"Damn, when you hide away from the world, you don't mess around. Do you really think you're safe here?"

"As long as everyone thinks I'm dead, I'm as safe as I'll ever be. But there will always be another General, another Geoffrey, another somebody who might not let it go. Someday, somebody is going to find out—you did."

"I had a lot at stake. Dak, I hate to ruin the moment, but what about the virus, what about the Ebola? Are they safe?" Montana referred to the camp behind them.

"I was wondering when that would come up. Maggie told me you knew." Dakota sighed and put his fish in a leather pouch. He leaned back on his arms and stretched his legs out in front of him. "They know, they all know. Walter told them. I was going to leave, but they wouldn't have it. As far as Maggie and I can figure out, Geoffrey forgot to factor in one minor thing."

"What is that?"

"He never programmed the virus to initiate at a set body temperature. He assumed anything above normal would initiate the flu and trigger the Ebola. He was wrong. It seems his little designer virus requires extremely high body temperatures. I go into seizures at a hundred and three. That brings my body temp down. I can't reach anything higher. Geoffrey doesn't realize it, but he actually did me a favor."

"How do you figure?"

"I'm not sure if Maggie told you this, but one of the reasons Michael died was we took away his reason to live."

Montana stretched out alongside his brother and shook his head. "Come again?"

"His longevity. The reason Michael lived so long was the fact that his body constantly had something to fight against. When we took that away, his normal aging process took over. Michael Ricco died of old age. Geoffrey solved that little problem for me. His designer flu keeps trying to do what it's meant to do, but I keep shutting it down."

"Meaning what, Dak?"

"Meaning that once every few months I get very sick. It only lasts a day or two, but I always will have something to fight against—Geoffrey made sure of that."

"Well, here's a little poetic justice for you. Geoffrey is dead."

Dak sat straight up and focused on Montana intently. "What? How?"

Montana smiled. "Ah, I get to tell you something you don't know."

"Come on, Montana, tell me."

"It's rather appropriate, actually. It would seem Geoffrey was visiting China a few months ago, some joint government research project using the information they obtained from you."

"Yeah?"

"He caught a nasty strain of avian influenza. Died before he made it back to the States."

"You're freaking kidding me, right?"

Montana laughed. "I couldn't make that up if I tried. Told you it was poetic justice."

"Damn, couldn't happen to a nicer guy."

Montana put his arm around Dakota's shoulder. "Yeah, still it is noticeably lacking in the personal touch of putting a bullet in his brain."

"Same old Montana."

Montana shook his head. "No, no I'm not."

The smile faded a little as Dakota nodded. "Yeah, I guess not. I am sorry, do you think you can forgive me?"

"Nothing to forgive, man. I gotcha' back. That's enough."

"What about you, Montana? What now?"

Montana stretched out on his back and watched the dawn break into day as he considered his answer. "A lot has happened in the last two years, Dak. I sold my half of the business to Ito. He took over the lease on my apartment, sold him the Jeep and the bike. Maggie gave me the tapes, the ones of Linney the night of the murder. I put them in. Almost watched them."

"You didn't?"

Montana looked out at the small ripples made by fish searching for breakfast and shook his head. "I shredded them. Figured I needed to trust myself when it came to Linney. Maybe she started out playing me, but that's not how it ended. She loved me, Dak, and if it looked like anything different on those tapes, then she was fighting for her life the only way she knew how." He gave a small shrug. "After what I thought happened to you, it didn't seem as important anymore. I took all my savings to come looking for you. I have nothing to go back to. I thought maybe I would hang around a while if that's all right. Maybe get to know my sister-in-law a little better, watch my nephew grow up."

Dakota's grin grew into a smile. "And your other niece or nephew."

"Maggie's pregnant?"

Dakota nodded. "She's due in the spring."

"You work fast."

"Gotta' lot of time on my hands."

Montana stood and held his hand out to Dakota. When he took it, Montana pulled him into a bone-crushing hug. "I love you, Dak. I missed you, but let me tell you, if I have to wear one of those getups…" He pulled back and motioned to Dakota's outfit. "It's a deal breaker."

Dakota laughed and swept his hand over his outfit. "Maggie thinks it makes me look sexy, like an Indian on the warpath, but for you, I think we can work something out."

They both stared at one another for a long moment before Montana broke the spell. "Next time you die on me, it better be for real, or I personally will kill you."

"Have to catch me first, man. Come on, I have an entire camp full of people who can't wait to meet you."

"Everyone acts as if you've been expecting me."

Dakota clapped his brother on the back. "Don't worry, we wouldn't have let you starve out there. Walter would have sent Moses after you before that happened."

Montana stopped. "Yeah, who the hell is that guy anyway? Certainly doesn't look like a Lakota."

"Ah, the stories I have to tell you…"

Two brothers separated by time and death, scars and pain, walked back to camp to embrace a family who might give them something neither thought they had a chance of obtaining.

Peace.

If only for a little while.

ABOUT ANN SIMKO

Through the Glass started out, interesting enough as a romance—Okay, let me stop laughing now. Seriously, I am not a romance writer, I found that out fast. I mean, I killed Montana's love interest in the first sentence and then I did what I love—torture my characters. I despise happy endings and adore bittersweet ones, I think I hit the mark here.

If you want to know what inspired the book as it stands, listen to the song Through Glass by Stone Sour. I can't tell you how many times I listened to this as I wrote.

This book is my favorite story of the series. I hope you agree. If you want to leave a comment, log on to annsimko.com and let me know what you think about what I did to my poor Dakota.

Ann's Website:

http://www.annsimko.com/

Reader eMail:

absimko@ptd.net

ABOUT THE COYOTE MOON SERIES

Book 1: *Fallen*

Available in ebook and print from Lyrical Press

Book 2: *Through the Glass*

Available in ebook and print from Lyrical Press

Book 3: *The Coyote's Song*

Coming soon from Lyrical Press

GO GREEN!

Save a tree read an Ebook.

Don't know what an Ebook is? You're not alone.
Visit www.lyricalpress.com and discover
the wonders of digital reading.

YOUR NEW FAVORITE AUTHOR
IS ONLY A CLICK AWAY!

LYRICAL PRESS
INCORPORATED
WWW.LYRICALPRESS.COM

Shop securely at www.onceuponabookstore.com

LaVergne, TN USA
20 June 2010
186732LV00001B/57/P